"Adriana Locke creates magic with unforgettable romances and captivating characters. She's a go-to author if I want to escape into a great read."

—*New York Times* bestselling author S.L. Scott

"Adriana Locke writes the most delicious heroes and sassy heroines who bring them to their knees. Her books are funny, raw, and heartfelt. She also has a great smile, but that's beside the point."

—*USA Today* bestselling author L.J. Shen

"No one does blue collar, small town, 'everyman' (and woman!) romance like Adriana Locke. She masterfully creates truly epic love stories for characters who could be your neighbor, your best friend— you! Each one is more addictive and heart-stoppingly romantic than the last."

—Bestselling author Kennedy Ryan

"Adriana's sharp prose, witty dialogue, and flawless blend of humor and steam meld together to create unputdownable, up-all-night reads!"

—*Wall Street Journal* bestselling author Winter Renshaw

Tangle

Dogwood Lane Series

Tumble
Tangle

Stand-Alone Novels

Sacrifice
Wherever It Leads
Written in the Scars
Battle of the Sexes
Lucky Number Eleven

A DOGWOOD LANE NOVEL

Tangle

ADRIANA LOCKE

Montlake
Romance

Published by Montlake Romance, Seattle

www.apub.com

Amazon, the Amazon logo, and Montlake Romance are trademarks of Amazon.com, Inc., or its affiliates.

ISBN-13: 9781503905283
ISBN-10: 1503905284

Cover design by Letitia Hasser

Cover photography by Wander Aguiar Photography

Printed in the United States of America

To Alexander, Aristotle, Achilles, and Ajax.
Eat all the doughnuts.
Share all the laughs.
Find all the love.

CHAPTER ONE

HALEY

"Tell me you have one." My purse hits the counter with a loud, unceremonious thud. "I'm in desperate need of a caramel-topped doughnut. Bonus points if it's cream-filled. Double bonus points if there are pecans on top."

My friend Claire looks at me from across the bar of the Dogwood Café. "That good of a morning, huh?"

"Something like that." The stool squeaks as I sit. The sound rips at my temple, adding to the frustration of the start to my day. "I'm going to need the biggest cup of coffee you can find too."

"The coffee I can do. The doughnut, though. That's going to be a problem."

"Come on, Claire," I say, sniffing the air. "You have one. I smell it."

"You can't smell it."

"You underestimate me and my senses."

She glances under the counter. Her attention settles on a spot near the end of the bar, where the doughnuts are kept beneath a heavy glass dome. They're a specialty at the Dogwood Café—handmade pieces of pure joy created by the owner's wife.

I live for these things. So does Claire, and the look in her eye tells me one of my favorites is left. The problem is, they're her favorite too.

"I'll jump the bar and get it myself," I warn.

Her laugh is loud, filling the mostly vacant dining room. "There's one left, but—"

"No buts. None," I say, talking fast so she can't interrupt me. "I. Need. That. Doughnut. Today has gotten off totally on the wrong foot, and I need something to smile about, okay?"

"You have me. We're friends. Smile away."

"Doughnuts make me smile. People don't."

I hold my hand out, palm up, and look her in the eye. She waits for me to crack. When a few long seconds pass and I haven't even blinked, she sighs.

"Someone bought it," she says. "For real."

Brushing a strand of my long black hair out of my face as if preparing for battle, I narrow my gaze. "No."

"No, what?"

"You aren't allowed to keep the doughnuts for yourself if a paying customer wants them."

"Haley—"

"No. I love you, Claire. I do," I say, shaking my head. "But not more than doughnuts."

"Haley—"

"And not more than doughnuts on a day like today." I wince as my brain decides to play back the morning for my mortification. "*Especially* on a day like today."

"It's sold."

I shoo her away. Like a child, I climb onto the stool, knees on the seat, and peer over the bar. Just as I suspected, perched on a platter—like the little gift from God it is—sits a glorious caramel-topped doughnut with the most perfect pecans I've ever seen.

The sight alone melts some of my stress. The way the icing glistens in the sunlight streaming through the windows makes me forget about the meeting I have in a few hours. Staring at the pecans, I almost forget my ex-boyfriend's stupid text messages this morning and how much our split still hurts even though I don't want it to.

"Want me to go ahead and grab it?" I ask. The words come out strangled because of my inverted position. When Claire doesn't answer, I look up.

She's looking behind me, smoothing out her blue apron. The flirty smile on her lips clearly isn't for me.

"Hey," I say in an attempt to draw her attention back my way. "Give it to me."

"If you insist."

I freeze.

The voice, all gravelly and deep, isn't Claire's. And unless she has become a ventriloquist with a penchant for leather-scented cologne that sends chills racing down my spine to my yoga-pant-covered behind—a behind that's up in the air . . .

Oh, crap.

My body teeter-totters over the bar as I try to find the internal switch from awe to action.

A swallow passes down my throat as I survey the situation from my precarious position. Claire's cheeks are tinted pink as she drops her gaze to mine. The giggle that's hidden by a twist of her lips tells me one thing I already thought to be true: whoever is behind me must be seriously good-looking to warrant the sparkle lighting up her face.

Lowering myself onto the stool, I keep my gaze focused on the oversize wooden fork adorning the wall behind Claire's bright-red curls. I wonder how close my cheeks are to matching her tresses.

"I'll take the doughnut to go, please," I say with a gulp.

"And I'll have mine here."

His voice must be inches behind me, and the proximity makes me jump. He chuckles before sitting down.

The richness of his scent blends with the honeyed twang of his voice, and I consider what will happen if I dissolve into the vinyl barstool. It's too early in the day for humiliating myself in front of cute strangers.

Can life come with a "Redo" button already?

I grab my bag and dig deep, as if the aforementioned button is buried at the bottom. Sorting through mountains of candy wrappers and receipts only reminds me how much I'm sucking at life right now, but it's better than looking at the guy who just saw my butt up in the air. In the thinnest yoga pants I own. With the brightest pink panties I have in my closet.

My wallet gets jolted a little harder than necessary as I realize how pointless wearing my pretty panties is today. No one will see them but me. That's what I get for making some stupid deal with my cousin Dane that I won't date for six months.

It's for my own good, I remind myself as I sling a tube of lip balm against my wallet. *The guys I pick are completely wrong for me.*

A muscled forearm extends across the bar, taking a cup of coffee from Claire. "Thank you," he says.

Hands still stuck in my purse, I look at Claire.

She grins. "Did you say you wanted coffee?"

I clear my throat, trying to ignore the pull of energy from the man beside me. "Yes, please. I'll take it with me."

She scoops up the doughnut. As soon as she's gone, the room seems to shrink. Fidgeting in my seat, knowing this guy just saw me in a very unflattering position, I start to stand.

"You aren't from around here either, I take it," he says before I can execute my plan to flee. "I mean, with your accent and all."

I consider pretending he isn't talking to me and ignoring him altogether, but that would be rude. And as things are going, his voice might be the highlight of my day. So I sit again.

"You mean I don't sound like I'm from Tennessee?" I ask, still not looking at him. "I'm shocked. I thought I had my drawl down pat."

He chuckles. "Sorry. You sound very midwestern, if I was guessing."

"Good call. I'm from Ohio. I've lived here a long time, though . . ." The words drift away, along with all coherent thought, as my gaze is snatched out of thin air. Despite ascertaining from Claire's reaction that he's cute, I'm wholly unprepared for the delicious package in front of me.

Staring back at me are the bluest eyes I've ever seen. They're the color of the sky on a winter day—crystal clear and bright. His brows are heavy, his lashes thick, and if I could find my voice, I'd compliment them.

Smooth, tanned skin is highlighted by a brilliant white smile. A sturdy jaw is softened by laugh lines at the corners of his full lips. There's confidence in his posture that somehow absorbs my shock, and the kindness in his smile puts me at ease.

"Ohio, huh?" he says. "I'm a Michigan fan. I hope you won't hold that against me."

"I'm not a sports fan. I hope you won't hold that against me."

His grin grows wider. "Fair enough."

What's not fair is how I can't remember what I'm doing here or what I have to do after. I untangle my gaze from his just in time to see Claire coming around the corner with my doughnut on a plate. Just like that, everything comes rushing back.

I didn't realize my shoulders had relaxed or the throb in my temple had eased, but I'm well aware when they slam back into me again.

"Did I forget to tell you I wanted that to go?" I ask, rubbing the side of my head.

"You told me," she says. She sets the plate down in front of him.

"Hey," I say, pointing at the plate. "That's mine."

He looks at the doughnut and then at me. I fully expect him to slide the plate my way. There's not a part of me, not a piece the size of one of those candied pecans, that thinks he won't.

5

But he doesn't.

Instead, he smirks.

"At the risk of you stabbing me with a fork, I beg to differ." He then tells Claire, "This looks delicious. Thank you."

"You are so welcome," Claire purrs.

I glare at my friend. "You can't give that to him because he's cute, Claire."

"Hey now," he interrupts with a furrowed brow. "I'm not sure I like 'cute.' Ruggedly handsome? Roguishly attractive, maybe?"

"Thief?" I offer.

He lifts his fork like he's taunting me but, proving not to be a total daredevil, doesn't touch the doughnut.

"Um, maybe I gave it to him because he ordered it first," Claire offers. "Get ahold of yourself, Haley."

That's it.

"Get ahold of myself?" The dam holding back the irritation that's been building all morning breaks in a spectacular display. I half stand and half sit on the stool and fire away at my friend. "Do you even know what's happened to me this morning, Claire?"

"No."

"Let me fill you in," I say through clenched teeth. "A smoke detector started chirping at four o'clock this morning because the battery went bad, despite changing them last week. Okay? And I was too short to reach it without climbing on a chair, and because it was four a.m. and I hadn't had coffee, I fell. Hit my knee, bumped my elbow, and I cried. Because I'm a baby."

Claire bites her bottom lip to keep from laughing.

"Then—"

"Hold up," he says.

"Hush, Doughnut Thief," I say, shushing him with a wave of my hand. "Then I couldn't make coffee because the town flushed the water lines yesterday and the water is still red. And then, because it just keeps getting better, I get a call from Sandra at the library, asking me to come in today, and I'm praying like heck it has nothing to do with the rumors that we're having budget cuts." I take a lungful of air. "I'm over today, and it's not even really started yet."

"Ouch," the man says, taking my need for oxygen as a cue to add his opinion. "That is a rough morning."

"Oh, it gets better," I insist, feeling my blood shoot through my veins. "Then Joel sent me a text."

Claire's brows shoot to the ceiling. "Joel the Hippie?"

"Stop calling him that."

"That's what Dane called him the entire time you dated him," she says.

"You dated a hippie?" the man asks. "That's surprising."

I glare at him. "Want to know what's surprising? I've managed to act like a lady and haven't taken that doughnut right off your plate. *That's* surprising."

He chuckles.

"This isn't funny." I bounce in my seat, trying not to beg while also trying not to snatch the pastry. It's not so much I need the doughnut itself; it's that I need the comfort of the carbs that will remind me of my mother's homemade cinnamon rolls and give me the illusion that everything is going to be okay. "My life is falling apart."

Ignoring my puppy-dog eyes, he digs his phone out of the pocket of his jeans. His fingers fly against the screen.

I take a moment to study him from the side. The light catches his neatly trimmed, sandy-brown hair. His face is freshly shaved, and I wonder vaguely what he would look like with a good three-day stubble.

For a moment, the doughnut is forgotten. In its place is a thought as delicious as the caramel icing—of the taste of the thief's lips against mine. My little daydream is halted when he slips his phone back into his pocket.

"How much do I owe you?" he asks Claire.

"A doughnut and coffee is four eighty-six," she says.

He fishes a ten-dollar bill from his wallet and places it on the counter. "Pay for her coffee, too, and then keep the change. Can I get this coffee to go, though?"

"Sure thing," Claire says.

She strolls to the cash register, leaving the thief and me alone. I struggle to fight the grin splitting my cheeks.

"Did you just buy my coffee?" I ask.

"Yes."

"You know what goes good with coffee . . ." I look at his plate and then back to him. All he does is laugh.

He gets to his feet, unfolding a body that's taller, and harder, than I expected. His jeans are coupled with a gray-and-black flannel that fits him well enough that I can see the lines of his body. The curve of his biceps, the dip of his waist, and the slight angle from his shoulder to his neck are divine.

"Are you finished?" he asks.

I zip a line from his boots to his face. "What do you mean?"

"I don't want to walk out of here until you've finished appreciating me." He grins. "If you're done, I do need to go."

A full-on blush covers my body, and when he laughs, I wonder if he's thinking it's the same color as my panties. This makes me blush more.

"You are not the gentleman I hoped you were," I say.

He smiles devilishly, assessing me as he shoves his wallet back into his pocket. Then, with a pained expression and a dose of hesitation for my benefit, he slides his plate in front of me. "Here. You can have my doughnut. I know it's not all you wanted, but it'll have to do. I'm late." He takes a cup from Claire for the road.

"I didn't hear anything you said after, 'You can have my doughnut,'" I say, sticking my finger in the middle of the pastry. "But thanks."

"They have forks, you know."

"I know. But I wanted to make sure you didn't ask for it back." A warmth spreads through my middle as he smiles. "Thank you for this."

"You're very welcome, Ohio." He heads to the door but stops before exiting. Looking at me over his shoulder, he narrows his eyes. The feel of his attention on me changes. It gets heavier. Not uncomfortable, but it makes me squirm nonetheless. "I'm Trevor Kelly, by the way. What's your name?"

"I'm Haley." My voice is breathier than I intend or expect, and if I weren't still flushed from getting caught staring at him, I might blush again. "Haley Raynor."

"It was nice to meet you." His features soften as he steps into the sunlight. "Oh. If I didn't mention it, you owe me for the doughnut."

And with a final grin that sinks me into my seat, he's gone.

CHAPTER TWO

HALEY

"If he turns around and walks right back in here, it won't be soon enough," Claire says.

"As long as he doesn't come to get his doughnut back." I swivel on the stool to face her. "By the way, I should fire you from being my friend."

"Why would you do something like that?"

"You knew he was here, and you let me climb on the bar and stick my butt up in the air."

She shrugs. "I didn't *let* you do anything."

"You didn't warn me, which means you let me by proxy. And as your best friend for the last eight years, I expect more."

"You kept cutting me off in your quest for a hit of caramel icing." She wags a finger my way. "This is your fault."

I make a show of dropping my jaw in faux shock. "You're blaming this on me?"

"Totally. I couldn't get a word in to save my soul."

"Let's just make a quick note that you didn't bother to blurt out 'hot guy' or 'sexy stranger.' Either of those two phrases would've gotten my attention."

Claire leans against the counter, a conspiratorial grin on her face. "I come to work every day and serve a bunch of old farmers wanting coffee. If you told me this morning I was going to meet the hottest guy I've ever seen in the flesh today, I would've called you a liar."

"Same." I swipe at the icing with my finger. "I wonder where he came from. There aren't any Kellys in Dogwood Lane, are there?"

"Lived here my whole life and haven't met a Kelly."

"I was going to say, if there's a family of men like that around here and you haven't introduced me to them by now, you're *definitely* not my friend anymore."

Icing hangs off my finger before I plop it in my mouth. A rush of sugar blitzes my tongue, and I make a concerted effort not to moan.

Claire hands me a fork. "Like you have a hard time meeting guys."

"Oh, I can meet guys all right. I just can't meet the right *kind* of guy." I lick my lips. "Any tips? Not that I'm looking, of course. I'll just note them down for later."

"You're desperate if you want tips from me." She holds out her wrist to show the word HAPPY inked on her skin. "I tattooed a guy's name on my body who makes his living, for a lack of a better word, in dive bars. A guy named Happy, to make it worse. Don't ask me for help."

"Good point."

I stuff my mouth with doughnut. It's thicker than usual and takes much longer to chew than I anticipate. By the time I swallow, Claire's refilling a couple of farmers' coffee cups by the door.

Taking another bite, I let myself calm down for the first time this morning. My eyes close. Air flows in and out of my lungs in a controlled fashion, just like the guru on one of my social media accounts showed her followers last week. I focus on putting the chaos of the day behind me and stepping forward with positivity and confidence. I envision restarting the day with purpose and focus.

Until Claire comes back.

"You know," she says, "watching you eat makes me think I do it wrong. I don't enjoy food as much as you."

Wiping my mouth with a napkin, I shrug. "Your loss."

"Somehow you have icing on your cheek." She points just under my eye. "How do you manage that?"

"It takes skill." I dab at the spot until Claire gives me a thumbs-up.

"I should get extra friend points for not letting you eat that in front of Trevor."

"What would it matter? We'll never see him again," I say.

"I have a sneaking suspicion that's not true. He asked for your name, Haley."

"So?"

"So guys don't do that. Just don't be surprised if Trevor Kelly circles back around to see you again. That's all."

His name being spoken seems to jolt his energy right back into the room. My body unconsciously leans toward where he was sitting. It takes all of two seconds to imagine him naked, hovering over me, with that delicious smirk I'm sure I'll remember later tonight when I go to bed. And probably tomorrow too.

Claire bursts out laughing. "I know what you just thought."

"I don't know what you're talking about," I say, shoveling in another bite. "I was thinking about how much I love breakfast."

And that's why we're friends. Claire's mind is as dirty as mine. Although I have no idea why she thinks Trevor Kelly would be back to find me. Yes, he asked for my name, but he knows where Claire works. And with her sweet, cherublike face, gorgeous hair, and awesome personality, it's not as if he wouldn't want to come to Claire again for coffee. I was someone he teased because, let's face it, I deserved it. *Kind of . . .* But Claire is a catch.

"See? I don't love breakfast that much. What's my problem?" She sighs.

I swallow, my mouth sticky from the sugar. "I think your problem is your attitude."

A rag launches my way. I duck, the white fabric shooting over my head and landing at the foot of the salad bar.

"What did Joel want, anyway?" Claire asks.

The mention of Joel's name zaps the Trevor-induced energy right out of me. I stab a bit of doughnut with a little more force than necessary and remember his text. He was sweet, asking how I was doing, and wanted to see if we could meet up for dinner. For a moment, it was like old times. The Joel I was infatuated with for almost a year. Then, lucky for me, I recalled the way he ghosted me for a full week before finally finding the balls to break up with me. Via text.

"What he told me he wanted or the truth?" I ask.

"The truth."

I drop the fork and look at Claire. "He wanted to have sex with me."

She makes a point of sighing, her head rolling around on her shoulders in frustration. "Of course he did. He's a hippie. Free love and all that."

"You'd be proud to know I told him to cuddle with some Matcha." I grab my coffee and pull it to my chest. "I mean, I was tempted to cave, but I held strong."

"I'm sorry, but I don't get what is tempting about him. He's a hippie, for the love of God."

I laugh. "He's not a hippie."

"Still."

"Still, I said no and . . . you know what?" I smile smugly. "It wasn't all that hard. And not because he's a hippie," I mock, getting that in there before she can, "but because this not-dating thing I'm doing is working."

"How many weeks have you gone now without a date?"

"Many, but it's mostly as a security precaution for me. Habits are hard to break, and I might've been addicted to dating, actually." I pause. "Can you be addicted to dating?"

She shrugs.

Adriana Locke

"Besides," I say, moving on, "if I win, I get to name Dane and Neely's baby."

Claire furrows her brows. "I didn't know Neely was pregnant. Wow. That was quick."

"She's not. At least, if she is, I don't know it." I lug my purse onto my lap and find my debit card. I slide it across the counter.

"I can't remember the last guy I saw you with, actually."

"I didn't think I'd make it this long. I think this is week seven. Eight, maybe." I make a face. "Anyway, it's amazing how much time you have on your hands when you're not worried about someone else's schedule and wants and all that crap."

"Yeah, but you don't just date. You fall in love. That's a whole other level of commitment."

She's right. It's a vicious cycle I've been in my entire life—meeting a guy, going on a few dates, and then attaching myself to him like my life depends on it. I read a book one rainy day at the library that said this is a habit of people who weren't shown enough attention as a child. I'm not sure about that. I had a great childhood—attentive parents, aunts, uncles, and cousins who loved me. I never felt attention-deprived.

The truth of the matter is I'm tired. And as much as I fight it and hate to admit it, Dane is right. I owe it to myself to step back from dating and focus on me for a while.

"I'm not looking for a committed relationship until I'm out of school," Claire says. "No guy is worth the distraction when I'm this close to finally graduating."

"I'm so proud of you," I tell her, wrinkling my nose. "I wish I would've figured out how to finish my degree when I moved here."

"You'd just lost your mother. Moved to a new place and were taking care of your cousin's baby, Haley," she says softly. "You did great."

I lift my fork, cut a chunk of doughnut, and fill my mouth. "Sure I did. I'm twenty-six. Work part time at the library. And am alone."

She shakes her head. "It's amazing no one has married you yet, with those impeccable table manners."

I fire her a look, making her laugh, before swallowing. "Well, no one is marrying me for a while. I have a bet to win with Dane."

"Are you still babysitting Mia?" Claire asks. "With Dane and Neely living together now, I wasn't sure."

"Yeah. I still grab her after school a lot, and she sleeps over a night or two a week. Actually, I need to run her leotard to Dane before I go to the library."

I think about Dane and smile. No one could ask for a better cousin. We're only a couple of years apart in age and fight more like siblings, but he's always been there for me. And despite our propensity for silly bets, he's kind and thoughtful. Neely is a fantastic fit for him, and I'm glad he's finally found the happiness he deserves.

Claire slides my card back to me. "Trevor paid for yours. Remember?"

His name elicits a shiver that runs down my spine. "Well, if nothing else good happens today, a hot guy bought my breakfast. I'll take it."

"You definitely made a better impression than I did," Claire says.

"Why? Did you say something super ridiculous before I got here?"

"Like telling him he charmed my panties right off me? Or how his smile made me want to strip in the middle of this diner?"

I cringe. "You didn't."

"No," she scoffs. "I didn't. Have a little faith, will you?"

"I seem to remember a weekend in Nashville where you did try to strip in the middle of a bar while shouting how the bartender made you want to . . ." I grin. "What was it? Come—"

"Stop," she says, flustered. "We don't need to remember that."

"Oh, I think we do."

"That was the tequila. Not me."

"So what about the time in Memphis when we—"

She waves me off. "Point made."

"Okay. So why do you think you made a bad impression?"

Claire's forearms rest on the bar as she looks at me. "I didn't say that, exactly. I just said you made a better one."

"Oh, I'm sure," I say with a snort. "I unknowingly sashayed my butt in his face. I begged him for his breakfast and called him a thief. That's a five-star impression right there."

"I think he found you . . . interesting."

"Probably unforgettable, and not for reasons I'd choose if I had the option." I stick my card in my wallet. "Oh well. Can't win them all, right?"

My friend shoves off the bar. Her head cocks to the side. There's something on her lips that she's afraid to say.

"When you look at me like that," I tell her, "I get scared."

"I was just thinking he's the kind of guy I could see you with."

I grab my coffee and take a long drink. Putting the cup between us helps a little, like it gives me a tiny bit of distance from her crazy yet tempting ideas.

She watches me pointedly ignore her. When I don't resume the conversation, she slides my plate away.

In a flash, I pull it back to me again to swipe the last of the caramel icing with my finger. "One—I'm on a hiatus."

"So?"

"So I'm not dating anyone. And two, I'll never see him again unless our coffee-and-doughnut urges and locations match up. That's highly unlikely. And three, if anyone would have a shot with him, it would be you."

She bursts into a fit of laughter that confuses me.

"Why are you laughing?" I ask.

"He didn't look at me like he wanted to smear that icing on my nipples and lick it off."

"Claire!"

She crosses her arms over her chest, completely undeterred. "It's true."

I squirm in my seat. The picture she painted is enough to make me want to go home and take a cold shower. But as I hear his laugh echo through my mind and wonder how rough or gentle his touch would be, I snap back to reality.

"I'll give you that he's gorgeous," I say.

"And sexy."

"And charming," I add.

"And he seems intelligent."

"And he can be kind," I admit, tapping the plate with my knuckle.

"So? What's the problem?" Claire asks.

I look at her. "That. All of it. That's the problem."

"For someone as smart as you, you're making no sense here."

Of course it makes no sense to her. It doesn't even make sense to me until I sit down and really am honest with myself. But when I am, I know I'd fall so in love with a guy like Trevor Kelly my head would spin.

I sigh. "I fell in love with Joel. And Henry. And Marcus. And however many before them. Things would not go well with Trevor, even if he were interested, which he's not. And if I were in the mind-set to want to hook up with someone, which I'm not . . ." My phone buzzes in my purse. I fish it out. A text sits on the screen from Dane.

"I gotta go," I say, getting to my feet.

Claire looks up as the door chimes. "I'll be right with you." She glances back to me. "Call me tonight. We can head to Mucker's for pizza."

"Will do, unless I lose my job today."

"Don't think like that," she says. "They probably want to give you a promotion."

I give her a smile for the compliment and head to the door.

"And if Trevor Kelly wants to be repaid for that doughnut, you better follow through," she calls after me.

"Bye, Claire." I step into the sunlight, feeling a little lighter than I did when I walked in. A gorgeous man—whom I'll never see again—gave me his doughnut today. Life is good.

CHAPTER THREE

TREVOR

"This is going to be interesting."

My words drift through the cab of my truck as I wait for a pickup loaded with hay to go through the intersection. Bales are stacked in the bed higher than the cab, held in place with only a few straps. The driver gives me a wave as he drives by, and I return the gesture, wondering if waving is a thing here. Because everyone does it. Every single person.

It's clear I'm not in the city anymore. These people take southern hospitality to a whole new level with the waving crap.

My eyes flip to my rearview mirror. I can't see the Dogwood Café anymore, and something about that makes me chuckle. Not that I can't see it, but rather that I'm still wishing I could.

Idiot.

Haley Raynor. Now there's a feisty, sassy girl I wouldn't mind spending some more time with. For someone so tiny, she sure had some attitude. I barely held in my laughter as she described her morning, but that look in her eyes when she saw *my* doughnut? Let's just say there are other parts of me that wouldn't mind that look directed at them. And it's better not to think about her yoga-pant-clad ass while driving either.

Clearly it's been a while since I've gotten laid.

My thoughts are broken when my brother's name pops up on the dash. I press a button to answer the incoming call.

"Hey, Jake," I say. "What's up?"

"Hey," he says. "How's the city no one knew existed until Dad married Meredith?"

I glance at the little building on my left. It's one of those miniature, freestanding buildings with a tiny front porch. It has an old-fashioned barber's pole spinning outside. The man on the porch waves as I pass. Naturally.

"Calling this a 'city' is a stretch. I'm not even sure it qualifies as a town," I say. "Maybe a village? Is that a thing?"

My older brother chuckles. "Why did I expect it to be exactly that?"

"Oh, I don't know. Because Meredith uses the word 'quaint' in every other sentence?"

"I really don't love her, you know," Jake says.

"Yeah, well, I'm not her biggest fan." I follow the navigation system and turn onto a highway leading out of town. "Just be glad you aren't the one assigned to making sure her dream house is completed to her exact specifications."

Jake sighs. "Trust me. I thank God every day. I'd go outta my mind if Dad sent me to some Podunk town for Meredith's benefit."

"But remember—this is for Dad, too, because when his wifey is happy, he's happy."

I can hear the sarcasm dripping off my words as I repeat Dad's favorite mantra of the last year and a half. Since he divorced Mom, he's thoroughly enjoyed himself, to put it mildly. Then he met Meredith, and he's a changed man. Or so he says. I call bullshit.

"Oh, spare me the rhetoric," Jake scoffs. "Dad doesn't love her. He loves her D-cups and the fact she's our age."

I ease my foot on the accelerator and think about what Jake just said. I've thought about it a lot, about whether Dad and his new wife are actually in love or she's a gold digger and he's getting played. My hope is the former. My head says it's probably the latter.

Either way, not my problem. Even though it kind of is since I'm the one here.

"You're probably right," I admit.

"Probably? I *am* right. And really, I don't blame him. Think what this does for his ego."

"Like his ego needs to be stroked."

He chuckles. "I doubt that's all she's stroking."

"Nice visual, Jake." I groan.

The navigation system tells me to take a right. My tires hit a gravel road, and dust billows around both sides of my truck. The only sign of life is a slow-moving tractor in the middle of a field. Beyond it rises a hill that appears to touch the clouds. Trees cover the mound, creating a striking picture against the bright-blue sky.

"What's the plan?" Jake asks.

"I went over everything this morning before I left home. All that's really left are Meredith's changes, unless I get on-site and see something's wrong." I work my neck back and forth. "I don't see any reason why the house can't be done before Dad's retirement party next weekend or shortly thereafter."

"And let me guess," Jake says. "You'll have to stay on-site the whole time."

"Probably, but it's just a few days. Two weeks max, and nothing should be affected in the office. Natalie has it squared away, and I can hopefully do a lot from here. I just told Dad I'd make sure it was perfect."

"Sure," he jokes. "That's why. It has nothing to do with Liz, right?"

My stomach knots as my head hits the seat. I grab the knob to turn off the heater, but it's not on. *Shit.*

I rub my forehead. "Believe it or not, I didn't expect her to take our . . . See? I don't even know what word to use to describe it."

"She accidentally-on-purpose ran into me yesterday at the gym, and let's just say she thought you were a lot more serious than you did."

I groan. Jake doesn't even try to mute his amusement.

"I'm so glad you find this funny," I say.

"It's funny because it's you, not me, and it's funnier because you say this every time. You'd think you'd learn."

"Learn what?" I bark. "That I have to make it clear I don't want to marry every woman I date? I do that. I lay out what I want, how I see things—all that shit. I set expectations. I couldn't be clearer if I had them sign a contract."

I swing the truck to the left, heading for the forested hill.

"Our father is an attorney. You could get one drawn up," Jake says with a chuckle. "Or just stop screwing with the crazy ones."

"The problem with that is you can't always tell the crazy ones. I didn't know Liz was nuts until I told her she wasn't getting the cock anymore." I ponder this. "Maybe it's my cock that makes them crazy."

Jake snorts. "Yeah. I'm sure it's that. Hang on for a sec."

He puts me on hold. I take a left and slide farther out of town, my mind drifting to Liz.

Liz did something that's never happened before: she scared me. In all my escapades, I've never met a woman who behaved like she did. Who nodded and smiled as I told her what was up—that we could see each other when I was in town. Fuck around. Have dinner. I thought she was cool with that.

Turns out she wasn't.

The way she sobbed when I told her our relationship had run its course was something I won't soon forget. The tears. The heaving. The proclamations that she may never be okay again. As if it's my fault she read entirely too much into every word I said and every action I took . . . except for the words and actions I meant for her to take to heart.

21

I'm used to women becoming attached. It happens. But I'm not used to *that*, and if she thinks she's going to guilt me into spending time with her, she's wrong. I don't need an extra arm or a woman stuck to my side. The thought of either makes me want to jump over a cliff. Variety is the spice of life, and I like my life spicy. *Like Haley. She'd give my life a bit of spice for a while, I bet.*

"I'm back," Jake says. "Shit hit the fan on the bridge project today. I'd stay out of here if I were you. I'm gonna go nuts this afternoon."

It's my turn to laugh. "Will do." I take in the greenery and solitude. "This is a good place to lie low. Slow down a bit."

"You mean sleep with one at a time."

"Believe it or not, I never get involved with more than one at a time. I do have morals, brother."

"Good. I don't," he jokes. "But I do want to thank you."

"Yeah? What for?"

"For dealing with the house so I don't have to. Even if it was for selfish reasons."

"Well, it was perfect timing. And even though it might've been a little selfish, I think I can save us some money. It's quite possible sending the CFO of a construction company to a jobsite might not be the most asinine thing in the world."

"You act like you don't know anything about construction," he scoffs. "You could've gotten your engineering degree instead of one in accounting and one in business administration. Then you could've taken over this side of things."

I smack my lips together. "Anyone can manage a house. Only one of us, meaning me, can add. Someone had to do the hard stuff."

"You're an asshole."

"True," I say.

Jake laughs. "All right. Call me later and fill me in on the house, and make sure I don't have a coronary after this management meeting today."

I start to respond, but my attention is pulled to my mirrors. A little black car flies up behind me and rides so close to my bumper I can't see it in my side mirrors. To repay the jerk behavior, I ease off the gas and slow my pace to a crawl.

The dust starts to settle as our speed decreases. The car behind me blares its horn.

"What's going on over there?" Jake asks.

"Oh, some asshole just flew up . . . on . . . me . . ." I reach up and adjust my mirror. A slow smile splits my cheeks. "It's her."

"It's who?"

"Her," I say, shaking my head. "What the hell?"

"Liz? She followed you down there?"

"What?" I ask, the sound of Liz's name shocking my system. "No. Not Liz. Haley."

"I'm confused," Jake admits. "Who's Haley?"

My grin grows wider. "Oh, just a sweet-as-hell woman I met in the café this morning."

"For fuck's sake, Trev. You just got to town."

"What can I say? Women love me."

"You could say all the things you just said, like how you need to slow down," he says, mocking me. "Or how you're putting the brakes on your conquests."

He continues to jabber on, but I tune out. Haley's hair has been piled on top of her head. She's biting a nail as she drifts back and noses into the other narrow lane to see if anything is coming. So I move my truck into the center of the road.

She honks.

I burst out laughing.

"I must've made an impression if she's following me already," I point out.

"You heard nothing I just said, did you?"

"Nope."

"Go add to your fan club and call me this afternoon," he says.

"Yeah. Will do. Later."

I end the call before he says goodbye.

My navigation tells me to take a right in two hundred feet. In a small break in the tree line is a barrel. A white board is attached to the front, bearing the words KELLY JOBSITE.

Part of me wants to do what I came here to do: check out the house and get some fresh air. The other part of me, the one led by my groin, wants to pull over and see what Haley wants.

That side wins.

Before I can do that, her turn signal indicates she's turning right too. And with no other lane in sight, it's obvious we're headed to the same place.

With a curious mind and a semihard cock, I pull into the driveway.

CHAPTER FOUR

TREVOR

"Good God," I mumble.

Dad's house stands in front of me, towering over the valley from its perch at the top of the hill. Even in its incomplete state, it's impressive, with arched windows affording what I'm certain is an incredible view. Over the solid, eight-foot door is a stained glass window that was custom made to Meredith's specifications.

It's over the top and ridiculous and, much to my chagrin, kind of awesome.

I pull my truck under a large pine tree next to a white pickup. Haley rolls to a stop behind me. It takes all of two seconds for her feet to hit the lawn. Her attention is momentarily redirected to a man leaning out a third-floor window, but snaps back to the truck in a hurry. She's absolutely adorable with the little scowl that wrinkles her lips as she marches my way.

Her unpainted fingernail pecks on the tinted glass.

Leaning back in my seat, stretching my legs out in front of me, I watch the way the sun caresses her face. A gentleness shines from her deep-brown eyes that lends an air of vulnerability to her otherwise animated expression. Her full lips are twisted as if she can barely stop herself from speaking, and the memory of her incessant rambling in the café makes me chuckle.

She pecks again. As I roll the window down, I wonder if she's always this amusing.

"What is wrong with you?" she asks. The question skips from her lips two seconds before she realizes who I am. Her eyes go wide, brows shooting to the sky, as two and two come together.

I grin. "Good to see you again too."

"What are you doing here?"

"It looks like I'm being stalked."

She steps away from the truck, a grin tickling her lips. "Oh, please."

"Care to explain it another way?"

"If anyone is stalking anyone, it's *you* stalking *me*," she says.

I touch my fingertip to my temple as if I'm mulling that over. "Yeah, there's a big problem with that theory, Ohio. I was at the café *and* this place first. That would make you following me. And if I remember correctly, you were kinda drooling over me this morning, which only lends truth to my hypothesis."

Her cheeks flush in the sweetest shade of pink. My fingers itch to reach out and touch her skin to see if it's warm, to feel the effect of my observation. Instead, I pick up a pen out of a cup holder and fiddle with it.

"Oh, I'm sorry, *Thief*," she says. "Did you think that drool was for you?"

"You're admitting you're a drooler? That's gross."

She shrugs. "I've been known to get a little excited about a doughnut."

"So I've seen." I open the door and step onto the lawn. "Your enthusiasm for pastries knows no bounds."

"You're just jealous I didn't get that excited over you."

I lean closer, my heartbeat picking up at the proximity of our bodies. A slight gasp parts her lips.

"You're so cute when you lie," I whisper.

Her mouth is open to fire back a response when the man from the window joins us. He's my height, well over six foot, and wears a carpenter's belt and a disarming smile.

"I'm taking it you two know each other," he says. He looks at me and extends a hand. "You must be Trevor."

"I am. You must be Dane," I say, giving his hand a firm shake.

"Nice to meet you," Dane says. "Matt, my brother, the one you've been talking to this week, will be here shortly. He's with our third hand, Penn, getting a few things from the lumberyard."

Haley waves her hands in front of her. "Wait. Wait. Hold up. How do you two know each other?"

"Trevor is here from Nashville to inspect the house," Dane explains. "This is going to be your dad's place, right?"

"It is," I say. "In case it's not obvious, my father is going through a midlife crisis."

Dane laughs, rubbing a hand over his head. "It doesn't matter to me as long as he pays my invoices."

"Lucky for you, my father's wife is a bit of a diva. I have a stack of additional projects that will result in a lot more invoices for you."

Haley cuts in. "Don't mind me, but your father's wife would be your stepmother, correct? Or am I missing something?"

"I have a hard time calling someone anything with the word 'mother' in it when she would've been eight when I was born."

Her head goes back and forth as she does the math. "Ooh, I see."

"Yeah. So I stick with 'my father's wife.' It doesn't seem as weird that way."

"That makes sense," Dane says. "So what kind of extra projects are we talking about?"

I suck in a breath and look at the sky. "Have you ever built a poodle spa?"

"A what?" Haley asks, unable to hide her laugh. "A poodle spa? Did you seriously just say that?"

"That's what she called it," I say, lowering my chin. "Sounds ridiculous, I know, but she's kind of . . . What do the kids call it these days? Extra? Yeah. Meredith's kind of extra."

Dane groans. "Mia says that." He looks at me and realizes I have no idea who Mia is. "She's my daughter. She's almost ten. Sometimes *she's* extra."

I can't help but chuckle at the look on his face, like he's in way over his head with a little girl. "She's ten, though, right? I bet she gets extra-extra when she's twenty."

"Dane is completely screwed with Mia." Haley elbows him in the ribs.

I take a step back as I witness Dane and Haley exchanging a knowing look. It's one of those looks that people who know each other intimately share.

Maybe I've misinterpreted her reactions to me. Is that possible?

Surely not.

"Dane has made me tell Mia boys are bad her whole life. You know how some people base their parenting strategy on a religion or a learning technique or something like that? When he hired me as Mia's nanny, my guiding principle was 'boys are bad.'"

"Yeah, you're the nanny." Dane groans. "I hate when you act like you're just an employee or something, cousin."

"Yeah, yeah, yeah," she says, bumping him with her shoulder.

I keep the relief washing over my features unnoticeable. "Cousin" is good. Logical. Keeps her available.

"Probably a good idea, teaching her boys are bad," I say.

"Oh, it's totally a good idea," Haley agrees. "Just like your dad's wife's poodle spa."

Dane shakes his head. "I'll be honest. I don't even know what that is."

"Me either, but she hashed it out on pink, scented paper, just for you," I say.

Haley's smile lights up her face. "I know, or presume, you aren't her biggest fan, but I think I'd love your dad's wife. I think I'd love anyone that wants to build a spa for their poodle. How sweet is that?"

"I have lots of ways of describing it, but sweet isn't on the short list," I tell her. "I don't get her obsession with dogs. She has their toenails painted and these little bows put in their hair. It's so strange."

Dane looks at me in horror. "You aren't kidding, then. She really wants a spa for her dogs?"

"Apparently. I have no idea why."

"I do," Haley says. "Think about it. It's smart. If you have a dog, you have to take it to the groomer's and have it washed and treated for fleas and stuff. It would be a lot easier to have that done at home."

"It would be easier to not have a dog," I say. "They're too much of a commitment."

She huffs. "Well, that says a lot about you."

"Your road rage says a lot about you."

"Oh no," Haley says, jabbing a finger my way. "You instigated that."

"How did I instigate anything when *you* flew up behind *me*?"

"And you slowed down to a crawl."

"A safe crawl," I toss her way.

Bantering with her like this is a game I could play all day. Not just because the way her eyes light up makes everything seem sunnier or because the way her lips turn toward the sky makes me want to laugh for no apparent reason. But also because it's not going to end with her feelings being hurt and I'm not going to be made to feel like a dick for joking around. Hell, she gives as good as she gets.

"And how do you two know each other?" Dane asks. "Because this is obviously not the first time you've met."

"I gave Haley a doughnut this morning," I say, as if that explains everything.

Dane chuckles. "Well, you may not have known her your whole life, but now you'll be friends forever."

"I'm not sure," I say, turning my head to the side. "I think she's kind of irritable. And definitely argumentative."

Haley scowls. "No, I'm not. But I'm not going to stand here and let you act like what happened on the road back there was my fault."

I look at Dane. "See what I mean?"

"Yeah, I get it," he says. "I don't know what to do with her half the time."

"I'm standing right here, thank you very much," Haley says. "But not for long. I do have to go. I have to change clothes before I go to the library."

"Do you have Mia's leotard?" Dane asks.

"Yup. It's in my car." She looks at me out of the corner of her eye. "I was too perturbed by a bad driver to remember to grab it."

"You drive like a bat out of Hell," I say.

"And you drive like a grandpa," she fires back.

"It's a gravel road."

She turns her entire body to face mine. "I was late."

"You'll never get there if you're in a coffin," I say, my body facing hers without thought. "Talk about permanent late-makers."

Dane breaks up the back-and-forth with a loud chuckle. "You two fight like married people."

"If that's what marriage is like, then I'm glad I'm off that path," Haley says.

My gaze drops to her hand to confirm there's no engagement ring on her finger. Still, her words prickle at me.

"Were you married before?" I ask. My tone stays unaffected. It hides the way my stomach clenches as I say the words.

"No," she says. "Not married. Never engaged. And now I'm on a dating hiatus."

"You're on a dating freeze? Does this have anything to do with the hippie?" I ask.

Dane winces. "Do I want to know how he knows about Joel?"

"He sent me a text." She rolls her eyes. "Apparently, he's lonely."

"If you have a date with him, I win," Dane warns. "And while I really wouldn't care if you dated someone you really liked, please don't let it be Joel."

I lean against my truck as Haley bites her lip. The back of my neck tightens as I watch her in this little standoff with Dane. I'd love to give my two cents about her dating this guy, a guy I don't know but still feel pretty opposed to for personal reasons.

Finally, after what feels like an eternity, she sighs. "No. I don't have a date with Joel. But I really do have to go. Wanna follow me to my car and grab Mia's outfit?"

"Sure," Dane says.

I watch them walk away, unable to make out the words of their conversation. Trickles of Haley's voice float on the breeze and twist around my gut.

Her brows furrow as she listens to something Dane's saying. She watches him as if she's hanging on every word. I take a step toward them, as if I have some right to interject myself into their conversation, before I stop. Because I don't. As comfortable and strangely familiar as it is with her, she's still a woman I met an hour ago.

Slipping my hands into my pockets, I shove off my truck and meander around the front of it. A massive horsefly is flattened on the grille. I bend down and inspect it like it's the most interesting thing in the world. Otherwise, I'll keep peeking over the side of the truck at Haley, and that's just weird.

"Hey, Trevor!" Haley's voice rings through the air.

I hop up like a damn bunny to see her leaning on the open car door, a hand on her hip.

"Yeah?" I ask, reflecting her smile back to her.

"If you're afraid of gravel roads, take a right when you leave here. It'll take you an extra ten minutes to get back to town, but you won't have to drive like a geezer."

"Don't you have somewhere to be?" I ask.

Her chest rises, as if reality just caught back up with her, and she nods. "See ya around."

"Later, Ohio," I say.

She climbs into the car, does a quick three-point turnaround, and is gone way too soon.

Dane trudges up the hill, an amused look on his face. "Do I need to worry about you?"

"Worry about me? Why?" I drag my gaze from the driveway to the man at my right.

"There's a certain look on your face that I happen to know intimately."

My brows pull together. "I don't know what you mean."

Dane wipes his forehead with the back of his hand. "She's a great girl. I love her like a little sister. She's taken care of my baby—hell, she's taken care of me—for the last few years."

"I can see her doing that."

"Yeah. She's feisty but as sweet as they come, and that sweetness gets her in trouble sometimes." He stands still, weighing his words. "Look, she can do what she wants. But you and I both know you're not here long, so don't play her out, okay? If you want a girl to entertain you while you're in town—"

"Hey," I say, holding my hands up. "I have no intentions of playing anything or anyone."

He doesn't look convinced. "Do what you will. She's a big girl. But if you do anything to make her cry"—he grins before heading up the hill—"I'll ruin your poodle spa."

"Hey, now," I say, following him. "Let's keep the poodle spa out of this."

He stops at the top of the hill and faces me. There's a hint of trepidation on his face. We watch each other closely.

"All joking aside," I say, "Haley's cool. And I respect you protecting her. But when it comes to me, you just have one thing to be worried about."

"What's that?"

I start toward the house, looking at Dane over my shoulder. "You're going to be in over your head on the puppy suite."

"The puppy suite?"

I step onto the stoop. "Wait until you see these sketches."

Dane mumbles under his breath as he steps inside. After a quick glance at the spot Haley's car occupied near the tree, I follow him.

CHAPTER FIVE

HALEY

I survey the desk littered with book requests, pens, and file folders. This space was the first spot in Dogwood Lane to feel like home. It feels like the end of an era as I toss my personal effects into my bag.

I was welcomed here with open arms the year Mia started all-day preschool. While I never considered I'd stay here forever, it was comfortable. Even though it was unsatisfying from time to time, I wasn't in a hurry to leave. I didn't even jet out of here after getting let go—I stuck around most of the day, helping to get things organized and making sure Sandra, my boss, knows where the files are that she will be needing. Now that I have to leave, my stomach is a little unsure.

"I'm so sorry, Haley," Sandra says. She stops at the front desk, her eyes full of concern. "I did not want to tell you I had to let you go. That's the hardest time I've ever had giving someone news like that."

"It's not your fault. The budget got cut, and to be honest with you, Sandra, I'd rather they trim some of us than shut the whole place down."

Her eyes fill with tears again. "I know. Me too. But I'm so scared that's what's going to happen, Haley. The town isn't growing anymore, and the tax base is shrinking. They just refuse to see the value in the library over filling potholes in the road."

I circle the desk and pull her into a hug. "It'll be all right. I know it. I don't know how, exactly, but I know it will."

Her perfume reminds me of my mother's, the soft fabric of her dress providing the comfort I imagine my mother would give me too. Losing Mom so long ago is a wound that's never quite healed.

"You are such a bright light in the world." Sandra pulls back and touches the side of my face. "If you ever need anything at all, you let me know. You hear me?"

"Of course. And if you need anything, you know where to find me."

I head around the desk and stuff my favorite mug rug into my bag. Sandra brushes her fingers over a waxy plant sitting next to it.

"I hope we don't kill these with you being gone," she says. "You're so good with them."

"Just don't water them too much. That's where you go wrong."

She laughs. "You know, I heard Jennifer is hiring at the flower shop."

"Really?" I look up. "I might check that out."

"It could be a good fit." Tears fill her eyes again. "We're going to miss you around here."

I move around the desk and hug her again. I know she's going to miss me, but I also know the tears are about a lot more than this being my last day. They're the result of a stressful day of letting go of people she cares about and feeling terrible about it.

I get it. I've thought about looking for a job a hundred times over the last couple of years—just something different and more challenging. But I didn't because I didn't want to hurt her feelings. Funny how that works.

"I'll come by to visit," I say, pulling back. "Besides, I've put so many romances on the shelves just because I wanted them, I have to come in to borrow them."

Sandra wipes her eyes. "I do the same thing, but with thrillers. Perks of the job."

"Thanks for everything, Sandra. Not just for the job but also for teaching me to crochet last winter. And that tip on hard-boiling eggs. Game changer right there."

"It's one of my best-kept secrets." The smile fades from her face as I hoist my bag onto my shoulder. "Take care of yourself. Come see me. And call me if you need anything."

With a final smile and a little nod, I head toward the front. Nathaniel, a little ginger-headed boy, sits on a tiny stool. He looks up from a book and waves. I raise my hand before looking away.

My heart twists in my chest as I push open the heavy doors. I rustle through my bag for my keys, and the cool air hits my face as I step outside.

"Hey."

I look up when I hear a familiar voice.

Trevor's truck idles up behind me, the engine purring as he puts it in park. One arm hangs out the window, his fingertips strumming against the black paint.

My heartbeat ramps up, purring right along with Trevor's truck's engine. I take in the glimmer of mischief in his eyes and drop my keys on the pavement.

"Before you say a word, I was just driving through town and saw the library," he says.

"That makes total sense," I say, picking up my key ring. My stomach somersaults at the smirk he throws my way. "You just drove by and found the library so interesting you pulled in. Got it. What book are you looking to check out? I have an in if you want to request something specific."

He bites his lip, a dimple settling into his left cheek. "I was thinking one on the best bed-and-breakfasts in the area might be helpful."

"Are you staying in town?"

"Yes. Meredith's changes are pretty overwhelming, and there are a lot of them. Dad and Meredith are hell-bent on moving in right after he retires in a couple of weeks, so I need to make sure there are no hiccups."

"Look at you, being all logical. I have to say, I had you pegged as someone more . . ."

I tap my chin, looking at him like I'm unsure how to describe my thoughts. The word I want is on the tip of my tongue. But the longer I look at the muscles that stretch from his shoulders up the sides of his neck and the way the skin bunches at the corners of his eyes when he's ready to laugh, the word seems to vanish into thin air.

"Someone what?" he prods.

"Someone more impulsive," I say, throwing out the first word that comes to me.

His eyes light up. "I think you're projecting. If I remember the details correctly, and trust me when I say not one slipped by me, you were the one bent over a bar this morning for a pastry."

I turn away as he laughs. My cheeks are on fire—not because of his words, but from the look on his face. Like he does remember what I looked like and maybe, just maybe, he didn't mind it.

"Guess I was right," I say, hitting the unlock button. My trinkets jingle inside my bag as I toss it in the back seat. "You aren't a gentleman."

When I turn around to face him again, the levity is gone. He's watching me with a somberness that roots me in place. "Can I ask how today went? Or is that something people who just met this morning don't ask?"

"Are you trying to be courteous now?"

He shrugs. "Not really. I just . . . wondered."

I lean against my car and tug my sweater around me. "Budget cuts made them get rid of all expendable items and positions, and I, unfortunately, am expendable."

"That's a terrible thing to say."

37

"It's not terrible if it's true." Sandra's comment about the flower shop flutters through my mind, carrying a bubble of excitement with it. "I like to think that when one door closes, another opens. I just have to find the door, I guess."

"Look at you, being all logical," he teases, throwing my words back at me.

"I don't know what else to do. This is an opportunity to do something else. That's how I have to look at it, and not like it's a strain on my doughnut budget."

He grins. "God forbid something hurts your doughnut affair."

"Right?"

He shifts in his seat, his fingers rewrapping around the steering wheel. "How about we have an early dinner and discuss this more in depth? I bet you're a little more sensitive than you're letting on, and being that I know a ton about budgets, I could probably make you feel good about everything before the night was said and done."

"Is that what you tell all the ladies?" I wink.

He laughs. "Touché."

Despite the way his offer tempts me and causes a flicker of excitement to jump in my belly, sharing a meal with him would be a giant, gorgeous distraction I don't need.

"I better not. I have a lot of thinking to do," I say. "As a matter of fact, I'm canceling on Claire tonight too. I just need to be alone for a while."

"Fair enough. But if you ever want to talk budgets, I'm your guy. Or if you want to go over ways to feel good . . ."

I laugh, rolling my eyes at his invitation. "I'm good. Thanks. I took some college classes in accounting, so I get it. Budgets are budgets."

"You're a math geek like me?"

"No," I scoff. "I just took some general classes. Dad is an accountant, so I had a built-in tutor."

"You were almost perfect."

"I've heard that a time or two. Thanks for the offer, though."

"Yeah. Sure." He cocks his head to the side. "What do you think you'll do from here?"

"Heck if I know. That's why I said I have a lot of thinking to do. The world is my oyster, even though I don't really understand that analogy."

He smiles brightly. "Well, if you've read *The Merry Wives of Windsor*, Shakespeare uses it to mean taking what you want by force or violence."

"And how did you know that?"

He laughs, pointing at himself. "Nerd. Remember?"

He gazes into the distance. I gaze at him. There's something even sexier about him now, something I can't quite shake.

Something that completely and utterly rules out me going anywhere alone with him right now.

"You're staring again."

I jump at his voice. "I wasn't staring," I lie. "I was thinking about something else."

"Oh, I'm sure you were."

"Actually," I say, thinking on my feet, "I was pondering this new chapter in my life."

He glances in his rearview mirror. A car pulls into the parking lot but takes a spot behind him. He turns his attention back to me and studies me for a long time, the weight of his attention on me almost cozy.

"What's your biggest dream?" he asks out of nowhere.

"I don't know. What's yours?"

His forehead creases as he pops his bottom lip between his teeth. He works it back and forth for a minute. "I think I'm living it. As lame as that sounds."

"Why?" I press.

"I'm my own boss, more or less. I deal with numbers all day. I work with my brother. Sometimes I get to go outside and play in the dirt."

He grins an easy, simple-yet-heated smile that turns my core into mush. "Sometimes I run into beautiful women who refuse to have dinner with me. Now your turn."

I swallow, trying to wrangle my wits from his grasp. "I'm not sure, to be honest. But you know what? I do need to go."

There's a cloud that passes over his eyes. It dims the sparkle only for a moment, but it's long enough for me to notice.

My stomach flops, wishing I could climb into his truck and continue this conversation. But what's the point in that?

"Fine," he teases, the light back in his eyes again. "Your loss."

Probably so.

I smack his arm, my palm connecting with his wrist. A giggle escapes my lips but gently rolls away as our eyes meet.

My hand drops to my side, still warm from the contact. I clear my throat.

"So," he says, clearing his, too, "when I rolled in, I saw a sign for the Dogwood Inn. Is that open?"

"Yeah. It's open most of the year. I bet you can find a room. Just plan on 1980s decor. It's way old school in there."

His eyes go wide. "What are my other options?"

"Drive about twenty minutes back the way you came into town and stay there." I shrug. "We have one place here. Just be glad it's not hunting season. You'd be out of luck."

"Seriously?"

"Seriously." I open my door and stick my keys in the ignition. "If you stay in town, just remember that everything closes before ten o'clock. If you need food or whatever, grab it while you can. And," I say, getting into my car, "if Lorene offers you a slice of pie, take it."

He puts his truck in drive. "Is that an innuendo?"

I snort. "Tell you what—you meet Lorene and then decide what I meant."

"Are you setting me up?"

I just laugh, imagining his face when he meets the ninety-year-old church pianist at the inn.

He leans out the window ever so slightly, his hand extended my way. "Are you sure I can't take you for some ice cream? Or pizza? Or whatever? All joking aside, I feel like you've had a rough day, and I just don't want you going home and feeling like crap."

My heartbeat picks up. The cab of my car feels overly warm as I sit beneath his gaze. "I'm sure. Thank you for offering, though."

His lips part as if he's going to say something, but they close. He switches his sight onto something in front of him before looking back at me again. "Drive like you have some sense."

"Try to go the speed limit."

He shakes his head and pulls away.

CHAPTER SIX

HALEY

"D o you want to take some of this home?" Dane asks. He holds up
the pan half-full of lasagna. "Neely made enough to feed a small
army. We have more than enough left."

"I'm so full that I never want to see lasagna again," I say, rubbing
my stomach. "It was really good, Neely."

She beams. "Thank you. It's my mom's recipe. It makes a mess of
the kitchen, but it's worth it."

"That's why you have Mia," I say, elbowing the little girl in the side.
"Make her clean it up."

"Hey," Mia protests. "I have homework to do."

Dane tugs her ponytail as he walks by. "Then you better put Haley's
phone down and get upstairs and do it. Otherwise, start rinsing the
dishes and putting them in the dishwasher."

Mia makes a face, drops my phone into my lap, and sprints up the
stairs. As her steps grow fainter, my heart squeezes.

When Dane proposed to Neely, he bought her Malone's Farm outside town. They'll be moving soon, starting their lives together. This
makes me ridiculously happy for them, but after today's events, it also
makes me feel a little sad. It's another chapter coming to a close.

"That's one way to get homework done," Dane says. He grabs the bag of trash by the door and takes it outside.

I get up from the table, grabbing my dishes and Mia's, and take them to the sink. As I rinse the plates, Neely opens the refrigerator. Out comes a bottle of wine.

"Want some?" she asks me. "This is from a winery in New York. My friend Grace and I used to try to go there once a month. This one is our favorite. It's super sweet."

"Wine makes me sappy." I put the plates in the dishwasher. "After the day I've had, I probably need to pass."

She sets the bottle on the counter and frowns. "Dane told me about the library. I'm sorry, Haley."

"Yeah, well, don't be sorry for me." I close the dishwasher and lean against it. "I just hope they don't close the doors forever. If the library goes, it'll feel like the heart of Dogwood Lane will be gone. Then what happens?"

"I don't know." She frowns. "What's next for you?"

"I'm not sure," I say.

Neely grabs a rag and wipes off the counter. "I feel your pain. There was a time not long ago when I wasn't sure what was next for me. But I found it, and I'm proof that sometimes you have to let go of any preconceived ideas about what's right for you and just let the universe take its course."

"That's true. I wish I would've finished a degree at some point. That would probably help."

"There's actually a big demand these days for jobs you don't need a degree for. Everyone clamored for diplomas for so long that there're shortages in a lot of areas."

"I'm not laying bricks or something," I say.

"Speaking of things getting laid," Neely says coyly, "Dane told me about a guy on the site today."

The twinkle in her eye grows as I shift my weight.

Trevor has been on my mind all evening. I've wondered more than a couple of times if I made the right decision by not going with him.

I'm curious if he got a room at the inn and what he had for his early dinner. What does a guy like that think about a boring night in Dogwood Lane?

I could've known all that had I gone with him, but I didn't. And I'm glad I said no. As much as the curiosity is killing me, it feels good to have stuck to my guns—especially with a guy like him.

My cheeks flush. "What's that have to do with me?"

"Oh, I don't know," Neely teases. "Dane said you two seemed to hit it off."

"I don't know about that," I say lightly. "I met him this morning, so by the time I saw him at the house, I guess you could say we established a rapport."

"Which is . . ."

I laugh. "Which doesn't lead to anyone getting laid."

Dane comes in and makes a face. "Let's not talk about you getting laid."

He moves through the kitchen, kissing the top of Neely's head as he helps clear the rest of the dinner dishes. They work quietly side by side, the respect and trust obvious between them.

That's what I want more than anything in the world—more than any job or loaded bank account. I want the look on Neely's face in this very moment. I want to know what *that* feels like, and not so much what getting dumped via text feels like.

"What are you thinking?" Neely asks, pouring herself a generous glass of wine.

"That dating is kind of like being in the Colosseum," I say. "One minute, the crowd is chanting your victory. The next second, a lion is rushing from the gate, ready to rip your heart out."

"You try too hard," Dane chimes in. "You try to make these assholes happy and sacrifice your happiness in the process."

"No one asked you," I say, reaching for the bottle of wine. I pour myself a small glass as I shove Dane's observation out of my head.

"For what it's worth, even though I wasn't asked," Dane says, "I think Trevor is a decent enough guy."

Neely whirls around with a gasp. "Did you just say he was nice? You never like people. Men, specifically."

"He and I talked some today," Dane says. "He's smart and made solid decisions about the job. Seemed pretty nice, and his family is loaded."

The back door opens, and Dane's best friend, Penn Etling, strolls in. "Who is loaded?" He runs a hand across his dark hair, his sleeve of colorful tattoos flexing in the light. "Haley's here. How's my girl?"

I laugh. "I'm not your girl, Penn."

"But you could be."

"You could also wipe the lipstick off your neck from whomever you were just sucking face with before you come trying to sweet-talk me," I say. His hand clamps his neck, his eyes going wide. "I'm just kidding. You fall for that every time."

"I was just surprised there was lipstick on my neck since I haven't sucked face, as you so eloquently put it, with anyone in a while," he says.

"So two hours?" Neely jokes.

"Try since last night."

Neely sets down her glass. "Penn, can you learn to knock? Please."

"I'll try. Old dog, new tricks, and all that." He spies the pan of lasagna on the table. "Why did no one invite me for dinner?"

"Because I've worked with you all day," Dane says. "I need a break."

"That's what my mom just told me too." He grabs a breadstick and hops onto the counter. "So what are we talking about?"

"Trevor, I think his name is," Neely says, keeping an eye on me. "What do you think about him, Penn?"

"I think he's staying in town tonight," Penn says. Half the breadstick goes into his mouth.

"He said he was going to see about getting a room at the Dogwood Inn," I offer. I pick at a crumb on the counter and try not to let it be known I'm interested.

Neely raises a brow. "Should we read anything into you having that information?"

"Ah, Haley. Don't break my heart," Penn says, a hand covering the Saint Christopher's necklace hanging from his neck.

"I didn't think you had a heart, Penn," I tease.

"Only for you, babe."

Neely laughs, taking a seat at the island next to Dane. "Do you have plans to see Trevor?"

"No," I say, ignoring Penn's fist pump. "He just mentioned it this afternoon at the library."

Dane holds up a hand. "Wait. He was at the library? You saw him this morning at the café, at the jobsite, and then at the library?"

"I'm jealous." Penn shoves the rest of the breadstick into his mouth. "Not fair."

"He was just driving by the library as I was about to leave. No big deal and not hard to do in this town," I say, staring at the crumb from Penn's breadstick in front of me.

While that's all true, it sounds different out loud. It could be construed that maybe, possibly, it wasn't a coincidence at the library. That maybe, possibly, he was looking for me.

I gulp as I look up.

My friends' stares are heavy, their smiles—everyone except Penn's—uncomfortable. I take a long drink of wine and look at my phone instead of dealing with them.

The home screen is locked with a picture of Mia and me at a church ice-cream social over the summer. She's sticking her blue-tinted tongue out at the camera as I make a duck face. And just like that, my thoughts go from the church to Lorene, and back to Trevor.

"Maybe you'll run into him again," Neely says carefully. "Like you said, it's not hard to do in this town."

"It doesn't matter if I do or don't."

"Damn right," Penn says. "He's not your type."

"Oh, really?" I ask, turning to face him. "What's my type, Penn?"

He looks down at his body, holding his arms out like he's giving himself a once-over. "I'd say five-ten. Stocky build. Dark hair. Tattoos. Charming."

"That puts you out of the running," Neely teases.

Penn grabs another breadstick and waves it toward her. "I've always liked you. Until now." He chomps off the end of the breadstick.

I take a lungful of air and let it out slowly. My insides are still buzzed with talk and thoughts of Trevor. But in a very un-Haley-like way, I'm not obsessed with it. And I didn't text Joel again today either. It's progress.

"You know what, Dane?" I ask. "You might be right. I might've tried so hard for guys to like me that I jumped into their arms."

"I don't recall you ever jumping into mine," Penn says. "Just saying."

"There's a reason for that," I tell him. "Maybe two. Or ten."

"I'm here when you need me," Penn says. "Now that we've settled that, I need to go. I'm meeting a girl in twenty."

Dane starts laughing. "And you wonder why no one takes you seriously, man."

"What?" he asks. "I would've called it off with her if Haley had taken me up on my offer." He looks at me. "You're always my first choice, babe."

"Gee, thanks."

"You're welcome. And if things don't work out and you wanna relieve some stress, you know where to find me." He grabs another breadstick, shoots me a wink, and disappears as quickly as he showed up.

Neely laughs. "That boy is a mess."

"Always," Dane grumbles.

I grab my phone and shove it in my pocket. "I'm going to say good night to Mia and then head home. I need a hot bath and a notepad."

"Um . . ." Neely raises a brow. "A notepad?"

"To take notes," I say. "In all honesty, I'm feeling excited. I need to get a plan together. Or two. Or three."

"Slow down, Tiger," Dane says.

"I have bills to pay. I just need to figure something out." I think once again of the flower shop and smile. "Hopefully this wine doesn't put me to sleep before I can get my head wrapped around everything."

"You drank three mouthfuls," Dane points out.

"I'm a lightweight."

"We might be out back when you come downstairs," Neely says. "I tried to restore an old table today, and I want to show Dane. I can't figure out what I'm doing wrong."

I head toward the stairs. "That's fine. I'll let myself out."

"See you later," Neely says.

"Thanks for dinner."

"Anytime."

I bound up the stairs, leaving their voices behind me.

❦

Trevor

My stomach growls. It's a loud, raucous-sounding gargle emitting from my gut, reminding me I haven't eaten anything since the protein bar before I left home this morning. Much to my dismay, the Dogwood Inn doesn't offer dinner.

I drop onto the white duvet covered in little purple flowers and look around the room. The walls are cream with a floral-print border. A television just a bit bigger than a large pizza box sits on top of a dresser that's currently white but that I'd bet my last dollar has at least five layers of paint beneath it.

It's so quiet I can hear myself breathe. There are no sirens, no car alarms, no dogs barking from a neighboring yard. I'm not sure what to do with myself.

Grabbing my phone out of my pocket, I dial my brother.

"Well," he says, answering on the second ring, "how's it going?"

"The site looks great, actually. The guys we hired are thorough as hell. I figured I'd get here and find a hundred corners cut, but there's not one I can find. Everything is done to a *T*."

Jake whistles. "That's shocking."

"I know, right?"

"A guy I know used them on a remodel a while back. Said they did a real good job, but you never know how that's gonna go," he says.

The bed moans as I stand. My shoes sink into the thick shag carpet as I plod my way over to the window.

A barn sits a few hundred yards back. A couple of horses stand in the field surrounding it, the breeze blowing their manes like something in a kids' movie.

"Where are you staying?" Jake asks.

"Got a room at an inn, believe it or not. I'm looking at a horse right now."

"Sounds terrible."

"Nah, it's not." I scratch my head. "Weirdly."

"I'm reading that pause to mean the real reason it's not terrible is pussy related," Jake says. "You already got one lined up, don't you?"

"No," I say quickly. "Nothing like that."

"You sure?"

My thumb brushes against my lip as I try not to laugh at myself. No, I'm not sure. But I'm not *not* sure either. All I know is staying here doesn't sound as bad as it might have this morning.

Maybe it's because I'm relieved not to have to deal with Liz. It's possible I don't want to go back and sit in an empty house. I really don't want to have dinner with Dad and Meredith and listen to her go on and on about her dogs and interior design. Any way you cut it, being here and staying busy for a few days seems preferable.

The chance of running into Haley again doesn't sound too bad either.

"You're totally not sure," Jake says.

I turn away from the window. "You know what? Fuck off."

Jake laughs. He knows me well enough to leave this alone.

"I kind of like it here," I say.

"No. Nope. You are not joining the dark side with Meredith. I refuse to let that happen."

I laugh. "I just mean it's not terrible. You might even like it."

"No. It's Meredith's place. I hate it on principle."

"Speaking of Meredith," I say. "You should've seen Dane's reaction to the poodle spa."

"It probably looked similar to mine when I heard about it. And we are not putting that in our portfolio." Jake groans. "It's almost embarrassing."

"Almost? Try again." I yawn, my arms stretching high over my head. "I need to go. I'm starving." A grin slips across my face as I think of Haley and her warning to get my stuff before ten.

"Tell her I said hi," Jake says.

"Who?"

"Whoever you're thinking about."

"You're outta your mind," I say with a laugh.

"I'm gonna be if I don't get out of this office soon." He blows out a hefty breath. "What does sunshine look like? I don't remember."

I lug my bag onto the bed and rummage through it. "Take a day off tomorrow and come up here. Get some sunshine, fresh air, check out the house."

"I have no interest in seeing Dad's love nest. Thanks."

"We're getting paid for it."

"Like we're charging him what we'd charge someone else. We're just covering costs and a little overhead."

A paperback I've been reading for a couple of weeks is buried at the bottom of my bag. I retrieve it and toss it on the bed. "That's your fault. I thought it was fine to charge him full price."

"Yeah, well, I'm trying to be the change I want to see in the world."

I chuckle. "And what change is that?"

"A world where everyone isn't ready to fuck you over."

Mom's face floats through my brain, and by the way Jake grumbles under his breath, I bet he's thinking of her too. Shaking it off, I redirect our conversation.

"If you change your mind about coming down here, let me know," I say.

"Nah, I'm good. I have enough messes here to keep me busy. The meeting this afternoon went better than expected, but I still have to rework an entire schedule."

"Suit yourself. I gotta go before the town shuts down." I get to my feet. "I'll send you some pictures of the Love Nest tomorrow."

"No. Don't. I don't need or want that visual."

I grab my keys and wallet off the nightstand and stick them in my pocket. Heading out the door, I switch off the light. "Talk to you later, Jake."

"Bye."

The door to my room shuts behind me.

CHAPTER SEVEN

TREVOR

My headlights shine on a hand-painted sign spelling out the words GRABER'S GROCERY in bright-red letters. It's the only thing open in town besides a gas station and a place called Mucker's. The latter is the size of a shoebox and looks packed.

I kill the engine and step onto the asphalt. The air hints at winter's rapid approach. I shove my hands into my pockets, letting a shiver roll down my spine as I walk into the small market.

There's one checkout line open. The girl working the lane has to be fresh out of high school. She looks at me, much to her current customer's dismay, before giving me a wide, warm smile as a welcome.

I wave, chuckling to myself that I beat her to it, and grab a cart.

The place is quiet. There are random shoppers here and there as I walk the length of the store. Country music from the nineties trickles through speakers nestled somewhere overhead as I try to locate a deli counter or a sandwich.

"Can I help you find anything?" A man crouched at the base of the cereal display takes off his hat.

"I'm just looking for a sandwich. I didn't realize there wasn't any fast food in this town until now. And the café is closed."

He grins, getting to his feet. "A burger chain tried to come in here a couple of years ago, but the town council ran them off. Said it would hurt local businesses, which I suppose meant the café and Mucker's, as that's all we have."

"Mucker's looked busy. Good food?"

"Yeah. Kinda famous for their pizza around here. And the Rocket Razzle, but those'll put you on your behind if you don't watch out."

"Good to know," I say. "So sandwich? I'm not picky. Just starving."

He nods. "Yeah. Sorry. Keep going down until you get to the dairy section, then swing a left. There'll be something over there to get you to morning."

"Thanks."

"Hey, no problem."

He goes back to stocking shelves as I head toward the dairy case. I spy a cooler loaded with sandwiches. A turkey and cheese appears to be my best option. Swiping a bag of chips and a stick of beef jerky, I make my way back to the front.

A jet-black ponytail sticks up above the candy rack in front of me—a ponytail I recognize.

My skin warms as I approach her quietly. Her hair is swishing back and forth, a phone to her ear, and I bet dimes to doughnuts she's giving someone else hell. I'm kind of jealous.

I quell a laugh as I take a wide berth around a frozen foods display. As I come up behind her, a smile instantly graces my lips.

"No," she says into the phone that's sandwiched between her ear and shoulder. "I had dinner with Dane and Neely. And Penn, actually." She shifts her weight on her sneakers as she listens. "No. I'm not sure, but there are always options." She listens again. "Well, that probably would be the best option, but the chance of that is zero."

Her laugh rolls straight to me, like she emitted the sound for my own personal enjoyment. It lifts the sides of my mouth as I listen to her rattle on.

"The answer is no," she says. "Now I gotta go. Someone is waiting on me." She laughs again, joggling her items in her arms. "No. *Not him.* I'm at Graber's. Goodbye, Claire."

She slips her phone off her shoulder and shoves it in the pocket of her hoodie.

I stand still, biting back a grin. There's something about the way she said that that makes me think she might have been talking about me. If Jake were here, he'd call it narcissism, but I'll take my chances.

"Not *him* who?" I ask.

She whirls around, her ponytail almost hitting me in the face. A look of shock flits across her face before it's replaced with a tongue-in-cheek smile. "It's you."

"It's me that's 'not him,' or it's me standing here?" I grin. "Because, clearly, this is me. But am I him?"

"You're kind of annoying. You know that?"

"I've heard that a time or two."

Her shoulders rise and fall. "They say if more than two people tell you something, it's probably true."

"Really? I've never heard that."

"Yeah, really. Maybe you should give it some thought."

"Like the thought you're giving . . . him? Whoever *him* might be?"

She places her items on the conveyor belt. "I love that you hear me talking about a guy and you immediately assume it's you."

"So you're saying I'm wrong?"

I shouldn't prod. I know better. It's futile, anyway, since I know the answer. If I weren't sure, the way she masks the nerves in her voice would tell me all I need to know. I'm him. And for reasons I don't care to ponder, I like it.

"Yes, you're wrong," she says. "I wasn't talking about you."

"Who were you talking about then?"

She crosses her arms over her chest. "If you must know, I was talking about Penn."

"Penn Etling? The guy I met at the jobsite today?" I think back to the stocky friend of Dane's who showed up with Dane's brother, Matt. "You expect me to believe you have something for *that guy?*"

"Who said anything about having a thing for him?"

"Uh, you did. With the little giggle you had when you were talking about him." I cock my head to the side and smirk. "You know, *him.* Whoever-he-was-not, named Penn."

With a roll of her eyes that almost looks painful, she turns away from me. "Hi, Shandi," she says to the girl ringing up her items. "How are you tonight?"

Shandi looks at me and bats her eyelashes. "Tonight is getting better."

"Please," Haley says, "don't flatter him. His ego is already too big for this building."

"Well, I mean, he is tall, dark, and handsome." Shandi looks at me and grins before looking back at Haley. "That's twelve dollars and eighty cents."

Haley mumbles something incoherent and sticks her card in the machine. It fires back a buzzing sound. She reinserts but it just buzzes in response. "What's the matter with this thing?"

"They updated our system," Shandi says. "Which is code for they broke it. It's been doing this all night."

Another attempt results in another buzz. Haley removes her card with an irritated flourish. "Well, I have no cash."

"Here," I say, sliding my items down the belt. "Ring up mine and I'll pay for both."

"That would be a negative, sir," Haley says.

"Why?"

"That would be two nice things you've done for me today, and I don't want to make this a thing."

"Make what a thing? Me doing nice things for you? Besides, this is the third thing. Doughnut. Coffee. Groceries."

She gives me a dirty look that makes me want to grab her and kiss the shit out of her.

"I'd like him to do nice things for me," Shandi whispers as she slides my items across the scanner. "With Haley's, that's nineteen forty."

I hand her a twenty and watch Haley's face twist.

"Well, look at that," I say, walking around her and lifting her bag. "I bought you dinner." Peeking inside, I raise a brow. "I hope a pint of ice cream and a container of strawberries isn't dinner."

"No, it's not," she says, taking the bag from me. "I had lasagna for dinner, thank you."

"With Penn?"

She raises a brow, taunting me. "I didn't have dinner with him, but I did see him at dinner."

"Interesting."

"Is it?" she asks, heading toward the doors.

Only because you're involved.

"Slightly," I say, following her. "Not as interesting as if you would've seen the hippie. That conversation would've been riveting."

She glances at me with mischievous eyes. "I didn't say I didn't talk to the hippie tonight."

"And . . ." I make a hurry-up motion with my hand. "Spill. I'm dying over here."

"I told him not to call again."

A boy pushing a line of carts cuts in front of us. We stop to give him room to get in the door.

"I'm less riveted than I thought I would be," I admit. "I really thought that conversation would go somewhere."

"Well, being that the relationship didn't go anywhere, I'm not sure why the conversation should. Besides, I'm on a dating hiatus, remember?"

"Yeah, about that. Let's discuss."

"Let's not."

"Come on," I goad. "A girl like you intentionally not dating has to have a good story behind it. What is it? You tired of beating men off with a stick?" I grin. "Or other things?"

She gasps like she's shocked, but it dissolves into a laugh. "You're impossible." Her bag swings at her side as she steps into the night air.

I stand next to the gumball machine and watch her walk away. A dose of satisfaction rumbles through my body. Whether it's from her turning down Joel or knowing she's turning down every guy who asks, I'm not sure. What I am sure of is that her ass looks amazing in those sweatpants.

She glances at me over her shoulder. I speed-walk to catch up.

The parking lot is dimly lit, more light coming from the full moon overhead than from the flickering halogen lamps above. We stop at my truck.

She peers up at me. Her face is void of any makeup. Little creases that I didn't see earlier today form at the corners of her eyes, and somehow, it makes her prettier.

"Thanks for picking up my tab," she says. "My dad always tells me to keep a twenty in my pocket, but I never do."

"Solid advice. My dad's advice isn't as good."

"What's he say?" she asks.

I unlock my truck and set my bag in the seat. "My favorite one might be to bewilder them with bullshit."

"What does that even mean?"

"Well, Dad's an attorney. He always told my brother and me that when you can't dazzle someone with facts, you bewilder them with bullshit. Just overwhelm them with so many opinions and so much misdirection that they don't even want to fight."

"That seems . . . helpful?" She laughs, shivering against the cold metal truck. "I think."

"It is if you have a line of bullshit ready."

"Do you?" She twists her lips.

"Sometimes. Depends on the topic at hand."

I watch her shiver again. I hold up a finger. Fishing around in the back seat, it's a long minute before I find what I'm looking for.

I climb back out. In my hand is a gray jacket. "Here."

She eyes me warily.

"Just take it," I say, shaking my head. "You're shivering."

"My car is right there." She motions a few spots over. "I could just go get in and turn on the heat."

"You could. But I don't see you moving that way." I shake the jacket as her eyes grow wide. "I'm kidding. Just put this on, will ya?"

She reaches cautiously, her fingers wrapping around the fabric. "If this is your way of making me owe you forever, I'll have you know I'm not a woman of my word and I don't feel obligated to make good on any outstanding debts."

"I figured as much."

She slips my jacket over her narrow shoulders. The fabric swamps her, hanging well past her hips and over her wrists. She holds up her hands. The sleeves bunch at her elbows, making her laugh. "I bet my dad would have something to say about wearing random men's jackets."

She snuggles into the fabric, pulling the collar closer to her face. I can imagine her huddled under blankets and watching a movie or bundled up outside and playing in the snow. Her eyes glisten like a girl who's had a good life, and I wonder what kind of family she comes from.

"What's your dad like?" I ask. "If you don't mind my prying."

"Well, like I told you before, he's an accountant. Very exact about things. Precise. Very busy." She groans. "He married my mother when they were eighteen years old, and they were married until she passed away."

"I'm sorry, Haley."

"Thanks. It was a long time ago." She leans against my truck again. "What about your dad? What's he like?"

"He's worked relentlessly ever since I can remember. Divorced my mom and married this new girl he says is the love of his life." I shrug. "We've butted heads a time or two, but he's a good guy. Would give you the shirt off his back if you needed it."

"You're a lot like him, huh?" Her voice is an octave lower than it's been. Her brows raise in surprise, like the question was offhand, but she doesn't retract it.

Under normal circumstances, I'm quick to point out the differences between Branson Kelly and myself. This time, I'm happy to take the comparison.

With a half grin, I look at the woman in front of me. "Are you saying I'm a good guy, Miss Raynor?"

"I'm saying you just gave me the shirt that wasn't on your back, but same thing."

We exchange a smile, a stripped-down gesture that makes me forget all about the cool air. Her breath is visible in the chill as she speaks.

"I better get going." She starts to shrug off my jacket, but I stop her. "No, keep that."

"I'm not going to keep it," she says. "Who knows if I'll ever see you again to give it back?"

Our eyes grip each other in the narrow space between us. Her movement slows as something unspoken passes in our gazes.

"This place is pretty small," I say. "We've run into each other four times today."

"Because you're stalking me."

I grin. "Maybe I'll stalk you tomorrow and get my jacket back."

She doesn't look convinced, but doesn't finish taking it off either.

"Go on," I press. "Get in your car so I can get in mine and leave. I don't have a jacket and I'm freezing."

She pulls the jacket around her as a soft smile graces her lips. "I'll leave it at the café if I don't see you tomorrow, okay?"

Despite the cold temperature, my body hums with a warmth that's hard to identify. There's no way I won't try to see her tomorrow, and I'm pretty sure she won't hide from running into me either. As insane as it sounds to be happy about this, I am.

"You do that. Now hurry up. I can't leave until I know you're in your car with the doors locked."

She shakes her head but turns toward her car. "This is Dogwood Lane, you know. Nothing bad happens here."

"You just jinxed the whole town, Haley. Good work."

Her laughter hangs in the air even after her door closes. I swear I can still hear it as I pull out behind her and turn the opposite way.

CHAPTER EIGHT
HALEY

"Yuck."

I toss the toast with grape jelly into the trash. The single bite sitting in my stomach feels like too much, and coupled with the ice cream I ate entirely too late last night when I couldn't sleep, it probably *is* too much.

That's what happens when my brain is too busy to let me sleep. I stay up and snack and wake up feeling gross.

Brushing my hands off over the sink, I gaze out the window. The sky is bright and clear. High, wispy clouds float by, allowing sunshine to filter through the trees.

The music playing on my computer changes songs. I do my best rendition of the cha-cha as I wipe the counter off with a damp rag, singing along to a tune I really don't know the words to.

Tossing the rag in the sink, I stop at my computer perched on the counter. Two tabs are open. The first has a listing of jobs in the area. The second has a list of degrees offered at the community college in Rockery, the next town over. I've toggled between the two of them all morning, trying to see if my gut will tell me which way to go. Besides churning with chocolate–peanut butter ice cream, it's relatively silent . . . except when I think about Sandra's comment about the flower shop. I made a decision last night to check it out today. It can't hurt.

My gaze rolls over the tiny kitchen. When the chairs are pulled out from the table, there's no room to walk. It's cozy and warm and perfect for me and Mia when she's around. The Realtor couldn't believe it was a selling point when I bought the place; she was fully expecting to have to try to gloss over the fact it was so small.

Trevor's jacket sits on the back of one of the chairs. I laugh out loud, thinking of the way it hung nearly to my knees and how I tripped coming into the house last night. My mind wants to keep going, circling around to the way he teased me in line at Graber's, but I stop myself.

I pick up the notepad I had last night. Between the rows of flowers I doodled while watching a travel show on television is a list of things I love. Coffee. Doughnuts. Books. Flowers. Naps. Well-defined abs. Trevor's cologne.

"Nope," I say, shaking my head. "Not going there. Let's focus on . . ." I scan the other side of the sheet—the one with more practical things listed—and ignore the burn in my belly. "A résumé. I need one, and I don't know how to do that."

My phone buzzes in my pocket. I set the notepad down and grab it. "Hello?"

"Are you busy?" Claire asks.

"Hello to you too."

"Hi. Hello, Haley. How is your morning, love?"

I laugh at her antics. "Oh, shut up. What's going on?"

"Is there any way in the universe you can bring me a hair tie?"

"Are you kidding me?"

"No," she whines. "This one is about to snap. I feel it, and I can't leave and grab another one because I'm the only one here for an hour or so. If this sucker breaks, I'll have to use one of the thick rubber bands in the office, and those get stuck in my hair and I have to rip them out and it hurts. Hey, can you hang on for a second?"

"Sure."

My heartbeat picks up as I slide my arms into Trevor's jacket. I burrow into the fleece lining, dragging in a lungful of air that washes a warmth to my cheeks. It smells like him, all masculine and divine. My thighs ache as I grab my keys off the table and a hair tie out of my purse and make my way out the door.

The air is cool against my face despite the late-morning sun. I tug the fabric around me a little tighter and head down the sidewalk, figuring the exercise might do me some good.

"I'm back," Claire says. "If I wouldn't have called you, no one would've needed a darn thing. I call you and—voilà!—people need coffee. I don't get it."

"Well, you *are* at work. It's not hard to believe people want coffee."

"You know what I mean." She groans. "Anyway, hair tie—you bringing me one or not?"

"You know I'm bringing you one. I'm already out the door."

"This is why I love you more than other people. You never fail."

"That's my purpose in life: never fail Claire."

"Attagirl." She laughs into the line. "Guess who came in this morning."

I wave at the neighbor man watching his dog pee in his front lawn. My lips twist in a smile because I know who she's talking about, but I'm not about to tell her that. "No clue."

She giggles. "Seems as though Trevor stayed in town last night."

The sound of his name splashes me with a warmth I can't explain. The coat suddenly is too hot.

I force myself to steady. "Oh."

"Why do I feel like this doesn't surprise you?"

"Because it doesn't," I say as offhandedly as I can muster.

"Because . . ."

"Because he might've mentioned that he needed to stay a few days until the house is solid," I say.

She sighs dreamily. "You should've seen him. He was adorable, Haley. He sat with Lorene. I overheard them talking about him staying at the inn. And if my eavesdropping skills are as good as I think they are, he did some projects for her this morning."

I imagine Trevor on a ladder, hanging a wreath on the inn's door, and little ninety-year-old Lorene watching him. It's a vision that's sweet and sexy, and it makes my insides go squishy.

"I bet Lorene is smitten," I say.

"Oh, she is. She kept patting his hand and telling him he was a good boy." Claire laughs.

I cross the street in front of the church with the musket balls from the Civil War lodged in the steeple. Across the street sits the post office, and next to it, Buds and Branches. Baskets of wine-colored mums line the steps leading into the flower shop.

My stride falters as I realize I have walked right to the shop and didn't even realize it.

"So what are you doing today, anyway?" Claire asks.

"Job hunting."

"You sound way too happy to be job hunting."

"Well, I guess I kind of am. Might be fun."

"What kind of thing are you considering?" she asks.

I look at the beautiful window of Buds and Branches, but something swishes in my stomach. It's as if I say it out loud, I'll jinx myself. "I'm thinking about being a chef."

"You can't cook."

I shrug. "Well, I'm not sure I'm actually qualified for anything at the moment, but I'll figure it out. I'm creating my best life over here. A little support would go a long way."

"I'm supportive," she protests. "I just want to make sure your best life is well rounded. And realistic." She pauses. "Nix the chef thing, Haley. Trust me on this."

I step around a broken piece of sidewalk. "You are kind of mean, you know that?"

"It was kind of mean to almost kill me with food poisoning too."

"There was a recall on spinach. That's not my fault. Furthermore," I say, "let's take a moment to realize no one has died of food poisoning from candy."

"Which is not food, which means you shouldn't be a chef. Case closed."

"Look," I say. "I didn't say I was sold on it. I said I'm looking at my options. Opening my mind to new possibilities."

The line muffles before Claire comes back. "A couple just walked in. Are you almost here?"

"Yes," I say, waving at my friend Jennifer, the owner of Buds and Branches, through the window. "But I'm going to say hi to Jennifer first, if that's okay."

"Beggars can't be choosers, right?"

I grin. "Right. I'll see you in a few. I need to drop off Trevor's jacket, anyway."

A not-so-subtle gasp shoots through the line. I imagine Claire's eyes going wide, her jaw hanging open. It makes me chuckle.

"Whoa, hold up. Did you just say you have Trevor's jacket?" she asks. "You have his clothes? Haley!"

"Relax." I laugh. "I borrowed it last night. It's fine."

"You were with him last night? Forget about you firing me from being your friend. If you are holding out, we're done here." She gasps again, this time for effect. "Spill it. And do it quick because some of the customers are staring at me and it's getting awkward."

"Oh, my gosh, Claire. Go to work."

"No. Not until you tell me what's up."

"I ran into him at Graber's last night and we got to talking in the parking lot and he let me borrow his jacket. It's no big deal."

"That's a huge deal. *Huge.*"

"It's not. Really." My stomach flutters as I snuggle into the fabric and let the feeling cuddle me. I wonder if he cuddles—*no.* "He was being nice. Besides, much to your dismay, it's not like that between us."

She snorts. "It's not pheromone-fueled? Fun? Sweet? Fated?"

"Will you stop?" I laugh. "You sound ridiculous. Now will you just go wait on your customers before we're both out of a job? You have tuition to pay for, may I remind you."

A long, hefty sigh hits my ear. "Fine."

"Fine. Talk to you soon."

"Bye."

Pressing open the door to Buds and Branches, I'm immediately hit with the scent of flowers. The light, romantic vibe of the building makes me smile. It reminds me of my mother.

My mom was such an optimist, always seeing the beauty and hope in things. She wore the prettiest floral perfume that smelled like roses still damp from the morning dew. She was the epitome of a lady and all that I hope to be someday.

Jennifer looks up from the desk. "Hey, you," she says, grinning wide. "What's going on?"

"Oh, not much," I say, slipping off Trevor's jacket. I think about hanging it on the hook by the door but don't really want to let it go. So I toss it over my arm instead. "I just thought I'd come by and see what you are doing. The fall decor looks amazing, Jen."

"Thanks." She looks back at the start of an arrangement in front of her. "I've had a heck of a time getting it together since Dana quit."

"She did? Why?"

She looks up from the bouquet she's working on. "She ran off with some guy she met on a dating app. I told her to be careful." She shakes her head. "Kids these days."

"Hey, at least she found love somehow. I might use a dating app when I go back into the fray."

"Don't do that," she says. "You don't need an app to find a nice guy."

"I need something," I mutter. "Anyway, I don't have time to worry about it right now. The library let me go yesterday, so all my attention is focused on that."

She drops her hand. A pair of scissors clatters against the tabletop. "I heard they didn't get the funding they were after." She frowns. "I'm sorry, Haley."

"Thanks. It sucks. But I slept in today, so silver linings, right?"

"I have to say, I'd love a couple of days off right now." She goes back to work on the flowers. "Tom wants to take me to Hawaii for our anniversary, but I can't leave this place. Especially not now with Dana gone. Besides," she huffs, "I'm barely in the black the way it is. If the place in Rockery would get caught up with the modern age and actually appeal to the area, I'd be in the red. But I can't close Buds and Branches, because I love it too much."

"I love this place too," I say.

"Hey," Jennifer says, shaking a rose at me. "You know what—"

She's cut off by a phone ringing in the back. She sighs, obviously annoyed.

"Would you mind watching the front for me for a second?" she asks. "That's my cell and it's probably Tom and he's probably irritated I didn't give him a straight answer on Hawaii last night. So this is going to take a second."

"Go. I got this," I say.

She disappears into the back.

I mosey around the store, stopping to smell the sweet roses and perfume-like gardenias. The blend of aromas is almost like a high. I could lose myself in the store for days, just like I could in a library.

Could I work here? Honestly? I look around the room and take in the beauty. I think I could. I think I could be happy here. *But is it possible?*

The arrangement Jen was working on sits on the desk. I venture over to it. It's a blend of multicolored Peruvian lilies, some of my favorite flowers. I pick up a few orange ones and find spots to nest them. When I step back, something still looks missing.

My attention is caught by a few gorgeous red roses in the cooler. I snag a couple of them and place them carefully into the mix.

"That looks wonderful," Jen says.

I look over my shoulder to see her leaning against the doorframe. "I hope you don't mind. I . . ." I shrug like a kid caught with their hand in the cookie jar. "I added the lilies and then thought the roses would be pretty. I can totally take them out if you want."

"Don't you dare." She comes up beside me and inspects it more closely. "It's perfect."

I clasp my hands together and smile. "I think so too."

"This will make someone very happy. Maybe someone will come in today and snag this for their wife."

"Do people still do that?" I ask. "I mean, I can't think of actually getting flowers from a guy before. I've even had them tell me they were a waste of money because they die." I pretend to cry. "No one remembers that flowers are a language of love."

"The good ones remember." She takes the vase and puts it in the front of the display cooler. "You know," she says, "I can always tell a couple that's going to make it just by watching them in here for a few minutes."

"You're kidding."

"No. I'm not."

"Then when I go back to dating, I'm bringing every guy in here for your take."

She laughs. "Oh, Haley."

"I mean it," I insist. "I'm too old to mess around with guys who don't want to bring me flowers." I think about what I just said. "You know what? I think I'm turning into my mother."

"I bet your mother was an amazing woman."

"My mom was . . . Yes. She was amazing," I say. "But let's go back to this telltale love thing. I'm fascinated. How do you know?"

She brushes bits of flower petals from the desk. "Tom and I have been married for almost twenty years. We learned to communicate somewhere over the last couple of decades, and the one thing I've learned is this: you say and hear the most when there aren't words exchanged."

"That is so counterintuitive."

"It is. But think about it." She plucks a tulip out of a display and brings it to her nose. "I can tell when a couple comes in to do their wedding flowers if they'll make it by how they act when no one is talking. Anyone can promise someone the world or pick a fight, right?"

"Absolutely."

"Those things mean nothing. But when I go in the back to do a quick mock-up of an arrangement and peek around the corner and see a couple laughing or comforting each other with a simple look—those are the ones that make it. You almost have to take the 'I love you' out of it to know they are in love, if that makes sense."

"Yeah. Kind of," I say, trying to wrap my head around it. I don't get too far when the door chimes behind me. I turn to see Gary Rambis walking in.

"Well, good morning, Haley," he says. "What brings you here?"

"I was just walking to the Dogwood Café and thought I'd come in to see Jen and the fall flowers. What about you?"

"I thought I'd take Amanda some flowers at lunch. Neely said her mom likes daisies," he says, jamming his hands in his pockets. "Today is our dating anniversary, and I thought I'd do a little something special for her." His brow furrows. "That's what you do, right? Or is that cheesy? I haven't done this in so long."

I giggle at how cute he is. "Flowers are never the wrong answer, Gary."

He wipes an invisible line of sweat from his brow. "Whew. I was afraid the rules had changed since I've done this."

"Nope. It was good seeing you," I tell him.

Looking up at Jennifer, I slip on Trevor's jacket again. My stomach starts to churn as I realize I haven't asked about a job yet. Anxiety hits me full on with every worst-case scenario playing through my mind like wildfire.

Then as I start toward the door, a whiff of roses tickles my nose. I stop and turn around.

"Hey, Jennifer," I say. "Can I ask you something?"

"Sure."

"Are you looking for help?"

I can feel my heartbeat in my throat. Avoiding Gary's gaze, I look at Jennifer as confidently as I can and pray this was a good decision.

She grins. "You know, I was going to bring that up to you earlier, and then Tom called. Are you interested?"

"Definitely. I mean, if you think I could do it."

She stands straight, a smile painted on her face. "Of course you could do it. You'd be great at it. I just need to talk to Tom about a few things first." She pauses and glances quickly at Gary. "I'll call you in a couple of days if that works for you?"

"Absolutely. Thanks, Jennifer." I give her a quick wave and step back outside.

The sun is a bit higher in the sky, my spirits right there with it. I almost skip down the road toward the Dogwood Café.

I glance down at Trevor's jacket hanging to my knees and laugh.

CHAPTER NINE

TREVOR

I shut the truck door behind me. "This is the only place to get lunch, huh?"

Penn is leaning against the side of his pickup. "If you want food it is. If you want—"

"Act like you got some sense, will ya, Penn?" Dane comes around the corner of Penn's truck, shaking his head. "Seriously."

"How do you know Trev's not looking for a piece of something other than pie?" Penn holds out his hands. "Just trying to give the guy options."

Dane looks at me in a silent apology. All I can do is laugh.

Spending the morning with these two plus Dane's brother, Matt, has been more than I expected. They're some of the hardest workers I've ever seen, but somehow manage to do it with a spirit of fun you just don't see when people are working for a living.

Penn claps me on the back. "Ignore Dane. Now that he's holed up with Neely, he's kind of boring. If you want to get to know the area *intimately*, let me know." He looks at Dane. "There. Did you like that phrasing better?"

Dane walks by, ignoring Penn.

"I love how you're all politically correct all of a sudden," Penn calls after him. "You used to be so much fun."

Dane flips him the bird, making us laugh.

Penn turns to me. "All joking aside, if you'll be in town long and want to meet some people, I'm your guy. There's a little get-together tonight at Brittney's. She's got a thing for me," he says, a twinkle in his eye. "But there'll be some others there."

"Thanks, man. But I'm gonna have to pass tonight."

Penn shrugs. "If you change your mind, you know how to find me."

We step onto the concrete patio in front of the Dogwood Café. Penn switches topics and rattles on about the plumbing subcontractor at the jobsite. I follow along until I see Haley through the window.

She's sitting at the bar, her back to us. Dane is standing next to her with his hand on the back of her chair. I watch as her shoulders rise and fall, a response to a question I can't hear. I don't realize I'm staring until Penn clears his throat.

"What was that?" I ask, pulling my gaze away from Haley.

Penn is watching me with an impish grin. "That one," he says, nodding toward Haley, "is a handful."

"What do you mean by that?"

He looks through the glass. "She's not like most girls around here. I give her hell, but only because she gives it right back. I don't know what I'd do if she actually gave me the time of day. Probably die with my cock in my hand."

She throws her head back, laughing at Dane, the ends of her hair brushing against the curve of her hip. She's even prettier when she's not trying to one-up me. The thought makes me chuckle.

"She probably knows that and uses it against you," I point out with a grin of my own.

Penn shrugs, like that explains everything there is to know about Haley. He slips his hands in his pockets as he watches her. "When Mia was born, Dane was all kinds of fucked up. He didn't know a damn thing about raising a baby. Then Haley came to town and kind of saved him, in a way."

"Dane seems to respect her," I say.

"He does. I think we all do. She's just too good of a girl." Penn twists his lips. "Even me, with the asshole gene I carry, wouldn't mess with her."

I look at him. "You're telling me that if she wanted to sleep with you, you'd turn her down?" I raise a brow. "You want me to believe that?"

"I don't want you to believe anything. I'm just telling you how it is. She spits a good game, but it's fake. On the other side of all that personality is a woman who's not as mean as she pretends to be." He runs a hand over his chin. "Damn it if she ain't gorgeous, though."

That she is. Sexy, too, even without trying.

He doesn't wait for a response. He opens the door and holds it for me.

The scent of hamburgers fills the air as I step inside the little restaurant. It's busier than yesterday, but still not packed by any means. Haley looks over her shoulder as Penn and I approach.

"I don't think the world can handle the two of you together," she says. She lets her sight linger on Penn for a long moment before flipping it to me. "Fancy running into you here."

I take the seat beside her. "Nice jacket."

"Some random guy let me wear it last night in a parking lot."

"Some random guy, huh? You must like something about him if you're wearing his clothes."

She rests her chin on her hand. "He has a couple of things going for him."

"I heard that. According to statistics, he's in the top tier of looks, makes decent money, and has a killer personality."

A snort rips through the air. "Is this Two Truths and a Lie?"

"No," I say. "But I am curious which one you'd lie about and say isn't true."

She drops her hand and laughs. "What are you doing here, anyway?"

"We've been at the site and thought we'd come down and grab some lunch."

I look over my shoulder to see Penn taking a bag from Claire. She hands two bags to Dane before looking at me.

"We have their lunch ready, and Matt's, because we know what they want and when they'll be here," Claire says to me. "If I'd have known you were coming in, I'd have had something ready for you too."

"Oh, that's okay. Don't worry about it." I grab a menu from between the napkin holder and ketchup bottle. "Can I get a bacon cheeseburger, no tomato, and a drink to go?"

"Sure thing," Claire says. She makes a point to glance at Haley, who makes a point not to look at her, before disappearing into the back. I wonder what that's about, but before I get too deep, Dane's hand clasps my shoulder.

"We're gonna head back," he says to me. "Matt should be back with the rest of the wood for the deck, so we'll get going on that."

"Sounds good. I'll come up later and see what's happening," I say.

He bites his lip as he glances down at Haley. "What are you doing today, Hay?"

"Well, I need to work on my résumé," she says, shifting in her seat. "Jennifer told me she'll call me in a couple of days, and I think it's promising, but I can't really waste time. If it doesn't work out, I need to have another iron in the fire."

"Who's Jennifer?" I ask. It's weird how people here seem to know absolutely everyone. They never use last names or reference them in any way other than "Jennifer," as if there's one "Jennifer" in the world.

Dane leans against Haley's chair. "I'm guessing Jennifer from the flower shop."

"Yup," Haley says with a contained grin.

"That would be awesome," Dane says. "You love flowers. It's down the road from your house. They'd probably pay as much as, maybe even more than, the library."

Her smile wavers. "But I don't know anything about flowers. I just like them."

Penn laughs. "I don't know anything about women. I just like them. Doesn't stop me."

Haley swats him. "No one is paying you for a service to know about women."

"You don't know that," Penn jokes.

Haley sighs, switching her attention back to Dane. "Anyway, it's really exciting, but I don't want to get my hopes up and then get let down. So the résumé it is. Unless, of course, you want to knock up your girlfriend so I can be a nanny again."

Dane walks backward toward the door. His hands are in front of him, the bags Claire gave him dangling in the air. "Give me time."

"I'm just saying," Penn says, keeping a safe distance from Dane. "If Neely was my girl, I wouldn't need a lot of ti—umph." He covers his stomach as Dane elbows him in a lightning-fast move. "I was kidding. Kind of."

"If you're both still alive later, I'll see you up there," I say, laughing as they continue to poke each other.

"Bye, guys," Haley says.

The door opens, filling the room with morning sun, before shutting again. Haley and I turn around to face the kitchen.

Her tongue is jammed in the side of her cheek. It's as if she's challenging me to speak first.

Challenge accepted.

"So . . ." I look at Haley.

"So . . ." Her tongue slips from her cheek as she looks at me. Her eyes are bright and lively, and I wonder if she wakes up this way. "I brought your jacket back."

"I see that."

She fixes her gaze on the oversize fork and spoon on the wall in front of her. "Thanks for letting me borrow it. I also ate all the ice cream last night. So thanks for that too."

"I'd say I see that, too, but I don't want to get smacked."

She fires a playful glare my way. "Smart move."

I settle in my seat and run my hands down my thighs. My jeans are smooth under my palms. I repeat the move a second time when I notice Haley's attention has turned to my hands.

"You know," she says, pulling her gaze to mine, "they say people come into your life for a reason."

"I've heard that. Not sure I agree with it, though." I take a drink from Claire. "Thanks."

She nods, a shit-eating grin on her face as she grabs the coffeepot and skirts away.

"Do you have any thoughts about it?" I ask.

"Yeah. I'm trying to decide what your reason is."

Leaning forward, I smirk. "Most women come up with the same reason for coming into my life."

"Of course you'd say that." She snorts, her perfect little pout pressing her lips together.

"Of course I'd be right." I toss her a wink as I sit back again. "But in this particular instance, I'm here because my father married a life-size doll who needs two hundred acres and four thousand square feet for him, her, and her two poodles, and I'm on vacation and can't sit still. It's pretty self-explanatory."

"You really don't like her, do you?"

"Meredith?" I shrug. "She's all right, I guess. Not the kind of woman I'd marry, but I didn't marry her."

She leans against the bar, resting her arms on the ledge. "If you were to get married, what kind of woman would you pick?"

"Are you asking me to go steady, Miss Raynor?"

"Hardly," she scoffs. "I'm just doing some market research."

I sit back in my seat and study her. I don't think I could ever think about Haley like I do Meredith or Liz. She's not like them at all. Come to think of it, she's not like any woman I've ever met. I just can't quite figure out why.

"I'm a bad person to research on because I'm not, nor will I ever likely be, in that particular market," I say.

She stares at me with an open mouth. A spattering of freckles covers the bridge of her nose and sprays over the tops of her cheeks. From this angle, she looks so much younger than what I'm guessing is her twenty-six, twenty-seven years.

"What?" I ask.

"You don't want to get married? Ever?"

"No. Not particularly." I roll my cup around in my hands. "I mean, if it happens, that's fine. Great. But it's not on the agenda."

"Why not?"

"Why would it be?" I ask her. "Why would you want to attach yourself to one person for the rest of your life?"

Her lashes flutter once. Twice. Three times before she shakes her head to rid it of the fog she seems to think is keeping her from understanding my point. "Because you're in love."

"That would work if you believed in love to start with."

A gasp escapes her throat. "You don't believe in love? What kind of animal are you?"

I think she's kidding with the animal comment, but I'm not sure.

My first reaction is to make some kind of sexual innuendo. To play it off and change the subject to something lighter. But the sheer shock written across her features locks me into this conversation I didn't start out to have.

"Fine," I say, blowing out a breath. "I believe in love. I really do. I just don't believe in one love for all of time."

She looks at me like I'm from outer space and don't understand what she's saying. "But that's what love is," she says slowly.

"Is it?" I take a brown paper bag from Claire, who wisely refrains from joining the conversation. She dips out, scooting into the dining area. "I don't know if I believe that. I mean, how can the twenty-six-year-old me know who the fifty-six-year-old me wants in life? It's ludicrous."

A steeliness settles over her eyes. "So this is your way of opting out of monogamy?"

"No. Why does it always have to go there?" I ask. "I've never cheated on a woman. Ever. Not even when I was a teenager with the sex drive of a monkey. One girl for me at a time. That's all I can handle." I pause and think about what I've said. "That's not the whole truth, if I'm honest. I firmly believe that cheating is an asshole move."

"Wow. So honorable."

"Not really. I watched my mom cheat on my dad, and I'm not a fan."

"Ah, so that's why you don't believe in love," she says. "I get it."

I bend my straw in half, watching it flip back up like a spring. I don't want to talk about my issues or about Mom. Both make me squeamish.

"What about you?" I ask. "Do you believe in some fated love like you see in movies?"

"Of course I do." She tugs my jacket around her waist in a subconscious move. "It's a basic human need—to love and be loved."

"That's where I think you're wrong. People need to be understood, not necessarily roped into buying flowers and chocolates."

She makes a face and turns her attention to the kitchen as a cook shouts an order is up. "It must suck to be so jaded about love."

"Or maybe it sucks to be so naive about it?"

"I don't think believing in one true love is being naive." She looks at me with a softness that feels like someone sent a rock through a slingshot and struck my chest. "I think believing you can go through life and not need love is naive."

There's something about what she says that prickles the back of my brain. It bothers me, irritates me, begs me to pay attention and dig deeper. But it's hard to do that when I have to spend so much energy telling myself not to reach for her and pull her into my arms.

"I didn't say you don't need love," I mutter. "I just said maybe getting different loves as you go through life may be more practical."

"That's sad."

"That's honesty."

She shakes her head. "You are the exact kind of guy who's broken my heart a dozen times. I should hate you on principle."

The softness in her eyes hardens as a shield locks in place. The need to touch her deepens, and I busy my hand with my cup to keep from making that connection—one I need more and more.

She looks at me out of the corner of her eye. I can't help but wonder what she sees when she looks at me.

"What kind of guy am I?" I ask finally.

She shrugs. "I don't know. Depends on the day."

"Today, then."

"I'd say today you're . . . charismatic. Cute."

"I hate that word," I grumble.

"Okay. How's 'unavailable' sound?"

"Fair enough." I stretch out my legs, my body tight. "For the record, you're the epitome of the women whose hearts I keep breaking."

"I'll play. What kind of girl am I?"

Every word that pops in my mind is one I can't say—one I shouldn't say. Words like "captivating" and "sexy" aren't going to help.

I twist my lips as she watches me and awaits my answer.

"Charming," I say, landing on the word closest to "charismatic" I can find. "Adorable."

"You make me sound like a little boy," she whines.

"Okay. How's 'available' sound?"

"Ugh," she groans. "See? Right there. That's the problem."

"What? That I go for the available ones? I'm sorry. I thought that was the right thing to do."

"No. That you say 'available' like it's a curse word. Like it makes us needy." Her eyes burn with an intensity that I can't look away from.

"Yes, I want to be in a relationship. Yes, I want to be loved and needed, and that's not a bad thing."

"No, it's not, theoretically. But it is when the proverbial 'you' thinks they're going to get those things from me when I'm crystal clear it's not going to happen." I sigh. "I don't like hurting people's feelings, Haley. I go into relationships with all my cards on the table, and I still walk out of it feeling like a prick."

She takes a napkin out of the container. Folding it over and over, her chest rises and falls faster. "For the record," she says, "I don't like wanting guys who don't want me in the same way. If I could figure out how to do that, I wouldn't do it either."

I turn away from her for both our sakes. "Seems pretty easy to me. Stay away from guys like me."

"Well, guys like you could not let girls like me in your bed."

"There go my plans for tonight," I joke.

We chuckle together. I barely hear the sound over the clatter of the kitchen, but somehow, it almost drowns it out too.

Although I've been clear and up front, I feel . . . disappointment. It's like the lines have been drawn, and I feel bereft because of it. But she's right. Guys like me should not let girls like Haley in my bed.

She gets to her feet slowly. Claire comes by and asks if she wants her lunch put on her tab. They have a quiet conversation as I busy myself with checking my nonexistent new text messages. I look up when Haley stands next to me.

"Here's your coat." She extends a hand, my jacket dangling from her fist. "Thanks again."

"No problem." I take it from her, watching the browns and golds in her eyes swirl together.

There's something I want to say, but I can't articulate it. When I don't say anything more, the light in her eyes dims, and she turns toward the door.

I could stop her if I tried. But I don't. What good would that do?

CHAPTER TEN

HALEY

The clock on the wall at Mucker's is shaped like a pizza. Each hour is marked with another topping. The seven is a pepperoni and the time Claire was supposed to meet me here for dinner twenty minutes ago.

I don't text her, because it's futile. She never texts me back.

The book in front of me, the one I borrowed from the library this afternoon, promises to make résumé writing easy. It lies—that, or I just have nothing to put on a list of qualifications.

I look up to see Claire's car pulling in front of the restaurant. She gets out, puts her purse on her shoulder, and starts toward the door. Then stops. She waves before talking with an animation I know means she won't make it inside for another twenty minutes.

My stomach rumbles. I turn to flag down Alexis to place an order, but when my gaze lands on Claire again, my hand falls to my side.

Trevor is standing next to my friend. He looks freshly showered and shaved. A green pullover hides some of the ridges of his body, and if I could stop looking at his face, I might be annoyed by that.

It's really disappointing that I didn't meet him six months ago. Back then, I didn't care whether I could get on the same page with a guy. I jumped in and hoped for the best. I just had to go and start making sense a bit too soon.

Trevor points toward the building as Claire laughs. She shakes her head and shrugs.

My pulse strums through my veins as I watch them talk like old friends and wish I were out there too. I grip the edges of the table, not sure whether to push back and stand or keep myself in place. The decision is made for me when Claire's eyes shift from Trevor through the window to me.

She makes a fist and brings it to her mouth. She fakes a cough before sticking out her bottom lip.

"What are you doing?" I mouth.

She fakes another cough. This time, she follows it with a laugh. She says something to Trevor again before climbing back in her car.

"What are you doing?" I ask, even though she can't hear me. My brows pull together as I watch my friend back out of the parking lot and venture off down the street.

My heart skips a beat at the exact moment the chimes ding on the front door. I don't have to look to know Trevor walked in. His gaze smacks the side of my face, covering me in a warmth that I didn't know I was missing. But at least now I know that this will lead absolutely nowhere. Girls like me—naive, willing for the wrong reasons—are a dime a dozen to Trevor Kelly. He made himself very clear earlier today. *I'd be his type if I were okay with a one-night or multiple-night stand only.* And that's not me. Not anymore.

He stops at my table.

"Claire said to tell you she was sick and that she'll call you tomorrow," he says. He shrugs with a nonchalance that makes me laugh. "She's also full of shit, but she didn't ask me to tell you that."

"I didn't need you to tell me that to know it."

"I figured as much." He takes in the little dining area. "This is even smaller than it looks."

"Most people sit outside. That," I say, pointing out the window behind me, "used to be a basketball court."

"I can see that."

"It's a really cool space. That big rock thing in the corner is a giant fireplace," I say. "They'll light fires on the weekends and bring out kerosene heaters. It's fun."

He grips the back of the chair across from me and scans the room again. The silence between us isn't awkward, but it's swirling with something I can't pinpoint. It's a vibe of uncertainty. I hate it.

I glance around him and notice Alexis refilling a drink, but her attention is on Trevor.

"That must get really old," I say.

"What?"

"Going in places and having women stare at you."

His shoulders relax as I feel him slide back into the easiness between us. "Who is staring now?"

I sweep the room quickly. "Oh, everyone."

"For what it's worth, I didn't notice. But thanks for telling me." He straightens his shirt with a grin. "Good to know I've still got it."

"Oh, please," I say with a sigh.

He laughs. "So can I sit with you?" He leans in. "I have a thing about eating alone."

"I'm pretty sure you wouldn't have to sit alone for long," I whisper.

He rolls his eyes but pulls out the chair. His body unfolds as he sits. And despite my ribbing of him, I completely understand why the lady in the corner is practically drooling.

There's an aura surrounding Trevor that's undeniable. It's also magnetic, pulling your attention toward him even if you don't want it to. It's a quiet confidence, an easygoing vibe like he could blend into the crowd if he weren't so damn attractive—a quality he doesn't carry around like a badge.

"What's this?" He turns my book to face him.

"I got that to help me figure out how to construct a résumé."

"There's an art to a well-crafted résumé," he says.

"Have I mentioned I'm unartistic?" I scrunch my face. "It's the most uncomfortable thing I've ever done."

He bites his lip. "I'm not going to say a word."

"I meant trying to sell myself."

"I'm still not touching that."

His laugh is free and light. The sound shoots right to my core. My entire body clenches, the unspoken innuendo impossible to ignore.

Alexis moseys up to the table. She gives me a quick once-over and then sets her sights on Trevor.

"What can I get for you two?" she asks. While the question may have sounded like it was aimed for both of us, it was clearly directed at him. "Would you like an appetizer?"

I sink back in my seat and wait for the flirting to begin. Much to my surprise, Trevor looks at me. "What do you want? Cheese sticks? Loaded fries?"

"I usually just get a pepperoni pizza," I say. "And an ice water."

He makes a face. "Really? After the doughnut, I thought you'd feel much stronger about this topic."

I glare, making him chuckle again.

He sets the menu down. "Give us a large pepperoni pizza and two ice waters. And toss some loaded fries on there, too, if you can."

"Sure." Alexis gives him her best smile. "Anything else?"

"No. Thank you." And as if Alexis isn't still standing there, he turns back to me. "So want my help?"

"With . . ."

He tries to hide a grin. "Your choice. But may I recommend making you uncomfortable? I know a lot of positions I can get you in that—"

"Stop," I say, my cheeks heating.

"Fine. With your résumé. Do you want my help?"

"I don't know. It's like head-butting a brick wall."

"Why?"

I shrug. "Because I don't know how to make it shine."

"Easy," he says. "Sell your best assets."

"I don't know what those are."

He leans back, crossing his arms over his chest. He's trying hard not to smile. "Want my input?"

"No," I say, refusing to look at him.

He sits up and clears his features of the amusement from before. "The key is to tell a potential employer why they should hire you. That's what you have to focus on—the 'why.'"

His phone beeps. He silences it and slides it next to the napkin holder without even looking at it. I want to ask him about it, but he just looks at me in a way that tells me not to. So I don't. Instead, I change the subject.

"How are you liking Dogwood Lane?" I ask. I don't mean it as some deep, thought-provoking question, but he seems to take it as one.

He considers my question. I expected an easy answer—that he can't wait to leave or that it's just what he thought it was going to be. Instead of spitting out something like that, he rests his elbows on the table and looks at me.

His gaze is warm on my face. It lights a flame inside my chest, the warmth radiating through my veins. He looks at me like he's interested in what I have to say, like my questions are worthy of consideration. It feels . . . nice. Very nice.

"I don't mind it, actually," he says. "It's amazing how much work I can get done when it's quiet, and it's so quiet at the house and the inn. Especially when Penn isn't around."

"He's loud," I say.

"Loud," he mouths, his eyes growing wide. He leans forward again. "Can I tell you a secret?"

"Sure."

"It's also kind of fun to be out there. Usually I'm cooped up in an office with reports and statements—which I love—but it's nice to get some fresh air and dig around in the dirt."

"See?" I say, pointing at him. "That's what I want. I want to do something I can't wait to do every day. Something that brings me real joy and makes others happy."

"You want a unicorn job."

"Yes. And I think there's one out there for me."

"Me too."

We sit back as Alexis puts drinks in front of us. She glares at me when Trevor doesn't give her the time of day. I smile back.

"I just need to figure out this stupid résumé," I say, pulling the book back to me. "It can't be as hard as I'm making it out to be."

I flip through the pages, skimming over examples of what you should include in your cover letter and pointers on interviews. The information makes my head spin.

"For the love of God," Trevor mutters.

He's staring at his phone. His jaw is locked as he swipes over the screen with his thumb.

"What is it?" I ask.

"Liz."

"Okay. Who's Liz?"

"An ex . . . not girlfriend, really. An ex-acquaintance is more like it."

I bite my tongue to keep from responding. Of course he has an *ex-acquaintance*. Probably a lot of them. Maybe even some current ones that he's not bringing up. And none of them are my business. So why I feel a little prickly about this right now is beyond me.

"She's called me six times since I've been sitting here," he says. "I feel like an asshole not answering her, but every time I do, she takes it as a sign I'm interested. I'm not."

I fold my hands on the book and take a deep breath. "Maybe she'll get the picture."

"She's texted me forty-one times in the last twenty-four hours." He lifts a brow. "Does it seem like she's getting the picture to you?"

"That's a lot," I admit.

"No shit."

"Did you date her long?"

"I saw her over three, maybe four, months. It wasn't serious. Not to me, anyway." He tosses his phone on the table. "Got any insight?"

I laugh. "On what? Liz?"

"Yeah. I don't want to hurt her feelings. I just don't want to be with her. How do I handle that without telling her to just fuck off?"

"Telling her to fuck off wouldn't be very nice," I point out. I think for a minute. "Okay, question: When was the last time you actually talked to her?"

"I don't know." He grabs his phone and scrolls. "Three days ago. Via text."

"That's your problem," I tell him.

"I shouldn't have texted her back. I knew it."

"No, you should've. You should text her right now, actually."

He looks at me like I'm nuts. "You're not understanding what I'm saying, Haley."

"No, you're not understanding what I'm saying, Trevor. You're just making it worse when you ignore her. In your mind, you're putting up a boundary. In her mind, you're playing hard to get." I release a breath. "People want what they can't have. The longer you go and then text her back here and there is a little crumb tossed her way, keeping her strung along. Trust me. Guys used to do it to me all the time, and I was as ready to eat it up as Liz."

He cocks his head to the side. His brows are heavy, pulled together by a crease in his forehead.

I twist in my seat, wondering why in the heck I just shared all that with him. It clearly came from a sensitive spot in my heart, and he's not stupid—he'll know. He'll know I'm sensitive, too, in my own way, and he'll probably run for the hills.

The big hill. The one with the massive house on it.

"If you knew it, why did you do it?" he asks.

"Because when you like the guy, it feels like hope. Like maybe they're reconsidering." I shrug. "Pathetic, I know. But I don't make the rules."

He shakes his head and takes the fries from Alexis. She tries to make small talk with him. He expertly wiggles his way out of it and focuses back on me. But when he looks at me this time, there's something in his eyes that makes me shift in my seat.

"What?" I ask.

"I have a proposition for you." He pops a fry in his mouth.

"Why does that worry me?"

He grins. "If there's one thing I loathe, it's eating out alone. It's a long story, and it goes back to some unresolved mommy issues that I don't want to get into. But I hate it."

I don't know how to respond to that. So I don't. I take a drink instead.

"Anyway, how about this: I'll help you with your résumé. Get your interview skills sharpened. Help you however you need it in this forging-a-new-path thing you're on."

I swallow. "Okay. You've piqued my curiosity. Go on."

His grin grows wider. "And in return, you have dinner with me while I'm in town. Which helps us both because I don't have to eat alone and we'll work on your stuff. We'll kill two birds with one stone."

"A résumé shouldn't take more than an hour if you know what you're doing," I point out. "I read that in a book."

"True. But I'll help you know what to say in an interview, and if you want me to look at some job listings, I can. And let's not forget it's a free meal and you're unemployed right now."

"That's low," I say with a laugh.

"I know," he says, wincing. "I apologize for the last one. That was low even for me."

"Is this just a way to get me to spend time with you?" I tease, ignoring the way my blood is roaring through my veins. "I mean, after the stalking and the jacket thing and then this, I'm noticing a trend, bud."

"I can't say it pains me to think I'll have to see you every night I'm here."

I sink into my seat as his words wash over me. My chest bounces as I withhold a gasp, and I press my thighs together so hard I think I might pull a muscle.

I'm torn between wanting to say yes and wanting to remember everything he said at the Dogwood Café—all the reasons why I should stay away from guys like him.

This is hard.

I grab a fry and pop it in my mouth. "I think this is a bad idea."

"And why is that?"

"What if I can't resist your charms and fall madly in love with you, like Alexis. Or Liz. Or the old lady with silver hair sitting in the corner with a mug of beer?"

Trevor looks over his shoulder. The lady flushes as Trevor waves at her before turning back to me.

"I guess that is something to consider," he says.

"I was joking!"

I know better than to think anything else could happen between us. But am I being foolish, subjecting myself to more time with him? He's handsome, yes, but he also has a dry wit that really appeals to me. And every time I see that dimple . . .

"So . . . ," he prods.

My resolve weakens as he uses that damn dimple as a weapon. Finding the part of my brain responsible for logic under all the sexual frustration is nearly impossible.

He takes a fry. I remind myself I've gone two months without a date. I'm strong. And I do need help with my résumé.

I can do this. I'm a big girl. Besides, he'll probably only be around for another few days, so surely I can handle that.

He watches me warily before grabbing a napkin out of the dispenser. He gets up and heads to the counter and comes back with a pen.

"What are you doing?" I ask.

"Patience, little Haley," he says, biting his bottom lip as he scrawls on the napkin.

I sip my water as I watch him. I nearly choke when he turns it around to face me. The bright-blue ink is in stark contrast to the white napkin. In bold letters it reads:

I, TREVOR KELLY, PROMISE NOT TO BREAK HALEY RAYNOR'S HEART.

"Fair enough." I take the pen and add my own line. When I spin it to face him, he laughs.

I, HALEY RAYNOR, PROMISE NOT TO FALL IN LOVE AND CLING TO TREVOR KELLY.

"Fair enough." He sticks out a hand. "Deal?"

I lay my palm in his and ignore the way my body sings at the contact. "Deal."

CHAPTER ELEVEN

TREVOR

"That looks really good," I say, walking around the deck to get another angle at Matt's handiwork. "I can't believe you built this on your own. That's some skill you have."

The deck is almost the same size as the first floor of the house. Despite its massive proportions, each board is laid perfectly. Each nail pounded to the top of the wood. It's an amazing study in craftsmanship, one I know Dad will love.

The early-morning sky is bright, the air crisp. The combination makes me feel alive as I stand beside Matt and breathe in the smell of pine.

He leans against the rail and surveys his work. "Thanks. Projects like these are my favorite."

"Pains in the ass?"

He laughs. "Well, sometimes. But I love the big-scale stuff with all kinds of pieces that make you really buckle down and dive in." He glances to the side of the house, smirking as he takes in Penn having a discussion with a six-panel door. "Any fool can hang a door."

"You know," I say, "when I first met Penn, I wasn't sure how things were going to play out."

"Same."

I laugh, turning back to Matt. "I really like him. He keeps things fun around here."

"Pretty sure that's the only reason Dane keeps him around some days." He shakes his head. "I'm kidding. Penn's a good guy. We've been best friends a long damn time."

"You guys remind me of me and my brother. Jake and I are close in age and have wanted to work together our entire lives."

"That's awesome. We did not."

I chuckle. "Well, we did. Jake is older, so he got to run the construction side of things. I'm the smarter one, so I took over the financials and engineering elements. Can't imagine working with anyone else."

Matt follows me down the steps and onto the lawn. "Dane and I took over for our father. It just sort of happened. One day Penn showed up and didn't leave, and now it's just what we do. Some days I want to kill them both, but that's probably normal, I reckon."

We stop on the top of the hill and take in the view. The evergreens mix with the last flush of fall colors in the peaks and valleys below, and I wonder what it would be like to wake up to this. When Dad first said they were building a house here, I thought he was crazy. I told him he'd lose his mind in the middle of the country. I think I might've been wrong.

"I bet you can see a hundred miles every direction," I say, my voice carried away by the breeze.

"Probably." Matt takes a pack of gum out of his back pocket. "You sticking around this weekend? A bunch of us are getting together at my house to watch football and shoot the shit. You're welcome to come, if you want."

"Thanks," I say, taking the proffered piece of gum. "I have to head to Nashville for my dad's retirement party, actually."

Haley's face pops into my mind, and I fight off a little bubble of irritation about leaving. I've grappled with the annoyance since last night, when I remembered Dad's retirement party as I was looking up places to take Haley to dinner tonight.

As if my brother senses my weakness, my phone rings in my pocket. I pull it out to see Jake's name.

"I need to take this," I say to Matt. "The deck looks great."

He points at me as if to say, "Okay," and heads toward Penn.

I swipe the screen. "Hey," I say. "What's happening?"

"Not much. Natalie gave me this week's checks to sign. I'll just say I have a lot more hesitation signing them when I know you haven't seen them."

"They're fine. Natalie sent me a spreadsheet this morning, and I went through it." I pause. "She's good, you know. You can trust her."

"I don't trust anyone who doesn't have my blood." He sighs. "Anyway, what's happening at the Love Nest?"

I look over the valley again. "Dad's got a helluva piece of property up here, Jake. You really should see it."

"I'm losing you, aren't I?"

I laugh. "No. I'm just standing on what feels like the top of the world and thought I'd relay that. You know, to make you jealous."

"I'm green with envy."

"Better than blue from blue balls."

"True enough," he says. "Speaking of misery, Liz RSVP'd to Dad's party today."

I hold my forehead with one hand and pretend he didn't just say that. "Did the caterer add those little potato things we talked about to the menu? I reminded Natalie about it this morning."

Jake's laughter spills through the line. "Are we not talking about Liz?"

"How did she get an invite?" I moan. "For fuck's sake. I don't even want to come back for the fucking thing to start with, and to have to come back to her?"

"Okay, let's slow down. Why don't you want to come back for the party?"

I hang my head, knowing I've just stepped in a proverbial pile of shit. Jake isn't going to let this go. Moreover, if I mention Haley, he won't let that go either, and at some point in time when I do see him, I'm not going to want this held over my head. Because it will be. It's what brothers do.

"How mad do you think Dad would be if I don't come?" I ask.

It's not a real question. Dad would blow a gasket and probably fire me from Kelly Construction, even though he has no say there. I don't want to let Dad down, but fuck if I'm ready to reenter the madness that is Nashville.

And Psycho Liz. Staying here would be much preferred at the moment.

"You can't skip it, Trev. This is the pinnacle of Dad's career."

"I know. I know." I look at the sky and feel the wind whisper across my face. "Is there a way we can revoke Liz's invitation?"

"That would be a no."

My temple throbs as I try to come to some solution to this fucked-up situation.

"Whose bright idea was it to invite her, anyway?" I ask.

"She got one because she was your supposed plus-one."

"Look what you get for assuming."

"I didn't assume jack shit. Natalie did. Your golden girl." He chuckles through the line. "There's nothing we can do about it without looking like assholes."

"You are an asshole. Do it."

He laughs. "I'm not revoking an invitation."

"She's called me four times today, Jake. How about I give her your number? I doubt she'd mind."

His chair squeaks. "Let's not get crazy."

"My point exactly."

I blow out a breath. There's a heaviness on my back I can't shake off. I have to go to this party. It was always the plan. I just . . . don't want to. And I pointedly ignore the real reason why.

"Your ass better be here," he warns.

"I will be. The party is at six?"

"Yeah. Dad's partner is taking him and Meredith out for drinks, and then he'll bring them home. Dad has no idea."

"I can't wait," I say, my voice dripping with sarcasm. Scratching my head, I pull the phone back to see another text from Liz.

"Hey, Jake. I gotta go. But I'll see you this weekend, all right?"

"You better. Be good, little brother."

"Will do. Later."

"Bye."

I end the call and then flip to my text messages.

Liz: Can't wait to see you this weekend. Since you didn't respond, I let Jake know I would be attending your father's party. Talk soon!

I thumb up through her messages, scrolling all the way back to the months I was seeing her. Notes about dinners we shared, the weekend we spent in Charlestown, and a recap of a few entertaining hours together in a hot tub in Chicago all pass by.

The further back I go, the more I expect to feel something—some connection or tenderness or another emotion that's not apathy. Only one thing happens.

Haley answers on the second ring. "Hey," she says. "I'm glad you called."

Just like that, the heaviness is lighter and a smile is on my face. "Oh, really?"

"Wait. Is this Trevor?"

"Uh, yeah."

"Sorry. I thought you were someone else."

"You did not," I say. But even as I say it, I hope it's not true.

She laughs. "What's up?"

I sigh. "I have a problem."

"How bad of a problem?"

"I don't know," I say, clasping a hand on the back of my neck. "How do you quantify that?"

"If a 'one' is you walk into a building and no one notices, and a 'ten' is the Dogwood Café is out of doughnuts, what are you?"

I shake my head, a smile etched on my face. "I'm not sure how to operate that scale. I feel like I need a handbook."

"Fine. What's wrong? But keep it snappy because I'm planning my best life over here."

Running a hand down my face, I try to stay serious. Yet every time I start to speak, I think of the way I'm sure her lips are pressed together in a challenge, and all I want to do is listen to her jabber.

"Liz just texted me that she's going to a party for my father this weekend. Do I tell her I don't want her there or just let it go and blow it off?"

"If you blow it off, she's going to think she's going to blow you."

I groan, wishing I'd never met Liz. And, maybe, that I'd found Dogwood Lane sooner.

"Did you ever text her back last night?" she asks.

I don't answer.

"See?" she pokes. "This is why I told you to respond last night. You should've been preemptive."

"Why can't she just forget about me? Wait," I say, stopping myself. "I know why she can't forget me."

"Oh, here we go." Haley sighs.

I walk to the back section of the yard, where the top of the hill starts to decline. From here, I can see a field of wildflowers tucked behind a line of trees, and I wonder what it would look like in the spring. "I bet you would like this view," I tell her.

"Where are you?"

"My dad's house."

"I've seen it. Remember? And it is breathtaking." She stops abruptly. "Can I tell you something, though?"

"Sure."

"That house is way too big. It's almost a city. I have no clue why anyone would need a house that big."

I look at the structure towering over me from behind. The wraparound deck only adds to the girth of the thing, and I wonder how many people Meredith will hire to clean this one.

"Big is a gentle way of putting it," I say. "I'd go with enormous."

"You still talking about the house?"

"Look at you," I tease. "Your mind going straight to the gutter. I'm shocked, but I love it."

"Yeah, well, I got a good night's sleep, so I'm a little feistier than normal today."

I imagine her lying in bed, hair sprawled out on the pillows. I wonder if she talks in her sleep and if she moves around like I imagine she does or if she lies quietly in one place.

"Thanks for the warning," I say.

"Speaking of warnings, where do you plan on running into me today?"

I laugh, facing the meadow again. I've thought about that very thing all day. It's a weird preoccupation. It's just so easy, so amusing, to be with her. I can't help it. "I thought I could actually pick you up properly tonight. I mean, you're having dinner with me, anyway."

The line goes quiet. She shuffles some papers, and I think I hear a door opening.

Her lack of response sends a weird vibe through my body. I pace a small circle and wait for her to respond.

I get nothing. The longer it goes, the more nervous I get. It's like there's actually a chance of getting shot down.

"Haley?" I say finally.

"You really meant that?" Her voice has an edge to it, the humor of a moment before gone.

My stomach twists. I switch the phone between my hands and take a deep breath. "Yeah, I meant it. I thought we had dinner plans. But if you don't want to—"

"No," she says quickly, "I do."

My shoulders fall back as my lungs expel the air they were holding. "Well, good. What time do you usually eat?"

"Whenever," she says. The caution in her tone is unmistakable.

"Okay. What do you like to eat? Besides doughnuts and ice cream."

"Anything, really."

"For a woman who's typically so opinionated, you're awfully quiet right now."

She laughs. "Sorry."

"Don't be sorry. Just answer the question."

"Fine. I like everything except sushi because raw fish just seems barbaric. Oh—I also don't love lobster rolls, although I wish I did because they're gorgeous. And I refuse to eat anything that was ever on the inside of an animal, but that doesn't really qualify as food, I don't think, so that probably doesn't matter. Otherwise, I like everything. Except hot dogs because I watched a show on them once and it ruined me for life."

My laugh rolls through the air. A flock of birds takes flight out of a grove of pines below. I watch them take to the sky and appreciate how free they are to go about their business without any chains to the ground.

"So basically you like steak and burgers," I say. "Got it."

She swallows hard. "I'll be ready at seven? Does that work for you?"

"Sounds perfect."

I think she's smiling by the way she takes a quick breath of air. This makes me grin like a loon.

"Can I ask you a question?" she asks.

"Sure."

"Where are we going?"

"I can't tell you," I say, grinning wider.

"Come on, Trevor. I need to know how to dress."

I turn toward my truck, wondering how long it is until seven.

"Pants. A shirt. Unless you like dresses, then that will work."

"That's no help." She groans.

"See you at seven," I say.

"Trevor—"

"Goodbye, Haley."

Tucking my phone in my pocket, I feel it chirp with another text.

Before speaking to Haley, I would have considered tossing the phone. Yet somehow, this little sprite from Nowhereville Lane waved her crazy magic wand, and I just don't care. This time, I don't even care a little.

"I also don't love lobster rolls, although I wish I did because they're gorgeous."

No, Miss Haley Raynor, you're the gorgeous one in this equation.

CHAPTER TWELVE

HALEY

You're going where?" Claire shouts through the phone. "I knew it! I knew there was something between you. My Spidey senses were telling me."

"You don't know anything," I say, taking a glimpse at myself in the mirror.

I don't either, except my stomach is sloshing like crazy, and there aren't any deep-breathing techniques that will stop it.

"Oh, but I do. I know you are an amazing catch, and Trevor Kelly is apparently a smart man. I didn't want to put too much pressure on the situation, especially knowing you're on your dating hiatus—which I support, by the way. I just could tell by the way he looked at you that he wanted to scoop you up."

Claire's enthusiasm, while appreciated, isn't helping me keep focused on what this is.

And what it isn't.

"This is not a date," I say evenly. "Please chill a little."

"He's picking you up for dinner. It's a date, Haley."

I swipe a container of lip balm off the counter and smear it on my lips. My stomach flips, knocking all my internal organs askew.

When he called today, I expected him to be making sure I knew he was kidding about the dinner thing. I knocked an entire glass of sweet tea over the notes I was taking on résumés when he said he was still planning on meeting me for a meal.

If he thought I would change my mind, he's wrong. I need the help on my résumé, especially since Jen hasn't called, and spending an evening bantering with him in the process isn't the worst way to pass some time.

You're not sharing a bed with him, I tell myself. *Just a meal.*

"This is why I almost didn't tell you," I say.

"Because I'd call you out?"

"No, because you'd jump to conclusions."

I adjust the silver-colored shirt with black stitching that flatters my curves but doesn't cling to them. With no idea where we're going, it's the most universally accepted outfit I could dig out in ten minutes. Ten minutes, because I put it off until the last minute so I didn't primp and make myself a nervous wreck. This outfit will work anywhere. And most importantly, it doesn't look like I'm trying too hard. Or like I think this is a date.

Because it's not.

It's not a date.

I've reminded myself of this a hundred times since he called. I've also second-guessed myself a hundred and one times about whether I can remember this when I'm sitting across a table from him. When we're intentionally alone. And he's there just to see me without an excuse—the résumé notwithstanding.

"I'm not jumping to conclusions," Claire says. "I'm basing this off definitions. He called you and asked you to dinner. That, by *every* definition in the book, is a date."

"We also made an agreement last night. It's a business arrangement, Claire. He's getting a dinner companion, and I'm getting help on my résumé. We both win."

"I think you're wrong," she counters. "He pointedly asked you to dinner."

"And told me on a napkin that he'll be sure not to make me fall in love with him." I tug on my shirt a little harder than necessary. "He lives in Nashville. Hours away. And he has no interest in a relationship, and I don't either."

"Really?" she asks.

"Yes, really," I huff. "This might look like a date, and if I'm being honest, it could feel like one if I let it. But it's not, and I'm not entertaining anything otherwise. I'm protecting my heart this time if it kills me."

I spin on my heel as the doorbell rings. Even though I was expecting it, my heart still races. "He's here."

My heart goes from racing to pounding in a matter of a few seconds. I take a couple of deep breaths, silently ridiculing myself for agreeing to this while also reminding myself to play it cool. And for the love of all that's holy, *breathe*.

"Okay, go," Claire gushes. "Wear your hair up, and if you didn't wear that emerald-green scoop neck—"

"Stop."

"You didn't, did you?" She sighs. "This is why you should've called me. I could've helped you get ready."

"Stop it, Claire. I'm not kidding." I take a deep breath and blow it out until the air flows smoothly from my lungs. "This isn't a date."

"Fine. It's not a date. But please have fun. And relax. And believe for a minute that this guy might just like you and that's perfectly okay."

My shoulders sag as the kindness of her words sprinkles over my soul. "I love you, Claire."

"I love you too. Now go have fun on your not-date. And call me after."

"Goodbye."

I end the call. Shoving my phone in my bag, I head down the hallway. Doing a quick check of my reflection in the mirror by the door, I wonder if I should've worn the green top.

Too late.

My hand wraps around the knob and I tug the door open.

"Hey," I say, leaning against the doorframe.

"Good evening."

His eyes twinkle, their blue matching the color of his button-down shirt perfectly. His sleeves are rolled to his elbows, displaying a watch that catches the light above. He's fresh and perfectly put together in a way that appears to have taken about a minute.

Damn him.

I smooth an imaginary wrinkle out of my shirt, the one I wish with certainty was the green scoop neck. My intentional lack of effort is biting me in the ass. Now I'll look like the frumpy girl with this gorgeous man, and there's nothing worse than looking like the girl on a date with a guy totally out of her league.

"I didn't know we were getting so spiffy for this," I say.

He chuckles. "Did you just use 'spiffy' in a sentence?"

"Yes. You have a problem with that?"

"No, no problem. I just haven't heard it in dialogue since my grandmother commented on my fifth-grade school pictures."

"That must've been ages ago," I crack, grabbing my keys off a little table by the door.

"Easy there. You aren't that much younger than me."

"You know, the more time I spend with you, the more amazed I am that women fall for you like they do," I lie. "Are you sure this is a real problem you have?"

He reaches behind me to shut the door. His forearm brushes against my side. It's like a live wire bites me, sending a ripple of uncontained energy through my veins. If he notices, he doesn't show it.

"Maybe Penn was right and you're just a unicorn that's oblivious to my charm." He stands straight and smirks. "Nah, just kidding. That's impossible."

I sigh, my body still humming from his touch. "This is going to be a long night."

"Better get it started, then."

We walk down the sidewalk to his freshly washed truck. I keep a couple of steps behind so I can check him out.

His light-brown hair is combed to the side, angled in a perfect, offset spike. The sandy color matches the leather in the belt wrapped around his trim waist, as well as the boots on his feet.

He carries himself with a confidence I've never known but always admired in the rare few I've seen who have it. It's as if the world could be ripping at him from all sides and he wouldn't even know it. I wonder how people develop that kind of self-assurance.

We reach the truck. He holds the door open for me.

"After you," he says, waving toward the cab.

"Thank you."

He waits until I'm settled before closing the door. By the time I'm buckled in, he slides into the seat next to me.

The cab fills with his cologne and mixes with the masculine energy rippling off him in soft waves. Between the two, I'm a little light-headed.

"On a serious note," he says, starting the engine, "you look very pretty tonight."

I look down at my shirt. "Thanks. I probably should've worn something else, but this will have to do."

"Why?"

"Why, what?"

"Why should you have worn something else?" He furrows a brow like he's not able to follow me.

"I just . . . I don't know," I admit, feeling slightly foolish.

"Let me give you a little insight into the mind of a man," he says, twisting to face me. "When a man tells you that you look pretty, he means it. And odds are it has very little to do with your shirt."

My body warms as I sink into the leather seat and forget all about the green scoop neck. I settle my gaze on the floorboard for a moment so he won't see me beaming. "Well, in that case, thank you. Again."

I look up and we exchange a smile. He shifts the truck in gear, and we head down the road.

Dogwood Lane rolls by at a leisurely pace. The pine trees appear to touch the candied pinks and oranges of the evening sky. We ride for a few minutes, country music playing softly through the speakers. It's a comfortable quiet, the kind that could lure you to a peaceful sleep if you wanted it to. I wonder how I can feel so alive and so calm at the same time.

He takes an exit on the highway that leads out of town.

"Did you hear from the flower shop job today?" he asks.

"No, actually. I didn't." I bite my lip.

"Maybe she got busy."

"I hope so." I look at him and accept the sweet smile he gives me. "The more I think about it, the more I really hope that works out. But hope is a scary thing, you know."

"I didn't know that."

I sigh. "Oh, it is. Hope is like the peak of a mountain. If the wind blows the right way, you fall into a beautiful meadow on one side. And if the wind knocks you the other way, there's snow and ice and no hot chocolate in sight."

He laughs. "You with the analogies."

"But you know what I'm saying. It's the precursor to disappointment a lot of the time."

"That's life, Haley."

"Yeah. I guess. But this time, I'm focusing on the meadow side of the mountain and letting myself have a little hope."

He watches me out of the corner of his eye. "What makes you like the flower shop so much?"

I try to put into words the fuzziness in my chest when I walk into the shop. The warmth that spreads over my body when I see flowers and how happy it makes me to see other people giving and receiving the simple joy of a single bud.

"It's one of the simplest sources of pleasure." As soon as I say it, I know I've walked into a minefield. He snickers. "Oh no," I say as his smirk spreads over his cheeks. "That's not what I meant."

"I was going to suggest you get out more," he cracks.

I try to play it off but feel my cheeks warm. "What I meant was I love how something so simple can just turn someone's day around. Flowers just make people smile." I rest my head on the seat and look at him. "At least they do me."

"I'm sure Jen will call," he says. "And if she doesn't, her loss. And I might've overheard the ladies in the bank today saying they were going to be hiring. Just a heads-up."

"Thank you," I say, pleased he was thinking of me today. "Guess I need to make sure to nail this résumé, huh?"

"You will. *We will*," he says. "We'll find your salable assets and play them up. It'll be easy."

I groan. "I don't know about that. I can't even figure out what pertinent skills I have to 'sell myself,' as you say."

"You have people skills," he offers. "I mean, I've seen you in action. You can be kind of a jerk to me, but others seem to like you well enough."

"Hey!"

He looks at me, stopping me in my tracks. His eyes are scrunched up at the sides, his lips curled in a soft way. My hand falls from the door as I feel my heart leap into my throat.

He looks back toward the road. "You have childcare skills," he says, clearing his throat. "That means you can keep things alive. And you probably filed books and stuff, too, right? That's office experience."

I study him from the side as he focuses on the road. I wonder what all he's done in his life, what experiences he's had. I imagine him with some six-year plan to becoming independently wealthy, and suddenly, I'm extremely out of place.

He catches me staring just before I tug my eyes off him. "What?" he asks.

"Nothing."

"No, what were you going to say?" He narrows his eyes with a lighthearted wink. "Say it."

"You shouldn't press. It's rude."

He pulls the truck up at a red light and stops. "You know I'm not going to let this go."

I blow out a breath and watch the cars pass in front of us. "I'm not saying this to be whiny, because no one likes a whiner, but it's just occurred to me that I've probably wasted the last handful of years of my life."

"First of all, you're right. No one likes a whiner."

"This is why I didn't want to tell you," I point out. "Next time, leave me alone."

He laughs, his cackle filling the truck. As annoyed as I want to be with him, I find myself laughing too.

He flips off the radio. "Second of all, I think it's hard to waste your life."

"I don't know," I say warily.

"Have you not learned anything in life?"

"No. I have learned things. A lot of them."

"Like?"

I roll my eyes but play along since I brought it up. "Like what it feels like to be twenty-six and have nothing to show for it but a few life lessons." I scrunch up my face. "I'm kidding. I'm just having a moment. It'll pass."

Trevor looks at me, his eyes bright. "I think what you're feeling is more normal than you realize."

"Really?"

"Yeah. This goes back to what I was saying about love and how people change all the time. Do you know how many people I went to college with who are doing something outside of their degree right now?"

"I'm guessing a lot."

"More than not, probably. I'd venture to say three-quarters of my friends who graduated with a four-year degree aren't using it right now."

"Are you using yours?"

"Damn right. I paid way too much money for that piece of paper." He laughs to himself. "Well, my dad did. But he just paid for it so I wouldn't bum off him forever. That was his biggest fear, I think."

I laugh as he pilots the truck around a bump in the road. His forearms flex, his jaw moving as he thinks about something unknown to me, and I'm struck by what else there is that I don't know about this man.

"I highly doubt anyone would ever think you're lazy," I say. "You seem very motivated."

He laughs, running a hand over his jaw. "I have to be. Jake would kill me otherwise."

"Is he married?"

"Nope. He agrees with me."

"On what?"

"That there's too much pressure to marry and settle down. It's like you just get a handle on your hormones, if you're lucky, and all of a sudden, you have to pick what you'll do for the rest of your life and who you'll mate with for the next fifty, sixty years. It's asinine."

"I hate the phrase 'mate with,'" I say, making a face. "I get this image . . ." I shiver. "I can't."

"What phrase should I use? 'Making love'?" He bats his eyelashes at me. "Let me give you a tip: never trust a guy who says he wants to make love to you."

"Why? It's so romantic." I bat my lashes back at him. "A little cabin in the woods with white sheets and rose petals sprinkled all around . . ."

I open my eyes to see him looking at me, unimpressed.

"When a guy is thinking about taking you to bed, they aren't thinking about whispering love notes in your ear." His hand moves discreetly to his groin. He shifts in his seat, moving his eyes back to the road. "They're thinking about the curves of your body and how you'll feel wrapped around them."

My thighs press together, my stomach clenching so hard I almost groan as I immediately picture him hovering over me. I divert my gaze from his and out the passenger's side window.

"Let me give you a tip," I say. "Talking like that won't help lessen a girl's attraction to you."

"Ah, do you like a little dirty talk, Miss Raynor?" He chuckles, grabbing my thigh. His fingertips press into the denim covering my legs in one swift movement. It's a reaction, a playful gesture he didn't preplan; the way his mouth hangs ever-so-slightly open at the contact makes it obvious.

My gaze flies to the spot where he's touching me. The embers aflame in my belly burn hotter. He pulls away, but it does nothing to quell the riot inside me.

This isn't a date. He's just a flirt. He lives in Nashville. This isn't a date. He probably talks like this with every girl. This isn't a date.

"We're here," he says, his voice a little rougher than before.

When I look up, I realize we are at Colby's Steakhouse in Rockery.

CHAPTER THIRTEEN

Trevor

A fter you," I say, holding the door open for Haley.
She strolls by me, her purse tossed over her shoulder like we do this every weekend. I usually hate it when a woman gets a certain level of comfort with me. It's always a precursor to particular behaviors—behaviors I have no interest in entertaining.

Strangely, this time, it just feels normal. Easy. All right. Nice.

"Reservation for Kelly," I say. I slide up beside Haley, putting thoughts of anything other than having her by my side out of my mind. Even if it's just for these couple of hours, I'm going to enjoy this weird sense of peace.

"Right this way." The hostess grabs two menus and escorts us through the restaurant.

The place is decorated like a log cabin with little country sayings and pictures on the walls. The booths are covered in a burnt-orange vinyl, probably to make it easier to clean up after the families filling most seats.

My hand goes to the small of Haley's back as we venture through the other patrons. She glances at me out of the corner of her eye and gives me a shy smile unlike the ones I usually get from her.

The scent of vanilla ripples off her body. It winds around me, almost luring me closer to her. My fingers press into the fabric of her shirt, craving the contact, as we approach an open booth in the back.

I remind myself to behave, to remember who she is and who she isn't. She's not a woman I'm taking out as a precursor to a quick fuck after. She's not that at all.

That might just be why I like her.

And that's just plain weird.

"Here you go." The menus are dropped on the table. "Your server is Delia, and she'll be with you in a few minutes."

"Sounds good."

I wait for Haley to sit before taking my seat across from her.

"I figured a steakhouse was a safe bet," I say, resting my forearms on the table. "With all the food issues you didn't have . . ."

She puts her purse on the chair beside her. "I didn't want to seem too picky. I hate when people list off all the things they refuse to eat. If it's a food allergy or something, I get it. That's different. But if you're just making my life hard by refusing to eat beef that's not grass fed . . ." She shakes her head. "I'm not into that kind of pickiness."

"Lorene promised me this was a good spot."

"Ah, I heard about you and Lorene," she says, leaning my way. "I heard through the grapevine you were doing chores for her and you took her to breakfast."

"You tell that grapevine named Claire to mind her own business," I joke. "But, yeah, I did take her to eat and moved some pictures around. She's very grandmotherly."

She grins. "That she is. Has she given you pie yet?"

"No, but I smelled something pretty amazing before I left the inn tonight. I have high hopes."

"If you want another dinner with me, you're going to have to bring me some of Lorene's pie. And don't try to get a counterfeit piece, because I'll know."

I laugh, watching her eyes dance. "I saw you with a doughnut. I can only imagine what you'd do over pie."

God, no, don't go there, Kelly. Watching her gorgeous lips surround the pie-filled fork would probably unman me. If she groaned one time . . .

"I'm not even going to pretend to be embarrassed by or dispute that," she says with a hint of defiance.

I grab a menu, needing to change the subject quick. "Have you been here before?"

"Yes, actually. And I love it here. The food is super good and not overpriced." She picks up her menu. "I can't eat food that costs more than what I make in a day."

I lower my menu. "So if I told you my favorite meal is a filet mignon with crab at Morris's Steakhouse in Nashville, you'd be . . ."

She lowers her menu too. "How much is it?"

"Oh, like a hundred bucks or something. With sides," I add in as her eyes go wide.

"That's ridiculous, Trevor."

"It's really good."

Her menu slowly rises until it covers her eyes.

"Are you judging me over there?" I ask. "I can feel your judginess through the menu, and I don't appreciate it."

"No. You waste your money however you feel necessary. No judgment here."

"You're a brat," I say with a laugh. *An adorable, beautiful brat. But still a brat.*

Our attention is drawn to the side as a woman with a name tag reading DELIA approaches. "Welcome," she says, pulling an order form out of her apron. "I'm Delia, as you can probably read. And pardon the ketchup I'm currently wearing. A three-year-old didn't appreciate the macaroni and cheese and let me know that with gusto."

Haley giggles. "No macaroni and cheese, then. Got it."

"Sorry." She blows her bangs out of her eyes. "So what can I start you off with tonight?"

I look across the table at the deep-brown eyes staring back at me. "What would you like?"

"I'll have a sweet tea. No lemon, please," she says.

"I'll have the same." I look at Delia briefly but swing my attention back to Haley when there's a little too much to read in Delia's gaze. "Do you want an appetizer?"

Haley considers this. "I don't think so. Not tonight. I'm still a little bothered by your filet-and-crab order."

"You are not."

"I am too," she insists. "And on another note, surf and turf has never made sense to me."

"You don't even know what's good."

She grins. "You should watch your word choice. I'm at dinner with *you*."

Delia, who I've forgotten is even standing there, laughs. "You two are adorable."

I look over at Haley. Her face is covered by the menu, and I wonder if it's to keep me from seeing her reaction to Delia's assumption—that we're a couple.

The word usually makes me want to vomit. It's a sign things are crossing the line to commitment, to responsibility, and those are two words I don't love. But thinking of it attached to Haley feels different. It's like we are just together, two people having dinner and enjoying ourselves. It's not as suffocating, and I might even like it if I thought about it long enough.

Which I won't.

"Apparently no appetizer and no surf and turf," I say. "My *adorable* dining partner is a little pickier than she let on."

"Got it." Delia stuffs her notepad in her apron. "I'll be back momentarily with your drinks. Try not to kill each other while I'm gone."

"I'll try," Haley says. "It's hard."

Yes, it is. I adjust in my seat as discreetly as I can, because it seems everything about this firecracker across from me turns me on. *Shit.*

Delia disappears into the dining area as I turn my attention back to the lady in front of me.

"Okay," she says. "Being serious. You picked a nice place. Thank you. But you could've taken me to Mucker's, and it would've been fine."

"I'll take that as a point in my favor."

She narrows her eyes, her lashes dark and thick. "You don't really mind dining alone, do you?"

"Actually, I do. For real," I say when she narrows her eyes even more. "I'm fine to eat alone at home or in my office. But I hate going into public and having a meal by myself."

"Why? Are you self-conscious?"

"Not really," I say. "I just . . . Fine. Maybe I am."

"You are not."

"Yes, I am," I insist. My foot taps against the floor as I decide whether to explain myself. I don't have to. It won't matter if I don't. But for some reason, I want her to understand. Maybe because I think she might care. "I had this thing happen in elementary school where all the moms came for this Mother's Day program. We made them hats with paper plates and buttons, and we had to memorize poems. They brought tea and cookies, and I was so excited to show off my hat and poem to my mom."

I force a swallow as my chest tightens like it did the day she didn't come to the program. The feeling of loneliness that swamped me while I hid in the coat closet at school, humiliated that my mom was the only one who didn't come, envelops me. Even Charlie's mom came that day, and she missed everything. I was only eight years old. I hate that

I still think about this nearly twenty years later. *Get your head back on tonight, Kelly.*

I clear my throat. "Then, you know, she didn't show up."

"Hey," Haley says, reaching for my hand. "I'm sorry. That was really inconsiderate of me."

"You didn't know."

"Yeah, but you tried to tell me and now I feel mean and I hate feeling mean."

"Haley," I deadpan, "you couldn't be mean if you tried."

"Oh, you don't know me very well," she promises. "I can be meaner than anyone you've ever met."

"Doubtful."

Delia appears out of thin air and sets our drinks in between us. She takes our orders, burgers for both, before disappearing again.

I fiddle with the saltshaker while Haley checks her phone. Mine has gone off a handful of times in my pocket, but I've ignored it.

As I watch her fingers fly on the keyboard, I wonder who she's chatting with and what she's saying. And in the same breath, I acknowledge it's none of my business. For both of our own goods.

"Did you bring your résumé?" I ask, clearing my throat. "We could take a look at it before the food comes."

Her fingers hover over the screen as she looks up at me. There's a wobbliness to her gaze, an uneasiness that makes me uneasy too.

"Yeah," she says. Her phone goes to the table, and she pulls an envelope out of her purse. Instead of opening it or giving it to me, she sets it carefully by her phone. "Can I ask you a question?"

"Shoot."

"This dinner thing—is it just for tonight? Or . . ."

She bites her lip as she waits for my reply. I bite mine, too, to keep from saying something stupid—really to keep from saying anything because anything I say will probably be stupid.

If she were any other girl, I'd know exactly how this plays out. But she's not. And I know how she feels about things, and I respect the hell out of it, even if I don't agree. If I press this thing between us, I'll be an asshole. But I want to. And that want gets worse every minute I'm around her.

"It's whatever you want it to be," I say. "I go to Nashville this weekend. After that, I'll probably just be in town a few days. A week at the most."

I slide all emotions out of my brain as I watch her lips twist.

"I see," she says.

"If you want to have dinner and chat about life and doughnuts while I'm here, that's awesome. And if you're not into it or have other plans or just want to tell me to fuck off, that's not awesome but okay. Ball is in your court, sweetheart."

I grimace as the stupidity I knew I'd come up with rolls off my tongue. Her eyes go wide as she absorbs the word, and I kick myself for letting it slip.

What's wrong with me?

She eyes me skeptically. "If we're going to spend time together, we need a few ground rules."

I sit back in my seat and take her in. I have no idea what she's getting at, but she's fucking adorable when she's trying to be serious. "Ground rules for what?"

"For this arrangement we have."

"Why?"

"Because all contracts have terms and conditions, do they not?"

I laugh. "You've lost it."

"Really?" She lifts a brow. "Isn't it you who's always saying women arrive at conclusions about relationships that you don't intend to happen?"

Leaning forward again, I watch as the proximity of my body to hers lights up her eyes. There's a wariness to it, but also a hunger that I both love and am leery of myself.

116

My body hums just having her near. She doesn't know that, but it's really the best argument for her case. She's said so herself—she falls in love easily. She may be sexy and funny and intelligent, but I'm not here to make anyone fall in love.

"Okay," I say. "You've made your point."

Relief washes over her face. "Good. You can even use these lessons later on real dates."

Real dates. This isn't a *real date* and I know that. But hearing her say it out loud is annoying.

I study her for a long time, not sure what to say. My normal spiel seems pointless—she's the one who's demanding boundaries, but the fact I'd go without them might mean I need them more than ever.

She sits up in her seat. "First rule is no touching."

There's no way I heard that right. My forehead creases. "What did you say?"

"No touching."

"Um, is this for you and me or for me to use in general?"

"Both." She squares her shoulders. "Or whatever relationships you don't want to commit anything to."

"What if I want to commit to sex later? I think you're confused about the purpose of dating, Haley. It's to touch."

She takes a straw out of the wrapper and slides it in her drink. "You have to be careful. Touching means something to a woman. One little brush of your hand or hand to the small of her back . . ." She pauses long enough to remind me that I touched her there walking in. "One moment like that, and it's tattooed on a woman's skin."

"So what you're really saying here is you're sitting there thinking about me touching you earlier?" I grin as my body temperature rises a couple of degrees. "Another point in my favor."

"No, it's not," she says, shifting in her seat. "It's not a point in your favor, because you didn't mean anything by it. You were just being flirty and doing what comes naturally."

"Right." *Wrong.*

"So no touching. Between us, anyway. Leave room for Jesus."

I scratch my head. "I've been to church my whole life, and I'm still gonna need an explanation on that one."

"It means if there isn't room between our bodies for another body, we're too close." She relaxes back in her seat, watching my reaction with amusement.

I'm pretty certain my jaw drops, because I feel air rushing in my mouth. "I'm not going to go around with a measuring stick and make sure there's room for Jesus between us."

She grins. "You don't have to measure. We're talking about the proverbial Jesus."

"I'm not comfortable talking about Jesus at all." *Especially when it has to do with my body not touching yours.* "Can we just agree I won't try to turn you on? Because that's what this is really about. And," I say as she starts to protest, "I don't want to do that. I mean, I'd happily *do that.* But I think doing that would make you upset in the long run, so we shouldn't."

She laughs, but I see her pupils dilate. I notice the uptick in the rise and fall of her chest and the way her fingers rewrap against the side of her glass.

This woman is going to kill me.

"You're rambling, Trevor."

"I know." I tug at the collar of my shirt. "What else you got?"

"The second thing is no compliments on appearance," she says.

"You have to be kidding me." My palm hits the table, rattling the saltshaker against the pepper mill. "You don't want me to tell you that you look pretty tonight?"

"I mean, you can say things in a general sense, but no particulars. No commenting on hair or eyes or anything like that."

"I thought women loved that." I balk. "I thought it was the gentlemanly thing to do."

"It is if you're on a date. If you're wanting to be a gentleman and see if a date can ultimately lead somewhere." She bridges her fingers together and rests her chin on her hands. "Is that what you want?"

"No."

"My point." She gives me a forced smile. "And the last thing is, no insinuation that there will be more happening—more dates, conversations, whatever. Take it a day at a time. A meal at a time, as it is between the two of us."

Somewhere between sitting down at the table and ordering drinks, I went wrong. I lost control. The power I usually hold in conversations and interactions with women flew right out of my pocket and into her sweet little hands.

And to make matters worse, there's a good chance I'm going to do something I never do: play by her rules.

What in the actual fuck?

I shake my head. "So no touching. No being polite. And no alluding to plans in the future. Am I right?"

"You got it." She smiles at Delia as she places our plates in front of us. "Trust me, Trevor. This is the way for us both to get what we're after."

She's probably right. In a super annoying, sensible, fucking logical adult way, she's probably right.

"I think this is dumb," I say. My fingers burn with the knowledge they won't get to touch her again. *And hell if I don't want to know how soft her skin is against me. How her tiny hand would fit in my large, calloused one. Shit.* "I think this is really dumb."

"And I think you're dumb."

I look up at her, and she's smiling the sweetest damn smile I can imagine. "I was wrong. You are mean."

"I told you."

I have a feeling I have no idea how *mean* she can be.

CHAPTER FOURTEEN

HALEY

"Am I supposed to assume we are not having dinner tomorrow?" Trevor slides me a sly smile.

The truck rolls back to Dogwood Lane beneath the bright silver stars. My stomach is full, both from the wonderful food and the ridiculous laughter. I can't remember a time when my cheeks ached from smiling so much.

Once he agreed to my guidelines, things normalized between us. There were jokes and stories and more innuendos than one conversation needed. But the best part was I could see in his eyes that he wanted to touch me as badly as I wanted him to . . . but he didn't. There's relief, and satisfaction, in all that.

He'll be gone soon, Haley. And you're okay with that, remember?

"No, actually, because that's against the guidelines," I say with a casual shrug.

"I hate your guidelines."

"I know." I try not to laugh. "But we didn't get to work on my résumé, so that is a sticking point. I fulfilled my end of the bargain. You didn't."

"That's so unlike me." He glances at me over his shoulder. "I always make sure I fulfill my end of the bargain before getting mine."

"Of course you do."

I settle back in the seat. The leather is warm from the heater Trevor turned on for me, and I yawn as we enter town.

"Sleepy?" he asks.

"No. Not really."

I turn my head to look at him. He's so handsome as he rests one hand on top of the steering wheel and strokes his chin with the other. There's something so inherently sexy about a man who's in control, and that's exactly how Trevor looks right now—in control.

I just need to be in control too.

"This is probably against a rule," he says, "but I enjoyed having dinner with you tonight."

"I enjoyed tonight too," I say honestly.

He presses his lips together. "Do women really overthink everything?"

"Yes. Women really overthink everything."

He looks at me. "Are you going home and overthinking everything we talked about tonight?"

I consider telling him the truth—that I started overthinking things way before he even showed up at my house. But if I do that, if I admit there's something to overthink, he might get the wrong impression. Whether that I'm somehow clinging to something that isn't there, or that I'm trying to get out of spending time with him, it doesn't matter. Either would be bad.

"Don't lie," he warns. "Or does that bout of silence give me the answer?"

"Yes," I admit. "I'll overthink things. But that really has nothing to do with you, so don't get the wrong idea."

"How does it have nothing to do with me?" He shakes his head. "Such an ego killer."

I ignore the ego part and answer his question. "Because I could be on a date with Penn right now—not that you and I are on a date—and I'd be overthinking it."

His jaw tenses, but he keeps his eyes glued to the road ahead. "I don't think Penn's a good choice for you."

"How would you know?"

"Because I'm a guy, for one. And I know what guys like Penn are thinking."

"Me too. He'll sleep with anything that lies still. This is not a secret."

"Exactly, which is why he's a bad choice for you."

"You're wrong," I tell him. He gives me a look that would make me shrivel if I cared. "Penn is not a bad choice. He's not a choice at all."

He makes a sound of satisfaction and bobs his head back and forth. "Well, I'm glad you see it my way."

I roll my eyes as my phone rings on my lap. I look down and see it's Jennifer. I eke out a breath and sit straight up.

"Hey," I say. "This is Jen from the flower shop. Do you mind if I answer it? It's rude, I know, but—"

"No. Get it. Absolutely. I'll be pissed if you don't."

I swipe the phone quickly and press it to my ear. "Hey, Jen."

"Haley, hi. I'm sorry for calling you so late."

"No, it's fine. I'm just coming back from Rockery, actually."

"Are you driving? Do you need to go?"

I glance at Trevor. He gives me a thumbs-up before turning his attention back to the road. "Nope. I'm sitting in a truck being chauffeured around."

Trevor makes a face at that. I fight not to laugh.

"Oh, okay." She clears her throat. "Tom and I sat down yesterday and had a heart-to-heart about the business and retirement and what we want out of life. You know those conversations always lead to tears."

I feel myself teeter-tottering on the edge of hope, the icy side of disappointment taunting me. My throat tightens as I hold on to the phone for dear life, and I wish I could reach for Trevor's hand.

"I bet that was hard," I say with a gulp. "How'd it go?"

"Well, we decided to close this weekend because Tom's aunt is coming to town, and we really want to spend time with her. She's a sweet lady, and we don't see her often enough to warrant spending all day at the shop."

"I can understand that."

"It's a part of Tom's issue with the shop to start with. It takes up so much of my time."

"I can understand that too."

"He'd actually floated it as potentially for sale to a Realtor last week, unbeknownst to me. So when I came to him with the idea of you helping me out, he came clean . . . and agreed this might work."

I swallow back a cheer. Remaining professional is hard when I just want to blurt out, *Did I get the job?* Trevor seems to see my struggle, because he chuckles quietly next to me. I fire a glare his way, and he makes a show of smoothing his face of any humor.

Bastard.

"So," Jen continues, "as a compromise to keeping it open, I agreed to a vacation in Hawaii for our anniversary in a couple of weeks. Which sounds so First World problem, I know." She laughs. "But it does lend me a problem in that I have no one to manage the shop while we're away."

I take a deep breath and focus on the lights that flow by the truck instead of on the way my spirits soar entirely too high.

"I was hoping you'd come in and do that for me," she says. "I don't know when you were thinking to start, but it would be the first of the week."

"Yes," I almost shout. "Of course. Oh, Jen, I'd love to."

"Great. You did an amazing job with the arrangement the other day, and your passion for flowers reminds me so much of my own. I can start you off two dollars more an hour than you were making at the library, which I talked to Sandra about today. I hope that's okay."

"Of course."

"Perfect. If you want to come in and train next week, you could officially start then."

I cover my face with my free hand. Squeezing my eyes shut, I try not to squeal. "Yes. I'd love that," I say.

"Great. Come by sometime Monday or Tuesday and we'll hash out the details. Welcome aboard, Haley."

"Thank you. Thank you so much."

She ends the call, and I let my phone drop to my lap.

"So?" Trevor asks. "You're killing me, woman."

I turn slowly to look at him. I can feel my eyes widen, the heater in the truck drying them out. "I got the job."

Trevor smiles the biggest smile I've seen him share as he grabs my leg and squeezes it. "Congratulations," he says. "That's awesome. Are you excited?"

"Yeah," I say, still in disbelief. "I'm kind of shocked, but, I mean, this is . . . amazing."

"It is amazing."

The truck pulls to the curb in front of my house. Trevor cuts the engine and climbs out while I search for my phone, which somehow dropped on the floor. By the time I've picked it up and have my bearings, he's opened the door.

He takes my hand, his palm warm and strong. I step out and follow him to the door.

"Guess I don't need that résumé," I say softly as we step onto the porch.

"I mean, maybe not now," he says. "But it's always a good thing to have on hand."

He runs his fingers through his hair. Peering down at me, his eyes sparkle in the moonlight, and I want to reach up and touch his face. And thank him for dinner. And the support. And making me feel so capable . . . and pretty.

"I think tomorrow calls for a celebration dinner," he says. His voice is soft in the night air, and despite the warm temperature, I shiver. "I know planning ahead is against the rules, but you'll have to cut me some slack on this one."

"Great," I say, giving in to the happiness I feel.

"It was that easy?"

"Who am I to tell you not to celebrate me? That's ridiculous."

He chuckles. He takes a step closer, his eyes locked on mine, and for a long moment, I think he's going to kiss me.

His head dips down, his cologne filling my nostrils, and I war with myself about whether to lift my chin and prepare to dissolve or to take a step back like the smart woman I am pretending to be.

If only he weren't so delicious, if spending time with him weren't so easy. Fun. Tempting.

The battle inside my brain takes a second too long. Trevor's lips quirk up as he leans away.

"I forgot about Jesus," he whispers.

I laugh. The frustrated, pent-up aggression is heavy in the notes, and it makes Trevor laugh too. I stick my key in the lock with a little more force than it requires and pop the door open.

"Tomorrow at seven?" he asks.

"Perfect."

He leans forward and presses the very edges of his lips to my cheek. My breathing slows, my heart thumping evenly in my chest as I feel the sparks shooting through my veins rattle off like a holiday fireworks show.

When he pulls back, he smiles. "Good night."

"Good night" is all I can say.

I watch him walk down the sidewalk and get to the front of his truck.

"Go in," he says. "Lock the door. Then I'll go."

I start to argue for the sake of arguing. But it turns out my voice won't work.

It's probably for the best.

I go inside and lock up and then peek through the window. He pulls away down the road, and I grin the entire time.

See you later, sexiest-friend-I've-ever-had-whom-I-can't-touch-and-it-makes-me-crazy-but-I-need-to-be-a-responsible-adult.

I lean against the wall. "I got the job." I grin even harder. "And I had dinner with Trevor Kelly. Not bad for a random day. Not bad at all."

CHAPTER FIFTEEN

HALEY

"Y̶ou did great, Mia!" I shout.

The handful of students still in Aerial's gym cheer as Mia lands her gymnastics trick. Neely watches from her office, a satisfied look on her face. I know Neely thinks she hit the jackpot by getting Mia as her soon-to-be stepdaughter. Mia loves gymnastics as much as Neely—a collegiate gymnast back in the day—always has.

My little buddy runs across the mats, her ponytail swishing back and forth, and wraps her arms around my waist. "I've been working on that forever. I was starting to give up."

"No," I gush. "You don't give up. It's not what we do."

"I know. I remembered that and it's why I didn't."

I give her another squeeze before she pulls away.

"Hey, Mia," Keyarah calls out. "Wanna go home with Madison and me and watch a movie?"

"Can I?" she asks Neely as she approaches.

"If it's okay with Susan."

Their mom gives Neely a thumbs-up. The trio of girls grab their things and skip outside, and just like that, the bustling gym is eerily silent.

"It's funny how quickly it gets quiet," I note.

"It goes from a hundred to one in an instant." She walks onto the mats and starts picking up towels. "Thanks for helping me out today. The girls wanted to practice their routines, and I couldn't be out here and in the office working on competition paperwork at the same time."

"I didn't do too bad," I joke, helping her pick up. "I mean, I've never tumbled a day in my life. But I was slightly impressive with my 'Point your toes!' comments here and there."

Neely laughs. "You've been a gym mom for years. You should've picked up something by now."

I hand Neely a couple of towels. "Thank you."

"For?"

"I've always had a fear that some woman would come into Dane's life and kick me out. You've been so lovely to me, and I really appreciate that."

"Oh, please," she says. "You are as important to that little girl as I ever will be. She loves you, Hay."

I rest my head on her shoulder. "Yeah, well, she can stop growing up and wanting to spend all her free time with her friends. I'm relegated to spending my time with Claire now if I want to see a friend, and Claire's probably going to get me arrested one day."

Neely laughs, patting me awkwardly on the head. "Maybe there'll be another little one for you to—"

"Oh, my God," I squeal, jerking my head off her shoulder. "Are you pregnant?"

"No," she says with a full-bellied laugh. "Could you have asked that any louder?"

"Yeah, I could've. You just scared the crap out of me."

She looks at the floor, her face a rosy color. "I hope to scare the crap out of you for real, soon. I mean, we aren't married yet or anything, and I'd like to do things in order if I can."

"I can plan a wedding over a weekend. I swear. And," I say, dragging out the word, "I just got a job at Buds and Branches. So I have the flowers covered."

"You did? Haley. That's wonderful."

"I know. I'm so excited. I can't wait to jump in and make beautiful arrangements and bouquets." I sway back and forth. "This is gonna be fantastic."

She laughs, tossing the towels in a bin. "It's really the perfect thing for you."

"I know . . ." My voice trails off as I glance at my watch. It's way later than I realized. "Hey, Neely. I gotta go."

"Oooh. Do you have a date?"

I laugh, heading for the door. "No. More like an appointment."

"You're smiling pretty smugly for a dental visit, girlfriend."

"It's not a dental visit, girlfriend," I say, mocking her. "You about done here?"

"Yup. I'll be locked up and gone within ten minutes. Go on. I'll be fine."

"Perfect. Bye."

"See ya."

The streetlights are just flickering on as I venture outside the gym. Pulling my hoodie tighter around me, I jog down the street and take a right. Blue, an old hound dog that's lived here longer than me, lies in the middle of the road. That he hasn't gotten hit is a testament to the drivers who traverse this road every day.

"Hey, bud," I say as I jog by on the sidewalk.

He lifts his head and then rests it on the ground again.

I jog up the little incline and, when I reach the top, see Trevor's truck. He's early tonight.

I haven't talked to him since he dropped me off last night. I considered sending him a quick text as I normally would after a date, just to say thanks for a nice meal. Then I remembered it wasn't a date and he hates texts if his response to Liz's is any indication, so I didn't. I just sat in the bathtub and replayed the slight kiss on the cheek over and over again.

I did exactly what I knew I would do. I overthought everything. What I didn't expect was the way my thoughts always circled back to the kiss on my cheek and how that made me so . . . happy.

He hops out of his truck as I get closer. The jeans he had on the day I met him make a reappearance. The "shirt" stretching over his broad shoulders is a heather-gray sweater that makes him look like one thing he isn't: cuddly.

"I thought you stood me up," he calls to me. "I got here about five minutes ago and you didn't answer the door."

"Because I wasn't home." My breath billows in front of me. I bounce on my toes to stay warm. "Do you want to come in? Because clearly I'm not ready to go with you yet."

"Sure."

We head up the sidewalk and I unlock the door.

"I love how you walk everywhere," he says.

"Small-town life." I flip on a light switch and shut the door behind him. "Welcome to my humble abode."

"I love this painting," he says, heading over to the one piece of art I own. "LaCassa had an art show in Nashville a few years back. I don't know shit about art, but this painting in particular stood out to me." He looks at me. "I love that you have it."

"I love that I have it too," I say. "I actually won it at a charity auction for kids' cancer. I got it super cheap. It was before anyone knew who LaCassa was. Honestly, I didn't know who he was either. I just didn't want to spend my money on something that would be gone in one fell swoop." I bite my lip. "Like filet mignon."

"Agree to disagree on the filet, but love that you got the LaCassa."

"Me too." I let my hair down and run my fingers through it. "It'll take me a few minutes to get changed if you still want to go to dinner."

He grips the back of my sofa. "I'm not supposed to comment on your appearance because you have stupid rules, but I think you look fine."

"Fine? Great," I mutter.

"God forbid I say something else and throw a wrench into your universe."

"It's your universe, too, pal," I say, jabbing him in the chest as I walk by. "You don't want me to end up like Liz, do you?"

He grimaces.

"See? Rules exist to protect you from me." I head to the kitchen, flipping on lights as I go. "I know those might be a new concept for you, but you're gonna have to deal." I turn around by the table and put my hand on my hip. "Now, do you want to go to dinner or not?"

He stands in front of me. "We're going to celebrate your job. So, yeah, we're going."

"What if we go out tomorrow and just make sandwiches here tonight because I just chased a bunch of ten-year-olds around a gym and I'm tired?"

"I think that would probably break a rule."

He takes another step to me, his grin growing wider. My heart skips a beat as I breathe him in.

Having him in my space cranks up the attraction I always feel toward him. His masculine presence surrounded by my more delicate things is an intoxicating mix I can't get a handle on.

"It doesn't," I say, catching my breath. "But how close you are definitely does."

"This room is the size of a shoebox. Not my fault."

I take a step back and look at him warily. "You were that boy in school who went through the handbook and just chipped away at everything with the word 'don't' in it, weren't you?"

"Something like that." He scoots past me and opens the refrigerator. "Okay. We can make sandwiches or order pizza. Your choice. I only see two slices of cheese, though, and I really don't want to fight you over dairy products."

I roll my eyes. "You are *so* funny."

"I wasn't joking."

Laughing, I grab my phone. "Fine. Pizza is always the right answer."

"Perfect."

"I'll order Mucker's. They deliver."

I make a quick call to Mucker's. It's hard to ignore the way he moves around the kitchen or how his back flexes in his shirt. I finally look at the wall so I can focus on the order. By the time I'm done, Trevor is in the living room with the television on.

"Make yourself at home," I say, tossing my phone on the coffee table.

He looks at me and grins. "I did. This place is really small, but it has great feng shui."

I plop down on the sofa beside him. "I agree. Although I'm not going to lie—you saying 'feng shui' kind of freaks me out."

"It was my mom's thing when I was growing up. We always had a plant in the east area of our house to promote health." He makes a face. "That sounds ridiculous."

"Yup. It does."

He shrugs and looks around the room. "So what do you usually do on random weekday nights?"

"Well, my 'normal' has really shifted lately."

"From?"

"I used to have Mia a lot," I say, curling my feet under me. "Or I'd be with a guy I was dating, whoever that was. Or I'd be reading."

"What about now?"

I snap the remote out of his hands to stop the incessant channel surfing. I key in the number to a channel on do-it-yourself repairs, figuring we could both enjoy that, and throw the remote into the chair next to me.

He balks. "Did you just take the remote from me?"

"Yeah."

"Well, okay then."

I laugh at the look on his face. "Now we can have a conversation."

"Weren't we having one before?" he asks.

"Yeah, but you were distracting."

He snickers. "I get that a lot."

I don't want to laugh, but I can't help it.

"So back to my question: What are you doing now?"

I consider giving him a bullshit answer, one to segue into something else. But as I take in the genuine sparkle in his eyes, I think he really wants to know. And that's refreshing.

"I've been focusing on me for a change. It's been nice." I wince. "I sound like a total asshole."

"No, you don't. You sound like you're self-actualizing."

"Self-actualizing, huh?"

"Yeah. Like you're aware of your potential and that you owe it to yourself to reach that."

"What about you?" I ask, getting comfortable next to him. "Are you self-actualizing?"

He winks. "I am self-actualized. I've reached my fullest potential. This is as good as it gets."

"Oh, please," I say. "You can't tell me you've reached your full potential in every sector of your life."

"Maybe I have."

I look at him blankly. "So what you're saying is that Liz is your fullest potential?"

He grimaces. "That's a different topic."

"It's not really," I prod.

"Yes, it is."

I cock my head to the side. "Then explain that to me, Mr. Self-Actualized."

He rolls his eyes and falls back into the cushions. "I don't define what fulfills me like most people."

"Oh, I forgot. You don't believe in love."

His arms come out to the sides, and he shrugs, as if to say, "Bingo."

We sit in a tricky silence. Love is a sticking point with both of us, and if I push, it could ruin the entire mood of the evening.

"Want some tea?" I ask, getting to my feet.

"Sure."

"Be right back."

He takes my unspoken request not to follow and stays sitting. I head to the kitchen and pour two glasses of tea, considering the whole time that I might not be as smart as I think I am. I could get in way over my head before I know it if I'm not careful. It feels too natural around him, too amiable, to remember all the danger that comes with a guy like him—a guy who's on the opposite side of the spectrum in terms of what he wants out of life.

By the time I get back, the television is off.

"Thanks," he says, taking a glass.

I sit on the couch, placing my glass on the coffee table. I pull my feet up beside me.

The room is quiet. I wonder vaguely if he can hear my heartbeat. I can't hear his over my own, but I can hear every whisper of a breath he takes.

"Can I tell you something?" he asks. His elbows rest on his knees, his head hanging.

"Of course."

"If I were going to define fulfillment like most people, I'd pick a woman a lot like you." He lifts his head just enough to see me from the side. "But don't take that the wrong way."

My body fills with a warmth that is fleeting. The look in his eyes is so full of caution that I back away. And what's worse is I don't want to back away. These aren't pickup lines. He knows he shouldn't be even saying them. Yet he is. And although I see caution, I also see an element of sadness. But again, I won't overthink that either. He'd pick a woman *like me*, but it won't be me.

"Can I ask what she would be like?" I ask.

"Intelligent. Funny as hell. An ability to hold her own. And she'd be gorgeous but not really have any idea how pretty she is."

He takes my feet and rests them on his knees. It's a break in the rules, but it feels too good to have the contact, so I let it go.

Grabbing my toes, he shakes my feet. "Don't overthink that."

"You know I'm going to," I admit. "But for the record, I think if you wanted to go after a woman like that, she'd be lucky to have you. More or less."

He grins. "That would depend on the day." He rubs the tops of my feet, looking at the darkened television. Questions drift across his face, and I wonder if he's going to share them with me.

I also wonder if he's going to admit he's enjoying this as much as I am. There are no pretenses, no clamor to have to be someone we aren't. But therein lies the problem—who we are just won't work together.

"Why are you so anti-relationship?" I ask. "And don't give me some bullshit answer like you always do."

"Just call me out, why don't you?"

"I did."

He readjusts my feet on his lap and thinks. "I suppose it's multifaceted."

"I have all the time in the world."

Falling back to the cushions, he presses my feet against his stomach. "It's a lot of things . . ."

"Which is what 'multifaceted' means."

He laughs, shaking his head. "I guess . . . I guess it's because I hurt a girl when I was younger. I thought I was in love with her, and one day, I realized I wasn't." He frowns. "I didn't want to marry her. I didn't want to have kids with her. I didn't want to do any of those things, although I loved her tremendously as a person."

I watch a host of emotions flood his face, and my heart breaks as I see the pain he keeps hidden. "I'm sorry, Trevor."

"She hurt herself." He stares at some point in space. "I know it's not my fault. And she's okay now. But it shook me really hard that by changing my mind, I caused that. It seemed so unfair. To both of us."

I pull my legs off his lap and scoot next to him. My heart pounds as I reach over and take his hand in mine. "That isn't fair. To either of you. And I'm truly sorry that happened."

"Me too." He squeezes my hand before removing his from mine. "But that's the main reason why I just don't want to promise something I'm not sure I can make good on."

"For the sake of conversation," I say, "that's what a relationship is, though. It's promising to try something together and see if it works. And if it doesn't, you part ways. And if it does, you have the option of going to the next level."

"Or," he says, "you just don't start the process to begin with."

The doorbell rings and I get to my feet, both relieved and saddened to stop our conversation. I pad across the floor and open it to let the delivery guy in. "Hold tight, Bobby. Let me grab my purse."

I head to the kitchen and retrieve my wallet. Before I'm back, Bobby is gone and Trevor is standing in the foyer with the food.

"I forgot to give you some of my own guidelines yesterday," he says. "The first one is this: it's never okay for you to buy your own food when you're with me."

"But we're at my house."

"Celebrating your new job." He carries the pizza into the kitchen and puts it on the table. "Now stop talking about weird stuff like relationships, and let's eat pizza."

"Okay." I grab some plates and napkins. When I turn around, his phone is in his hand.

"I've been thinking a lot about what you said about handling Liz," he says.

The sound of her name makes me want to flinch. "What about it?"

"She's going to be at my dad's party this weekend. I can't uninvite her or not attend myself. So although I can't undo the fact that she'll be there, I can be up front about what it won't be."

I pass a swallow down my throat. "True."

"How's this?" he asks. "I just sent this to Liz: 'If you come, please bring a plus-one, as I will be. See you there.' Sound good?"

Does it sound good? For Liz to hear that, yes. He needs to set that boundary with her. It sounds good, but my foolish heart needs to ignore the burning sensation in my throat and the million questions I have as to who is going with him to a place Liz will be. But I'm not about to ask that.

"Sounds great," I say and hand him a plate. "Let's eat."

CHAPTER SIXTEEN

TREVOR

This is probably the worst idea I've ever had. And to be honest, I've had some doozies. Like the one that I came up with last night at the inn. It's the one that started this whole train wreck of terrible ideas.

Terrible and potentially amazing.

But it's logical, and logical is what you fall back on when you aren't sure. Logic never fails.

I hope.

I angle my head from side to side as I head into Dogwood Lane, trying to work some of the tension out. The back of my neck feels like a rubber band has been stretched through it and someone is pulling it taut. The pain is irritating and only adds to my discomfort about this whole day.

Lorene fixed me a breakfast of bacon and eggs, even though breakfast isn't included with the room. I made sure to fix her leaky faucet in the kitchen while she prepped the meal. I've enjoyed chatting with her over the last few days, but today I just wanted to get out of there and take care of business.

I stop at an intersection and wait for a school bus. I fire a text to Jake with my idea and answer a few questions we left unresolved after

I got back from Haley's last night. The messages go through, and I toss my phone out of my reach and wait for it.

One. Two. Thr—I don't get to "three" before the phone rings with as many unread messages. Like a firing squad, they come in so quickly I know any peace I had with Jake is dead. He'll use one of those texts to fire me up for the foreseeable future.

I hate the line Haley's drawn. Her stupid refusal to let me touch her or treat her the way I want to is maddening, and I'm not sure if I like her despite, or because of, it.

I drive up her street, swerving around the dog that doesn't appear to have moved since last night. He blinks, so he's alive but apparently really comfortable in the middle of the road.

The sun sits high in the sky, almost directly overhead. My fingers tap a beat against the steering wheel as I pull up to Haley's.

I don't want to feel this desperate. I've not wanted to do something I know I shouldn't like this for a long time.

I've clearly lost my damn mind.

As if my brain has taken control and put me on autopilot, I shut off the truck. Open the door. Get out and lock it behind me. Before I know it, I'm ringing Haley's doorbell with a flood of excitement hitting my veins.

"I'm coming," she hollers from inside the house.

I shove my hands in my pockets and wait for the door to swing open. When it does, I'm glad I'm not able to reach for her.

A pair of short shorts barely covers her legs, and a white tank top stretches across her breasts. I realize I've never seen her this stripped down. What I came here for? It's gone. No clue.

"Hey," she says, pulling her brows together. "What are you doing here?"

"Um . . ."

"We didn't discuss dinner, and assuming is against the rules. But even if I do agree to spare you a meal alone, it's like noon."

I nod like a freaking idiot.

She leans her head against the door. "Trevor? Are you okay?"

"Me? Yeah. For sure." I clear my throat. "I just came by to talk to you."

She steps back and opens the door. Surprise is written across her beautiful face. "Okay. Come on in."

The house smells like blueberries as I enter. I give her a quizzical look.

"I baked muffins this morning," she says as if she knows the question. "It was Story Hour at the library, and the kids always ask for my muffins." She shrugs. "I'm a sucker."

"That's really nice of you," I say.

"Even mean girls have their moments." She tosses me a wink. "So what brings you by in the daylight?"

I take a deep breath and head to the living room. The space is familiar and cozy, and without being asked, I sit on the sofa like I belong there. She sits beside me.

I give myself one more chance to come to my senses and stop this madness. While this idea may seem perfectly fine on paper, it's not.

I know this.

I feel this.

I can't help this.

All I can do is ask and then act like an adult either way.

Clearing my throat, I rest my elbows on my knees. "I want to ask you something."

"You're needy. You know that?"

"Me?"

"Yeah. You and your not wanting to eat alone. Need for fancy foods that are extremely overpriced. Need to show up unexpectedly with a question and not just call like normal people." She starts to laugh but stops when I fail to join. "What's going on, Trevor?"

"Well," I say, wincing, "I'm here to break another rule."

"Oh, geez," she says. "Here we go. What now?"

She looks so sweet with her hair piled on top of her head and her lips tinted blue from the berries. If I go through with this, I'm going to have a hell of a time behaving myself.

But can I?

I hope so.

"I need a favor." I look at her solemnly.

She eyes me with the care of a woman who knows better. "A favor like a slice of leftover pizza? Or a favor like give my opinion of the poodle spa? How's that coming, by the way?"

"Lovely." I sigh at her attempt at redirection. "It's a favor like . . . come to Nashville with me this weekend."

Her eyes almost fall out of her head. I shift in my seat, worried I've overstepped.

"What did you just say?" she asks.

I clear my throat. "Come to Nashville with me. *Please.*"

She tears her eyes from mine and gazes into the distance. Her guard is up, and I want to yank it down and have the vulnerable, sweet Haley back. But the protective mode is on because of me, and I hate that.

Before I can say anything else, she gets to her feet.

"I'm not sure I understand," she says. "You're talking about the party that you told your ex-whatever to go to with a plus-one because you . . . you . . ."

"Look," I say, getting to my feet, too, "I know this sounds stupid, but it's not *just* about Liz."

She crosses her arms in front of her. "Then what's it about?"

"The retirement party is a big deal." I say it like she should give a shit, like saying this should convince her right here and now to agree to go.

"What's that have to do with me?" she asks.

She raises a brow, showing me a crack in her tough-girl veneer that gives me hope. And as much as I'm grateful for that, I'm also grateful to see her holding on to her guns for a minute. That will serve her well with guys like me. Just not with me. I hate it with me.

"You know how pathetic I am at eating on my own," I say. "Don't make me go to a party all by myself."

She laughs. "It's a party with your family."

I reach for her out of instinct. She stills at the contact. My hand falls from her shoulder as I shrug, but I don't miss the goose bumps on her skin as my fingers slowly drag down her silky-smooth arm.

She blushes. "Trevor, look . . ."

"I know. I know, I know, I know," I say. "But I need a plus-one because I don't want to go alone."

"Take Liz."

"You're so funny," I say, narrowing my eyes.

She laughs. "You're afraid of Meredith, aren't you? That's the truth."

"I'm terrified." I stick out my bottom lip. "Just please go with me. I know this a huge thing to ask of you, but this is a big deal."

"It's a big deal to whom?"

"To me." I look her straight in the eye. "Please go. It'll be fun. I promise."

She paces the room, fidgeting with her hair. I want to scoop her up and kiss the shit out of her, and that makes me want to run out of here like my head is on fire.

I don't understand this wanting to be with her like this. I really don't understand wanting to do it, because if something bad happens, it'll ruin this friendship we've struck up out of nowhere—a friendship that keeps surprising me daily. Each day I want to see her. Spend time with her. Fight with her.

It's a weird dynamic. It works in a way I haven't experienced before. This is uncharted territory and I don't know what to do.

"Trevor," she says. She stops moving in a circle and faces me. "Let me be polite at first and tell you that I'm honored you'd take me around your family. That means a lot."

"But . . ." My heart sinks.

"But this is ridiculous."

"Why?"

She laughs an almost angry kind of chuckle. "We've done an amazing job at not messing up this . . . camaraderie? . . . that we have with one another. We've been adults. We've acknowledged how messy this could get, and we've avoided it, partly in thanks to my guidelines that you hate."

"I do hate them."

I want to touch you.

"But you want me to go away for the weekend with you?"

I want to kiss you.

"Around your family? Your friends?"

I want to claim you as mine.

"Where would we stay? How will you explain . . . us? Being together but not *together*? Wouldn't that be super weird?"

I don't give a fuck.

I shake my head to free myself from the irritation. Her questions are relevant. They're smart. And I'll have to answer, but I'm not sure how.

"Okay, in order . . ." I pause, trying to get my mind way out of the gutter. "Yes, I want you to go, and yes, my family will be there. We'd stay at a hotel, and I'd make sure you have your own room. And I'll tell people to fuck off if they demand to put some kind of label on us."

"You make it sound so easy."

"It would be easy. Isn't it always easy when we're together?"

"Yes," she says. "But I put a lot of energy into keeping it that way. Into not letting you get too close. Into reminding myself our little dinner events aren't dates. I tell myself constantly that you and I are friends, because you don't want a girl like me and I don't want a guy like you."

My jaw locks in place. To hell with the fact that she's right. I don't want her to be right. I want her to want me the same way I'm wanting her, even though I know it's fucking stupid. And unfair. And illogical.

But she doesn't. And I shouldn't.

"There's one to make me feel good," I grumble.

She sighs, defeated. "You know what I mean. When I decide to take a risk on a guy again, I want it to be someone emotionally available and someone who can support me. Someone who wants me and maybe could even love me someday." She swallows hard. "That guy, by your own admission, isn't you."

"Well, by your own admission," I fire back, "you aren't the girl who can go to dinner, fuck all night, and then leave the next morning and not care if I call or not."

By her sudden flinch, I realize that came across a lot harsher than intended.

"I'm sorry, Haley. I—"

"No. You're right. I'm not her. And I wouldn't want to be her if I could."

And I wouldn't want you to be.

She crosses her arms over her chest and steels herself my way. She gives back bravado, but I can see that my jab hurt. Yet she fires back with passion and grit, and motherfucker if it doesn't make me want her more.

I feel like my skin is too small for my body and I'm crammed into this little space so tight I can't breathe. Stretching my neck, wincing from the pressure across the backs of my shoulders, I try to relax.

The fact this is hard makes me pissy because hard isn't what we are, and what we are is something I haven't had with a woman before. If asking her to go with me is going to change that, then I shouldn't have done it.

I have to fix this.

I turn around and she's right in front of me, her dark eyes swirling with an emotion she tries to hide on her face.

"Fine," she says.

"Fine what?"

"Fine, I'll go. But make damn sure I have my own room because the guidelines are still intact."

My face breaks into an ear-to-ear smile. "You're afraid of seeing me naked, aren't you?"

She flushes. "If I see you naked, I'll call a cab and come home and bill you the fee. Because I'm not going to make myself miserable. Got me?"

"Yes, madam."

She extends a hand and I shake it before tugging on it gently and pulling her into my chest. She lets herself fall into my arms.

Her breath hiccups as she looks up at me with wide eyes. My body freezes, relishing the contact of her skin against mine.

God, I want her.

"Jesus has no room," she says, although she doesn't make an attempt to step back.

"Yeah. I'm aware."

"Then what are you doing?"

"Seeing something," I say with a smile.

"Seeing what?"

Seeing how much I can torture myself, it seems.

I stare into her eyes. The hunger for her that gnaws at me is reflected in her eyes. It would take a half of a second to kiss her like she deserves to be kissed.

I could do that. I want to do that more than I've ever wanted to kiss anyone. But hidden just behind that need is a vulnerability I can't ignore and one I'd hurt, and I can't do that. I won't. Even if it kills me.

I kiss her cheek. Stepping back, I head to the door.

"Seeing what?" she calls after me, a hint of franticness in her voice.

"Seeing *that*. Be ready at noon tomorrow. If you have a fancy dress, take it. If not, we'll get you one in Nashville."

I stop at the door and pull it open. I look at her over my shoulder. "Thanks, Haley."

"You're a giant pain in the butt, you know that?"

Her narrowed eyes give up to a sparkling grin that makes everything all right again.

"It's been said," I say. "It's also been said I have a giant—"

"Stop." She covers her face. "Just go so I can figure out what just happened here."

You and me both, Miss Haley Raynor.

With a laugh, I step onto the porch and shut the door behind me.

I pause on the sidewalk and look up at the sky. *What the hell did I just do? And why the fuck does it feel so right?*

CHAPTER SEVENTEEN

HALEY

"Can we call this one a date?" Claire lies on my bed, tossing a piece of popcorn in the air and trying to catch it in her mouth. It bounces off her cheek and falls to my comforter. "It includes family. I think that makes a difference."

"I think if I get in my bed next time and there's popcorn in it, there will be a difference."

"You mean, you'll be salty?" She laughs at her own joke. "That was good. My comedic timing is getting better and better."

Shaking my head at her, I fold the green scoop neck shirt and add it to my suitcase. "I think that's a stretch."

She grins and throws another piece up and misses on purpose. "Oops."

"Sometimes I wonder why I like you."

"No, you don't." She groans as she sits up. "I'm loyal and smart, and I'll be able to clean your teeth for free unless I fail this last class. Don't forget how expensive dental hygiene is. I'll be a big asset to you soon."

I roll my eyes. "How did you do on the paper you were working on last week?"

"Good. I think. Oh. Big news." She gives me her cheesiest grin. "I have an informal interview with a dentist office in Rockery. I shadowed a dentist there a few months ago, and they called and said they'd like to talk to me. Cool, huh?"

"Look at you. Taking over the world one tooth at a time."

She presses her lips together. "Bad joke, Hay. Bad joke."

"Yeah. Whatever." I head to my closet and sort through the rack. My suitcase is stuffed as it is, but I feel underprepared.

"You know, they have stores in Nashville if you forget something." She shoves some popcorn in her mouth. "You don't have to take everything you own."

I bury my head in my hands, the excitement, anxiety, and giddiness overwhelming me.

"It's gonna be fine," she says. "It'll actually be better than fine."

"How do you know?" The words come out muffled through my fingers. I lift my head to look at my friend. "What if it goes terribly?"

"How could it be terrible? You like the guy. He likes you. You're going to some schmancy party that will include free booze. If things do go bad, just drink until you forget about it."

I grab a shirt off a hanger and hold it up to me. "Oh, that's a responsible answer."

"That's not a responsible choice of a shirt." She makes a face as she hops off the bed. "I know this one is comfortable, and I'm all about comfort. But it does nothing for your shape, or your boobs, and if you're going to spend the weekend with Trevor, at least put some effort in."

Whining, I toss the shirt on the floor. My bottom lip sticks out as I sink onto the edge of my mattress. *Why bother? Why bother putting effort in?* The bag of popcorn rustles against my side and a few kernels spill out. I'm too preoccupied to give Claire crap about it.

It's like a bad meme where the math equations are all jumbled together on top of someone's head. Best- and worst-case scenarios swirl around. That's what I am—a big mess of thoughts I can't segregate into manageable chunks.

Claire sits beside me. "Now is the time I have to do the one thing I really don't love doing."

"You're going to exercise?"

"Lord, no," she says, clutching her chest. "Don't scare me like that."

My chest vibrates with a chuckle I can't quite eke out.

She puts her hand on my shoulder. "I'm going to be serious. What's really wrong right now?"

"What do you mean?"

"I mean, I don't know what to do with you right now. You've gone with other guys to a family dinner here and there. This isn't something new. I'm not sure why you're so freaked out about it."

"I'm not freaked out about it," I lie.

"Okay. I don't know why you're making such a big deal out of putting together a suitcase." She chews her fingernail, scrutinizing me from the side. "Or do I know why?"

I sigh. "Claire . . ."

"Talk to me."

"I don't want to," I say.

"Don't act like you're eleven."

"Ugh."

I hang my head, feeling my heart strum against my ribs. Everything is on the tip of my tongue, but I'm scared if I put my thoughts and feelings into the universe, it'll make them real. Then I can't take them back. Then I'll hear how dumb they sound, and I'll want to climb under the covers and cry.

I've worked so hard to get here—to the place where I'm able to get up in the morning and have coffee and worry about me. There isn't a guy playing games with my head or a job on the line that I'm tiptoeing around. I have a job at the flower shop and not a thing in the world to worry about outside my own interests, and there's such an unexpected relief in that. I don't want to lose it.

Most of all, I don't want to break my own heart. If that's what happens with Trevor, it's on me. I know what I'm getting into. In some ways, it feels like diving into a shark tank and hoping not to get eaten alive. But for some reason, I'm willing to risk it.

I get off the bed. Walking to the window, I peer out into the neighbor's backyard. "I think . . ." I force a swallow. "I think I could really like Trevor, Claire."

"I know, buddy."

"And I think . . . I think if I don't go on this trip, he and I can stay friends. And if I go, things might change between us, and I've never had something with a guy that felt normal after things got serious."

"But is that what you're worried about?" she asks gently. "Losing him as a friend? Maybe it is. And if it is, that's great. But if it's not, I do think you need to be honest with yourself."

I turn to face her. "It is. Partly."

"Do you think he doesn't like you in the way you might like him?"

His smile rips through my mind, accompanied by his laugh, and I feel it light me up from the inside out.

Does he? He without a doubt wanted to kiss me. The way he looked at me as he leaned down, my breath captured by the intensity of his gaze, leaves me frazzled just thinking about it. I've never felt wanted, needed—craved—more than I did in that moment on my porch. But that means he wanted to be with me. Not that he wanted me. When I pair that with the truths he's shared about his feelings on love, I have my answer.

"No," I admit, my voice shaky. "I think he does *like* me like I might like him. But I also know that doesn't matter."

Hearing that out loud is sobering. The words seem to hang over our heads, not disappearing into the past like some words do.

I blow out a breath, trying to rid myself of the heaviness of the moment. I go back to the closet and sort through the clothes. Shirt after shirt goes by, none of which I really see. All I can see is Trevor's face lowering to kiss my cheek. All I can feel is the way my heart wants me to let it happen even though it knows the pain of the inevitable destruction.

"I don't think you give the guy enough credit," Claire says.

"It's not about credit. It's about what he's told me from the start he believes and wants and accepts as his truth, and all those things don't mesh with mine." I yank a mustard-colored dress off a hanger and add it to the suitcase.

"Are you falling in love with him, Haley?"

"No," I say, my head snapping to hers. "That's not what I'm saying. I'm saying I don't want to get to that point because he doesn't even believe in love. Not like I do. Not like you get married and build a family and dedicate yourself to that."

"But . . . ," she prods.

My shoulders fall. "But he's pretty great."

"Yeah. We've known that from day one."

"Yeah," I say quietly.

Claire gets to her feet, a look of resolve on her face. "Here's what I think you do: Go to Nashville. Have a blast. Follow your heart but don't lose your head."

"Right." I groan. "He looks at me or stands too close, and I just want to forget my heart and head and let my body take over."

"Can't blame you there. But," she says, grabbing the bag of popcorn and putting the clip back on it, "I also know you're smart. And super strong. And whether you know it or not, you'll do what's right for you."

"I haven't always done that."

She considers this. "No, you haven't. One word: Joel." She laughs. "But you've changed lately. I like this new you."

We exchange a smile before she takes the mustard dress out of the suitcase and puts it back on the hanger. "You aren't taking that. It makes you look ashy."

"I love that," I say, breathing in a sigh of relief.

"Yeah, and I love you." She puts it back in the closet. "So back in the closet it goes . . ."

I lug the suitcase up and set it on the bed. It's loaded to the max with a little of every color, fabric, length, and degree of sophistication I own. "I, once again, have no idea what to wear," I say, remembering dinner at the steakhouse. I wince. "I'll be damned if I show up to a place with his ex, or exes, and look like crap."

Oh, God. What if there is more than one Liz there? What if several of his past cling-ons are there? He'll have slept with all of them.

I can't do this.

"I'm not sure you could look like crap. And that's probably what he thinks too." Claire tosses my hair like I'm a child. "Stand up."

"Why?" I ask as I get to my feet. "You know, maybe I should call this off."

Claire takes my hand and walks me to the mirror over my dresser. "Look at yourself."

I do and then look at her.

"At you. Not me," she says, bumping my shoulder.

"Fine. Now what?"

"That girl you're looking at is pretty great. She's so pretty it hurts to be seen with her. And so smart that her gorgeous friend comes to her with language arts homework because she's the only person in town who knows what alliteration is."

I laugh. "That's not true."

"Shhh." Claire brings a finger to her lips. "She's also caring and kind and is probably a great kisser."

"Oh, my gosh, Claire."

"And," she says, pointing back to the mirror, "she deserves to be happy in whatever way she wants to define that, and she should absolutely not accept anything less."

My emotions get the best of me. I blink back tears. "Thanks, friend."

"Have fun this weekend. Enjoy getting dressed up and drinking champagne and being around Trevor." She looks at me through the mirror again. "And for the love of God, if he wants to touch you, let him."

I step away from the mirror.

"What time is he picking you up?" she asks.

"In about an hour." Panic sweeps over me and I sit back on the bed. I'm not ready for this in so many ways. "I need to jump in the shower."

She grabs the popcorn and tucks it under her arm. "I'm going to get out of here so you can do all the things. Get your shower. Shave. Wear the good perfume. And call me if you need anything." She heads for the door. "And I'm taking the popcorn. It'll be stale by the time you get home, anyway."

"Bye, Claire."

Her footsteps grow more distant before the door pops closed. Before I know it, I'm alone. I glance at the clock. Forty-five minutes to go.

Taking a deep breath, I look at myself in the mirror again.

"You are going to be fine."

"She deserves to be happy in whatever way she wants to define that, and she should absolutely not accept anything less."

Thank God for Claire.

I head to the shower.

CHAPTER EIGHTEEN

TREVOR

"This is incredible." Haley walks slowly into the suite at the Bellader Hotel. She spins in the middle of the great room, her jaw slack. "I mean, this is gorgeous."

I lean against the wall and watch her turn another slow circle. Her hair hangs down, having dried on the drive to Nashville. There's not a drop of makeup on her face, which I find amusing. I'd almost guess she's making an effort to appear unattractive.

If I wanted to assist her in that endeavor, I'd point out how fucking beautiful she is without all that shit. I'm a man, and I'm a visual guy. I'd tell her she's gorgeous, even more so when she's stripped of makeup. And I might tell her that's what I've imagined—but without clothing— while lying in bed at night jacking off, since the day I met her.

But I don't.

"The view from here is as gorgeous as it always is," I say.

She faces me and raises a brow, getting the innuendo. "That's against the rules, Kelly."

I smirk, walking through the great room. "We were talking about the room, were we not?" I stop next to her and watch a dose of embarrassment flicker through her eyes. "I mean, if I were able, I'd tell you how everything in this room sort of fades when you're in it, but that might get me smacked. Apparently, being nice is frowned upon these days."

She's not sure how to respond. Instead of making her react, I walk away.

The windows making up the back wall overlooking downtown Nashville are one of my favorite things about the hotel. It feels like you're in the clouds. Like nothing can bother you. Like no one can touch you.

I don't have to look to know Haley is standing beside me. My body is aware of every move she makes. I continue to look across the city and not at her because if I do, I don't know what I'll say. Only that it won't be helpful.

I peek at her out of the corner of my eye. She's looking at me with a smirk of her own.

"What?" I ask.

"I was thinking."

"That's what I'm afraid of."

She laughs, her voice breaking the stillness of the air. "How much longer until the party?"

I glance at my watch. "We have a couple of hours. It'll take thirty minutes to get to Dad's if traffic isn't bad."

Her jaw drops. "The party is at his house?"

"Is that a problem?"

"No. I just . . . I didn't know. I had it pictured to be at the hotel or at the office or something."

There's a heavy dose of trepidation on her face. In lieu of kissing it out of her, I coax her back with a joke. "Don't worry. This house isn't nearly as big as the one in Dogwood Lane."

She laughs, her shoulders falling. "If your dad has two houses the size of the Taj Mahal, I'm going home. It's not even fair."

"I thought you didn't want a house that big?"

She shakes her head as she looks out the window. "I don't."

As I watch her, I realize how much of her is a blank space to me. Suddenly, I want to know everything, to fill the hole with every bit of information I can get about her.

"What would you like?" I ask. "If you could have anything in the entire universe, what would it be?"

She takes a while to answer, but that's okay with me. I'm perfectly content with having a few moments to take her in.

Her nails have been painted a pale pink color, and I wonder if she has them painted often or if she did it just for tonight. For me. The thought makes my cock twitch in my pants, and I can't adjust it or she'll see. Thankfully, she's preoccupied with my question.

"See that ridgeline?" She points to a spot in the distance. It's past the last tall buildings of Nashville, in an area where the hills begin to form. "I'd put a little place somewhere like that. With a great view of the sunrise and a field with tons of wildflowers. There'd be a room with windows like this and a woodstove because there's nothing more romantic than that. And a claw-foot bathtub nestled in a corner and tons and tons of bookshelves."

"And?"

"And that's it." She shrugs. "I don't really know what else someone could want."

"A Viking range. Heated floors. A poodle spa," I say, rattling off a few items from Meredith's list.

She grins. "None of that matters to me." She folds her arms over her chest and looks back at the city. "I would like to trip over kids' toys. And have a little oven I can bake cookies in. And a hammock for the trees for springtime."

I don't know what I was expecting, but it wasn't that. It wasn't something so fresh and simple.

"I love the way you say 'that's it' and then ramble on more things than you start with."

She grins. "What's yours? And I'll assume the Viking range and heated floors are a given."

I shove my hands in my pockets to keep from pulling her to me while I think about her question. *What kind of house would I like?*

A few weeks ago, my answer would've been simple. Something clean. Modern. Organized. Lots of stone and steel with wooden beams in the downstairs.

Now, I'm not sure. My taste in architecture hasn't changed—I still prefer a modern look over a rustic aesthetic. But maybe the change is in the feel of the place.

I read once in a magazine that Jake had lying around that a person's personal space mirrors their internal thoughts. It made sense. Mom's house was always a crazy jumble of things. Dad's was an attempt at being a trendsetter but missing the mark. Jake's is clean, thanks to a housekeeper, and mine checks off every box. But Haley's is different.

Her space is warm and inviting. It doesn't need a large square footage like Mom's to be interesting or the newest trends like Dad's to be relevant. You can tell someone lives there, someone does shit they love there, someone orchestrates a full life out of that little space.

And that has me thinking. What do I want?

I'm not so sure. Now the perfect place seems less and less about the place itself. Less about the view or the insulation of the space or the accessibility to my job.

It feels more and more about . . . something else.

Ideas like that will fuck a man up. *Just like what happened to my dad.*

I shrug. "I don't know. I do love a good heated floor in the winter."

She gives me a look. "You would."

"Hey, what's that supposed to mean?" I chuckle.

"It means you're a bit of a diva, I think." She laughs at me, not with me, and turns toward the room on the opposite end of the suite. "I need to get ready. This hair isn't going to fix itself."

I think about calling after her and telling her she's goddamn beautiful. I also consider offering to have someone from the spa downstairs come up and help her. But as she slides me a grin as she closes the door to her bedroom, separate from mine at her request, I think better of it.

I want her to go with me tonight just the way she is. Like a beautiful woman that I'm lucky likes me enough to be my friend. To humor me and my crazy ideas. To let me into her world, even if for a minute.

With a grin, I stride across the room into my bedroom. I leave my door open, just in case.

�

"Wide under narrow," I say.

I watch myself attempt a tie in the mirror. It's not something I've ever been particularly good at. There's usually a woman somewhere who is all too happy to help me get it right, and I'm all too happy to let them.

My fingers fumble with the smooth fabric of the tie. I clumsily attempt to pull the wide end up over the narrow. The material falls from my fingers. I sigh. This feels all too reminiscent of prom, and feeling like a teenager has me worried about the success of this evening.

I look at my reflection and wonder if I really need the tie. My charcoal-colored dress pants and crisp white button-down look nice enough. I wasn't going to wear my watch, but I can't stand the sleeves buttoned at my wrists, so the watch adds a little something to the blank space of my forearms.

Running a hand through my hair, I keep half an eye on the door. Haley exited her room a few minutes ago. I haven't seen her yet. That's probably why I can't tie a motherfucking tie any better than a ten-year-old boy.

A knock sounds softly through the room. I spin on my heel and see Haley standing in the doorway. I nearly fall over.

Her hair is half-up, pieces of her jet-black tresses falling all over the place in loose waves. A deep-blue dress covers her body. The neckline is wide, the fabric kissing the rounds of her breasts in a subdued way. There's a little tie at her waist that showcases the narrow circumference of her body. The bottom section comes together in the front like two separate pieces of fabric, leaving a little slit as a tease to men like me.

And if I have to fight them all tonight, every damn one of them, I will.

Mark my motherfucking words.

"Haley," I say carefully.

"Hi," she says back. She plays with a strand of hair, her doe eyes drawing me in.

I mosey her way. It's mostly to give myself time not to overreact. If this were any other woman, I'd have the dress off her already and be between her thighs.

But it's not.

This is Haley. She's more than that—more than a quick lay. But how much more, I don't know. I don't know if I even want to know.

She twirls the lock of hair around her finger, her lips forming a perfect bud. My body screams, my restraint slipping as I get close.

There's a slight shift in her posture, her body leaning my way. A hunger skims the surface of her gaze and cuts me like a knife.

I force a swallow as I approach her. "I have bad news," I say.

She drops the strand of hair. "What's wrong?"

Stepping in front of her, my body boxing hers against the wall, I breathe in her sweet, natural scent. "I'm going to break some rules right now."

She gasps softly as she looks up. "Trevor . . ."

"First," I say before she can object without hearing me out, "you look absolutely stunning. Just *fucking amazing*, Haley." The words come out soft with a grit that makes her cheeks flush. "I don't care whether I'm supposed to say it or not, but *wow*."

She giggles, lifting her chin. "Are you trying to be charming?"

"I'm not trying to do anything but tell you how beautiful you look tonight."

I step closer. Her chest rises and falls in deep movements. I can hear her breath flowing past her muted-pink lips. Each intake of air draws my attention to her mouth, and I want to capture it with my own.

"Thank you," she whispers. Her tongue darts across her bottom lip, leaving a coat of wetness behind.

I can't take it.

"Also," I say, my voice ragged, "I'm going to touch you."

Her eyes widen, her breathing going uneven as I bring my hand to her face. I cup her cheek in my palm, her skin smooth and warm. She looks me in the eye, holding my gaze, before nestling her face in my hand. She grabs my wrist, pinning my hand to her with locked fingers.

My blood soars through my veins. All my senses are overwhelmed. I can barely breathe, let alone filter all the warning lights going off in my brain.

I inch closer until her back is against the wall. My head is screaming with directions, my pulse strumming in preparation for the explosion it hopes is coming.

My legs straddle hers, one on either side, as I lower my lips toward her. She rises up to meet me.

My hand goes to the side of her neck, the edges of my tie flirting with the top of her cleavage. I can barely think anything rational as my cock stretches the fabric of my pants.

Knock, knock!

"Motherfucker," I growl, much to her amusement.

Haley sags against the wall. Her shoulders drop as the adrenaline of the minute before disappears.

She laughs, straightening out her dress as I take a step back. "Saved by the bell . . . hop."

I'm too irritated to comment on her joke. Nothing about this is funny to me.

"Sorry," she says, hiding a smile. "I just . . . That's probably for the best, right?"

"Sure." I march through the room. Making it to the door, I don't trust myself to answer it for fear I'll just start throwing punches. "Can I help you?" I ask through the wood.

"Yes. Mr. Kelly?"

"Yes."

"I apologize for the intrusion. I have your complimentary champagne, sir."

"What the fuck," I grumble. When I swing the door open, a man with a cart holding an ice bucket and a bottle of chilled champagne awaits me.

"For you, sir."

I snap my wallet out of my pocket and pull some bills out—how many, I don't know. I don't even care. I exchange them for the champagne.

"Thank you," I say before retreating back inside.

Haley is standing at the windows with her back to me. I leave the tray and slowly make my way toward her. She has one hand at her chin, brushing a finger across her lips as she gazes across Nashville.

She could be a picture from a magazine. Or an image from my dreams. Or a vision of impossibility.

I stop a few feet behind her and try to wrap my brain around the emotions flooding me. *Is it just testosterone? Is it wanting what I can't and shouldn't have? Or is this itch, this confusion like I've never felt—this war between wanting to do what I want but also what's right—because it's her?*

She turns around, a smile hovering on her lips. "Were you really going to kiss me?"

"Were you really going to let me?"

"Yes," she says.

"Then yes."

She walks my way. Her shoulders are thrown back, her chin held high in a bout of confidence I've not seen from her before. The closer she gets, the louder the alerts get in my head. Just as she reaches me, she walks on by.

My mind scrambles to process her diversion. "Hey. Where are you going?"

"It's time to leave. You said it would take thirty minutes to get there, right?" She grabs a navy-and-silver clutch off the sofa. "We need to get moving."

"What about the champagne?"

"We can enjoy it when we get back."

I narrow my eyes as my hands go back to my tie. I jerk on it a little harder than necessary, flipping the ends over with a flourish. She watches me and laughs at my state of undoing.

"You need help?" she asks.

"If you're wanting to go to this party, don't touch me," I warn.

She giggles, her eyes sparkling. It relaxes me enough to get the tie made. Once I'm good to go, I hold a hand out for her. She looks at me as if I'm challenging her somehow but gives in and lets me have her hand.

A flood of pride that she trusts me washes through my veins. I start toward the door, but she tugs me back. I stop and look at her.

"Trevor?" She gives my hand a gentle squeeze.

"What?"

She bites her lip. "What if I don't know what to say to these people?"

I've seen her charm anybody she's with, and she does it effortlessly, so her concern doesn't make sense to me. If she takes her wicked wit with her, she'll be just fine.

I pull her to the door.

"Just bewilder them with bullshit, babe," I say.

Her laugh fills the hallway.

And quite possibly my heart.

CHAPTER NINETEEN

TREVOR

W hat's wrong?" Haley asks.
I help her out of the truck and shut the door behind her. Her features look soft in the solar-lit backyard. Hedges and rosebushes line the parking area. It's just me and her.

Cars line the street and drive leading to the house, though. And as Haley awaits an answer, laughter and music drift from the house as the partygoers prepare to celebrate my father's retirement.

The juxtaposition of the two scenarios is striking. As I stand in the middle of the asphalt, Haley on my left and the party on my right, I'm rocked with the realization that this is the epitome of the difference between Dogwood Lane and Nashville. Between Haley and Liz. Between predictability and variety. And for the first time in my life, I'm not clear on which I prefer.

"Trevor?" My name rolls off her lips with a consideration that doesn't help my mental state. It's not like women usually say it. There's no rush to go do something or whine that she's not getting her way. She sounds like she actually cares. Like she actually wants to know what I'm thinking.

"Just thinking we'll sneak in the kitchen door and avoid the masses for a while." I offer her my hand and am pleasantly surprised when she takes it without hesitation. "I'm going to have to beat men away from you tonight, so I'll keep you to myself while I can."

She laughs, her lashes fluttering. "Damn you. Don't be so charming."

"Why?"

"Because it makes me like you, and this whole thing is a lot easier when I remember it's all a facade." She pulls her eyes away from mine quickly. The smile she fights to keep on her face wobbles. "It's all good."

My pace slows. She glances over her shoulder, dropping my hand.

I open my mouth to refute her words. To tell her this entire thing isn't a facade, that she is lovely. That I am already regretting the alpha attitude I'm going to give these cocksuckers when they try to hit on her. But as I dig into her body language, I realize what she's *really* saying.

Shit.

"Haley . . ." My words trail off as I try to find a rebuttal that fits. Finding ample words to describe how I feel—that I do want her only for me yet don't want the responsibility of that either—proves harder than I expect.

"There's a man staring at us from the window." She brushes a lock of hair off her shoulder. "Let's either go in or get out of here, because it's awkward."

"I could be convinced to leave."

She swats me on the arm. "You aren't leaving. You dragged me all the way here and made me put on makeup and this dress. Now we're going in, even if it's for ten minutes."

"Fine." I return her smile as we head to the house. "But for the record, I would've been just as proud to walk in here with you if you were wearing no makeup and your black yoga pants and pink panties."

I pull open the door.

"You're never letting me live that down, are you, Thief?" She groans as she walks by.

"Probably not, Ohio."

The kitchen is all white-and-black marble with stainless steel appliances. Pink decorations give the place a pop of color and a hint that my dad has officially lost all control of his manhood. *Well done, Meredith.*

"I was beginning to think you seriously weren't coming . . . *Holy shit.*" Jake stops in the middle of Dad's kitchen, a glass of bourbon in hand. His eyes go wide, a smile I've seen a million times on his face shining like an open invitation as he takes in Haley.

I roll my eyes at my brother and wonder how inappropriate it would be to get him in a headlock in the middle of a party.

"So this is her," Jake says, finally removing his gaze from Haley.

"Jake . . . ," I warn.

Haley elbows me in the side. "I'm her? I mean, I'm her, but am I *her*?" When I look down, she winks. "I'm *her*, aren't I?"

"I love that my brother brings up a woman and, all of a sudden, it's you," I say, fighting a grin.

"Well, you *were* him." She brushes a strand of hair off her shoulder again. "And now I'm *her*. Funny how things work."

We share a moment, the outside world lost to the joke only we understand. Partygoers laugh in the next room. Caterers slip into the kitchen to check on hors d'oeuvres. Glasses clink together in toasts, and none of it breaks through the moment Haley and I have.

Until my dumbass brother clears his throat.

"I'm Jacob Kelly, Trevor's brother," he says to Haley. "You can call me Jake."

"It's nice to meet you, Jake," Haley says. "Your brother has said a lot about you."

I have no clue what she's talking about. I'm not even sure I've mentioned him more than a couple of times. But she's standing next to me, looking like every man's dream girl, so who am I to pick things apart?

"I hope it was all good," Jake says.

He slides a look my way, letting me know he approves of my plus-one. I try to play it cool, to keep the cheek-to-cheek grin wiped from my face, but it's hard. Maybe even impossible. Although we're in our late twenties slash early thirties, there's still little else that compares with getting your big brother's approval. It's ridiculous and stupid and, yet, very true. But of course he would be impressed with Haley, and not just because she's hot. She has this vibe that speaks of welcome, and it's something so rare and stunning it's no wonder my brother is equally smitten so quickly.

"Oh, it was," Haley gushes. "He said he loves working with you."

Jake looks at me, pleasantly surprised.

"He also said you're terrible at math so you got the fun job, and now he has to pull most of the weight." She keeps her gaze fixed on Jake. "He's a little bothered by that. You should probably keep that in the back of your mind."

"I did not say that," I say. Mouth ajar, I half laugh. "What are you talking about, lady?"

She raises a brow, clearly amused at my defense. "That's exactly what you said. More or less."

"I bet you did." Jake looks at me, playing along with Haley. "Tell you what, Haley. Find me later and I'll tell you some truths about your boy here."

"Jake, you're dead to me," I say.

He grabs his glass off the island and heads toward the foyer. "I'll take my chances."

As soon as he's out of sight, I close in on Haley. Her body squares to mine as if they're in sync. She angles her chin so she's looking me right in the eye as I step within inches of her.

Her words from earlier ring through my memory, and I have half a notion to take her by the hand and pull her out of here.

She takes a deep breath. "Let's have fun tonight, okay?"

"Is that an innuendo?"

She laughs, shaking her head. "No. I know what I said a minute ago is still rolling around in that head of yours, and I didn't mean it the way it probably came out."

"Haley—"

"No, Trevor. I want you to enjoy the party with your family tonight. Don't worry that I'm getting clingy or reading too much into this." She forces a swallow. "I know my role."

"What's that?"

"To protect you from Meredith and Liz." She tries to shrug it off, to make light of how she feels, but I know her well enough now to see right through it. "Just wanted you to know I know that."

I give her a sideways glance and consider telling her that her presence here truly has nothing to do with anyone but me. If I do that, there's a chance she'll overthink it, and I don't want her to do that. I want her to enjoy her evening.

"You're going to be trouble, aren't you?" I ask.

"I actually think it's Jake who's going to be trouble," she says, her attention stolen by Jake's voice from the foyer. "I wonder what little tidbits he can share with me."

"Don't believe anything he says."

I look over my shoulder as Jake's voice rings through the house. "Ladies and gentlemen, may I have your attention, please? On behalf of Trevor and myself, we'd like to thank you all for coming to celebrate our father and his illustrious career at Astelford and Mills. Seeing the respect and support you all have for Branson Kelly means the world to us. Now, if you will, the car with the man of the hour is pulling in."

Headlights stream through the windows. My father's friends congregate in the entry, packing the large room like a sardine can until bodies are spilling into the kitchen.

"Come on," I say, taking Haley's hand and pulling her away from the masses. We stop near the table as Jake winds his way through the room. He mouths something I don't have to lip-read to know is about Haley and, most likely, filthy.

I shake my head as I turn to see Haley watching me with a crooked brow.

The crowd erupts into cheers and congratulatory exclamations, making Haley step closer to me so I can hear her. "What was that about?"

"Dad is here," I say, hoping to avoid it.

"No, the look you just gave Jake."

I laugh. "Oh, that. He's just a dumbass."

"I think he's nice," she says, stepping to the side to let a handful of people through.

"You would," I tease.

"What's that supposed to mean?"

"It means—"

"Hey, Trev!" My father's voice booms through the room. "Was all this your idea?"

"Aren't all the good ones mine?" I meet my father a few steps away. He pulls me into a hug. "Jake wanted to take you out for pizza."

Jake smacks me on the back as he joins us. "I did not."

Dad laughs, shaking Jake's hand and giving him a half hug. "Your best quality is that you listen to your brother."

"See?" I say. "Listen to me."

"Fuck off," Jake says with a laugh.

I reach for Haley's hand and pull her close to my side. Dad's face lights up, and as much as I hate to admit it, there's an approval there that makes me proud.

"Dad, I would like you to meet Haley Raynor. Haley, this is my father, Branson Kelly."

Haley stands tall, a smile on her face. Anyone watching would see it as a sign of confidence. They would be wrong.

A breath whispers through the air with a hesitancy I notice. Her jaw is tense, her lips not parted in the arch that means she's amused or relaxed. I lay my hand on the small of her back, not sure if it's her or me who needs the support.

"It's nice to meet you, Mr. Kelly," she says.

My father is intrigued. He looks at me for a long moment before shifting his weight and gaze back to Haley. "Please, call me Branson."

"Of course," she says. "Congratulations on your career."

He nods, taking in my arm behind her. "I'm delighted Trevor brought you this evening. I've heard so many wonderful things about you."

I balk. The man is lying through his teeth. I've never said a word about her to him. He didn't even know she existed until this moment.

"That's very sweet of you to say," Haley says. "And I appreciate you saying that to make your son look good. Nice touch." She winks at my dad.

"Hey," I object. "Maybe I did say nice things about you."

"Yeah. Maybe," she says, teasing me.

Jake chokes on his drink and excuses himself, knocking me in the back as he goes. "You've finally met your match. I cannot wait to see this play out."

My dad's chest rumbles, his eyes twinkling with mirth. "You must meet my wife." He looks around the room. "Meredith, sweetheart. Come here, please."

Meredith looks beautiful, as usual, and just as devoted to my dad as she joins us. Her hand slips under his elbow as she takes in Haley and me.

I hold my breath, my fingers flexing against Haley. "Meredith, this is Haley Raynor. Haley, this is my father's wife, Meredith."

"It's so nice to meet you," Meredith says. Her attention focuses solely on Haley. "Have you been here long? Did anyone offer you a drink?"

"I'm fine. Thank you," Haley says. "Your home is so beautiful. Both of them, actually."

Meredith's face lights up. "Have you seen our home in Dogwood Lane?"

"Yes. I live there. My cousins, Dane and Matt, are building it, actually."

Meredith releases my father and stands next to Haley. "They are so wonderful. I talk to Dane quite a bit with little tweaks to things. He's so sweet."

"He is," Haley agrees.

"He thinks I'm a little weird with the requests for my dogs, but they're my babies," Meredith says. "He's a darling for just going with the flow, though."

"If he says anything to you, ask him about his cat when he was a little boy. He'll shut right up," Haley says.

Everyone laughs.

I scan the little circle around us and stand a little taller. I've brought women to gatherings with my family before. Lots of times, actually. But standing here in my dad's house and watching Haley fit right in makes me relax.

There's no worry about what she'll say or that she'll complain about something later. She just laughs at my dad's stupid jokes and humors Meredith's questions and does it with a smile.

Dear sweet Jesus.

"Tell me about you, Haley," Meredith inquires. "You live in Dogwood Lane, so what do I need to know about the town? My grandfather had a home there, and I used to visit it as a child and just fell in love with the town."

"Me too. I've lived there almost eight years now, and I can't imagine living anywhere else."

My dad's eyes snap to mine. There are so many questions lingering between us, questions I don't have answers for, that I look away.

"You'll have to come see me when you're in town," Haley tells her. "I'll be starting at Buds and Branches this week."

"A flower shop? Is that what that is?" Meredith asks as Haley nods. "I love flowers. I could sit in a flower shop all day and just play."

Haley grins. "Really? Because that's how I feel. Flowers make me so, so happy."

"My dad was a landscape architect," Meredith says. "The last project he designed was a botanical garden. Plants, flowers, shrubs, trees—he loved it all and passed that down to me."

I look at my dad. I have no idea what's happening right now. How is Meredith, the extra of all extras, best-friending Haley, the simplest, most un-extra girl I know?

Dad shrugs. "Let's get a drink and find your brother." He leans down toward Meredith, and they share a tiny, intimate moment that surprises me. He kisses her briefly on the lips, and I'm surprised by the love I see reflected in her eyes for him.

I'm not sure what to make of all this, but I'm jerked back to reality by Haley's hand on my chest. "It's fine," she says.

Meredith looks at me. "Don't worry about Haley. I want to tell her all about my greenhouse."

I look at Haley, a quizzical look on my face. "You want to go with me? I hate leaving you here alone."

"Go," she says with a laugh. "Meredith said 'greenhouse' and I'm all ears."

"Okay."

Looking into her eyes, all I want to do is kiss her like Dad did his wife. But I don't want her to think I'd only be kissing her as a part of an act, a facade for God knows who right now. I won't do that to her. *When I kiss her, I'll take my time.* But I need to touch her, so I stroke the backs of my knuckles down her soft cheek and then head across the room.

"Thank you for this tonight. Not necessary, son, but thank you. The presents were overkill, though," Dad says in between sips of whiskey.

"Yeah," I say, my eyes not leaving Haley. "We told them on the invite to donate to the Children's Hospital. Apparently, your friends don't take instructions well."

He chuckles. "There's a big one in red paper. I'm curious what it is."

"That's from Meredith. I could tell you what it is, but she kind of scares me."

Dad claps my shoulder as he laughs again. "Always pick a woman who scares you a little. They keep you in line that way."

I take a drink from a server as he walks by. "I don't want to be kept in line."

"You will. When you meet the right woman, you'll appreciate the help in making sure you don't screw up your life."

Haley laughs as she and Meredith walk to the table. They sit, Haley's mouth going a mile a minute.

I'm not surprised she fits in here, but I am surprised at how seamlessly she's done it. As she sits with my father's wife like they're old friends, I wonder what it would be like to walk in here on a Sunday afternoon to this. Or on Christmas Eve with a few kids playing on the floor and a few hundred rolls of wrapping paper strewn around.

I shiver. Dad laughs. I drink half the liquor in my glass.

"I think," Dad says carefully, "that you got me the best gift out of everyone."

My attention is dragged from Haley at the table to my father. "Uh, I didn't bring you anything. Sorry."

"No, you did." He smiles coyly.

"You mean the party? You're welcome."

"I mean that look in your eye, son."

I scoff. "There's no look in my eye, old man."

"As you just so kindly pointed out, I wasn't born yesterday." He tosses me a wink, one of those gestures that dads do that lets you know they're way smarter than you.

I'm not sure what he sees in my eye, and I'm completely sure I don't want to be *kept in line* by a woman. I like spice and variety, and that will do me for years to come. But Dad did too. He had a revolving door after the divorce from Mom. Until Meredith.

Seeing him and Meredith standing together, seeing how their love seemed so similar . . . genuine, has made me wonder. He's truly happy, and I think Meredith is too. *Maybe he needed the right person to step in and open his eyes.* As Dad moves away to talk to other guests, my eyes naturally swing to Haley.

I think about taking her home tomorrow.

That she doesn't need résumé help anymore.

That the house is wrapping up and doesn't need me anymore.

That there's no reason for me not to walk away anymore.

CHAPTER TWENTY
HALEY

"This is the time I usually check out of these parties." A man saunters up to the kitchen island and takes a caramelized fig with bacon. He's cute in a basic kind of way and has a friendly smile. "But I'm here for these things."

I laugh as he takes a bite and pretends to melt. "Those are so good. I think I've eaten ten tonight. Or fifteen."

"This is my eighth, so not far behind you."

I smile at him, grateful for the distraction. The party has gone on for what feels like forever. My feet are starting to hurt in my heels, and I'd kill someone for a hot bath and a book.

I'd also kill for Trevor to come back.

For the most part, Trevor has been the perfect partner for tonight. Attentive, always ensuring I'm not left out in conversations, making me feel as though I belong here. I'd almost convinced myself he is right and that maybe, just maybe, some of the doting tonight isn't because he wants his family to believe we are together.

Almost.

"There's a fig cocktail around here somewhere too," I offer.

"What is it with these people and figs?" He laughs. "Must be a thing for rich people because I've never been to a party with figs. Or caviar tartlets. Did you even know tartlets were a thing?"

"I did not," I say. "I'll be honest, and don't judge me for this, but most of the parties I attend feature the combination pizza rolls."

He chokes, grabbing a napkin and covering his mouth. His eyes water as he catches his breath. "I love that you specified the combination ones. Everyone always goes for the plain pepperoni."

"Right?" I say, scanning the area for Trevor. "I usually go for pepperoni pizza, but the combination pizza rolls are where it's at."

"I concur." He plops the rest of the bite in his mouth.

I swish the water around my glass as he chews. My stomach is uneasy. I think it has less to do with the figs and more to do with Trevor.

A striking woman in a red dress arrived about an hour ago. I caught her staring at me while talking to an edgy-looking Jake. Then a little while ago, unless I'm paranoid, I caught Trevor following her outside.

It was Liz. It had to be.

I take a deep breath and force the image from my mind. I was, after all, brought here because of her. Maybe it was less to keep her away and more to make her jealous. After all, I haven't known Trevor very long. Maybe he saw me as an easy solution to what's really going on with him and Liz.

You don't need to worry about this, Haley. You won't see him after tomorrow. He'll drop you off, Branson's house will be done, and that will be that.

Jake walks up. He takes in Fig Boy and me and chooses to stand between us.

"How are you tonight, Haley?" he asks.

"I'm good."

He lifts a brow, calling me out without actually saying anything. I lift mine right back, as if to ask him if he knows, why is he asking.

"You should be," Jake says pointedly.

"Oh, I am. We've been having a fascinating conversation about our culinary tastes. Right . . ."

"I'm Noah. I work with Jake and Trevor."

"Ah," I say. "Noah and I have the same taste, it seems."

Jake's jaw twitches. He opens his mouth as if to say something but stops short of actually speaking.

"How do you guys know one another?" Noah asks.

Jake holds his hand out. "Why don't you explain it, Haley?"

"Sure." I set my water on the counter. I tried to prepare an answer to this question on the way here, but every time I thought about it, Trevor said something and sidetracked me. Here I am with no Trevor and no response. "I'm a friend of the family," I say. "Kelly Construction is doing business with my family in Dogwood Lane."

"Oh, yeah. I heard about that in the office last week," Noah says. "I guess the carpenters down there are unbelievable."

I note that to tell Dane. "Yes, they are."

Jake turns so that Noah can't see him. "Friend of the family, huh?"

"Makes sense to me."

"Let's see if this makes sense . . ." He fires a mischievous grin my way before excusing himself.

I lift my water glass again, unsure what he meant. The vessel almost slips from my grasp as a hand plants firmly on my hip from behind.

Trevor's cologne floods my senses as I look into Noah's eyes. He glances over my head before letting his gaze fall back on me.

My body roars in response to Trevor's fingers biting into my skin. White noise rushes over my ears as I try to step out of his grasp.

Not happening.

Trevor holds me in place, my back to his front.

"Hey, Trevor," Noah says.

"Hi, Noah."

Noah's lips twist. "Friend of the family, huh?"

"Yes," I say, ignoring Trevor's body pressed to mine. Not being able to see his face, to read him, to have some idea what he's thinking, makes me crazy. "He needed a plus-one, and since our families are doing business right now, we thought it would be fun."

Trevor's fingers flex, ruffling the fabric of my dress between us.

"Are you having fun, Haley?" The sweetness in Trevor's voice is for my benefit. Being that he just spent a decent amount of time alone with Red Dress, he can take that sweetness and shove it.

Yes, I'm jealous. I'm mad. I'm frustrated with myself. Trevor, Jake, and even Fig Boy because he ate the last caramelized fig.

"I am," I say, giving it right back to him. "Noah and I have a lot in common."

"Is that right?"

Noah takes his drink and a big step back. "Not that much, really. Just an affinity for pizza rolls." He forces a swallow. "I'll see you in the office next week, Trevor. Nice to meet you, Haley."

"You too, Noah," I say.

Trevor stands even closer to me, if that's possible. A vibration ripples from him, sinking into my body. As I absorb his irritation, I do my best to project my own.

"Are *you* having fun, Trevor?" I ask, staring straight ahead.

I don't know what I hope he says. I don't even know where I'm going with this question. I only know I have to say something to break the ice and figure out what he's thinking.

"Not as much as you." His tone is rough. The rawness in the way he says the words scrapes over my skin. "I know you saw me with Liz."

I've heard him talk about her a number of times. But hearing him say her name now that I have a face to put with it—a memory of the two of them together—makes it a different animal.

Before, she was an obsessed ex he didn't have any desire to see. Now, she's a knockout he sneaks around with at parties.

What isn't any different is my non-relationship with him, and I'll be damned if he thinks I'm going to chase after him like Liz.

His head dips to the side of mine. His breath is hot on my neck. "She didn't appreciate me bringing you here."

"Then I guess your plan worked."

His chest shakes behind me. I hear his tongue swipe across his lips as he suppresses a chuckle. "What was my plan, exactly?" His hips roll ever-so-slightly. His cock sweeps over my behind. "I seem to forget."

My insides tighten so hard it knocks the wind out of me. I find a black-and-white pencil sketch on the wall above the table and glue my eyes to it, hoping to find some balance.

Jake comes around the corner, locking eyes with me for a split second before glancing up at his brother. "Hey, Trev. Dad wants to see us real quick."

I heave a sigh of relief. "You better go."

Before I can react, Trevor takes my hand and pulls me with him. It takes me two steps to match his one.

My heart shoves blood down my veins at double the speed it should. That, in combination with Trevor's hand against mine, makes me a little light-headed, and I'm glad when we stop in front of Branson.

"What's up?" Trevor asks as we reach his father. Branson stands next to Jake, each of them with a glass in his hand.

I try to slip my hand from Trevor's. He grips it harder. I want to yank it from his and would if it wouldn't cause a scene.

"This is incredible," Branson says. "You two are the best."

"Thanks, Dad," Jake says.

The three Kelly men stand in a row. Jake and Trevor bear a striking resemblance to their father, with strong jawlines and heavy brows and a subdued charisma that's magnetic.

My hand still in Trevor's, I plead silently with him to let it go. Every time I try to slip it away, he squeezes it tighter.

Emotions all over the place, I try to focus on Branson as he talks to his sons. His eyes crinkle at the corners when he speaks, like Trevor's do, and there's a lilt to his voice, much like Jake's.

Branson searches the room until his eyes land on Meredith. His entire persona changes. It's like his heart opens so fully that it spills into the room around us.

I look at Trevor and wonder if he has that in him. If he met the right person and could allow himself to believe in crazy things like love, like his father so obviously does.

If he could do that with me.

My heartbeat slows as Trevor casts me a small smile.

"And thank you for coming, Haley," Branson says, pulling me back to the moment. "Meredith and I hope you'll join us for dinner when we get situated in your neck of the woods."

"I'd like that," I say.

He looks at his sons. "Now, I'm going to chat with my guests until they leave and then properly celebrate my retirement by taking Meredith upstairs and—"

"Yeah. That's enough, Dad." Jake groans.

Branson laughs, giving his sons a final handshake, and leaves to join his wife.

Jake slips a hand in his pocket and looks at his brother. "I'll wrap this up if you two need to go."

"We're fine," I say. I remove my hand from Trevor's as discreetly as I can. "We can absolutely stay and help you clean up, if you'd like."

"No, we can't," Trevor says.

I look up at him, nonplussed. "Yes. We can."

Jake laughs. "You're losing your touch, Trev."

Instead of ribbing him back, Trevor locks his jaw.

"On that note"—Jake points at Trevor—"I'm going to go check on the guests. While I could kick your ass, I don't really want to do it tonight."

"Good night, Jake," I say.

"If I don't see you again, it was nice to meet you, Haley."

"Same here."

Jake slips into a small crowd that's laughing behind us. It takes all of two seconds for Trevor to spin me around to face him.

"What's wrong?" he asks.

"Nothing."

"Don't lie to me."

"I'm not." I set my jaw too. "Why does something have to be wrong?"

His Adam's apple moves in his throat as his eyes heat.

I squirm, my dress too hot. Too tight. Too everything.

"I need some fresh air," I say.

He takes my hand again. "I'll take you."

"I can go alone."

"Yup," he says, pulling me toward the door.

With a flick of the handle, it swings open. A moment later, we're outside. The sky is dark, the moon and stars bright. I close my eyes and feel the cool air on my face. When I open my eyes, Trevor is in front of me.

"You give good advice," he says, his voice soft.

"Why?"

"I was honest with Liz."

The sound of her name on his lips is like nails on a chalkboard. I'm not even sure what he had to be honest with her about.

"I thought you said you were very clear with her from the start?" I ask.

He looks at the ground, slipping both hands in his pockets. "I was. Sort of." He raises his eyes to mine. "I heard what you said about people wanting what they can't have. And how maybe she's misinterpreting my behavior as playing hard to get."

I run my hands up and down my arms. "And?"

"And I talked to her tonight. I told her I probably suck at communication. That I wasn't playing games with her. She's a great person and she'll make a great companion for someone, but that someone isn't me."

What?

My hands falter. His eyes meet mine. They make me forget about the temperature and the stars and how eight caramelized figs are seven too many. All I can focus on is the sincerity in his beautiful blue eyes.

"She said seeing you with me tonight helped," he says.

"I'm glad."

He grins. "She said I never looked at her like I look at you."

My stomach drops to my knees as I catch the heaviness of his words. I don't know what to say to that or if I heard it right or if it means anything other than he thinks I'm crazy.

My mind races and my mouth can't catch up. "I—"

My words are stolen by his lips touching mine. A rush of helplessness washes over me as I sink into his arms. He pulls me so close to his strong, hard body that we may as well be one. As I go limp, the world outside his lips blurs.

He tastes like the sting of bourbon and the sweetness of Coke, and of the hundred fantasies I've had of this exact moment. Only those daydreams weren't nearly as satisfying as having Trevor Kelly in the flesh.

My lips part, giving him permission to do all the things he's telling me without words he wants to do. He slips his tongue inside, gentle but demanding, like he can't wait a moment longer.

His nose nudges mine, his hands cup my face. He makes contact in every way possible as we kiss under the moonlight.

Breathless, I pull back. He rests his forehead against mine, and I'm not sure if his groan is because I stopped the act or because it happened at all.

I suck in a lungful of air, every cell in my body tingling. He locks his hands at the small of my back and keeps his forehead touching mine.

"There's no room for Jesus." It's a dumb thing to say, but it's all I can come up with.

He chuckles but makes no apologies or room.

"Why did you do that?" I ask.

"Did you hate it, Ohio?"

"No."

"Then why ask?"

My pulse gallops as I lean back.

Screw the rules and the fear and the chance he'll break my heart. He might. Judging by how I reacted to seeing him with Liz, he could. But as hard as I tried not to be, I'm interested in this thing with him, whatever it is. The only hope I have that he might be interested, too, is Liz's words. How ironic.

"She said I never looked at her the way I look at you."

This is a risk—a huge one—but we're here. I'm here. And . . . I want to be.

"Because if you're gonna kiss me like that, I need a warning. Hey!" I say as he jerks me around.

He has my hand tucked in his and is leading me toward the truck. We pass the truck and continue down a little solar-lit walkway. At the end of the path sits a small outbuilding with an arched room and floor-to-ceiling glass walls.

He unlocks the door with a four-digit code, and we step inside. The lock is engaged with a sharp snap. There's a rustle behind me as Trevor searches for a light. And then softly, small, twinkly lights glow around the room.

Plants fill the space. There are some on tables, some on the floor, some hanging from the ceiling. Little Christmas lights dangle in different places, giving just enough light to not trip and fall.

"The greenhouse," I whisper. "Oh, my God. This is unreal."

Trevor steps in front of me. His shoulders are back, his eyes broody. He takes my face in his hands.

I gasp, unprepared for the contact. "What are you doing?"

"I'm warning you," he says softly. "I'm going to kiss you."

CHAPTER TWENTY-ONE

HALEY

I stand under the soft glow of a string of lights. My arm slides against a slick, waxy leaf as I back away slowly from Trevor.

He's eating me alive with his eyes. Sizzling the sides of my face where his thumbs gently stroke my skin. Setting my body ablaze as it becomes apparent he's on the verge of losing control.

I ache. Every piece of my body demands contact from this ridiculously good-looking man. With every press of the pad of his thumb, another ripple of want shoots through my veins.

I'm not sure if the humming sound pulsing around me is coming from the greenhouse or inside my body, but the continuous pressure quickens my thoughts.

I want him. I want him here and now, and whatever happens after, I'll deal.

And that's it.

"*I'm* warning *you,*" I tell him. The lines around his eyes bend as he narrows them. "If you start kissing me this time, you better not stop."

He pulls my face to his, crashing his mouth to mine. His hands drop to the sides of my neck, then to my shoulders, before they scale the length of my back.

I moan into his mouth as he slides his tongue inside. My hands plant on his chest, my fingers flexing against his pecs.

He groans, the sound barreling to my core. It cinches my lower belly, and I buckle with the strain.

His hands find the underneath of my behind and cup my ass. He jostles me forward until our bodies are pancaked together, and the only way we'd be more connected is if he were inside me.

I tremble at the thought, feeling his tongue dip inside my mouth again. He explores me like he has every right and permission to stake claim to my body.

"Trevor," I whisper as his lips drag along my jaw. He lays kisses one at a time down my neck and then up again until he's nestled behind my ear. He nibbles my earlobe, pulling it with his teeth, and I think I'm going to explode.

My body sags against his. His fingers bite into my skin, the tips close enough to my opening to tease, but not close enough to do any good.

A shot of adrenaline soars through my frame, and I become acutely aware of my situation. I'm going to do this or I'm not.

Trevor takes a step back, his breathing ragged and heavy. His chest rises and falls like he's run a mile but is ready, and willing, to run another should I request it.

"Hey," I say, fighting to catch my breath.

"Hey, what?"

"I thought I told you not to stop."

He grins, a sexy smirk showing off the dimple in his left cheek. His mouth opens and his tongue touches his top lip. "If I keep kissing you, it won't be kisses anymore."

He looks at me like I'm the only thing in the world. It's heady—intoxicating, even. The feeling is so strong that nothing matters in this moment but Trevor and me.

I saunter toward him. "What, exactly, would it be?"

"I'd lift that beautiful dress right over your head until you were standing in front of me in your panties and bra."

My hands shake as I keep eye contact and bend forward. I can hear my breath in the silence as I grasp the edge of my dress. It's joined by a gasp from him as I lift the fabric up and over my head.

Warm air caresses my skin. His gaze nearly melts it. A bulge stretches the fabric of his pants. Knowing I've turned him on this much drives me crazy.

"Now what?" I ask, holding the fabric out for him to take.

"My God, Haley." He forces a swallow. "I can't believe you're standing here in front of me like this."

"You want to go back to the rules now?"

He snatches the dress from my hand and tosses it to the side, making me giggle.

My heels dig into the soft earthen floor as I take the three steps between us. I grab the buckle of his belt and, with a shaky hand, unlatch it.

He stands still, his hands at his side, as I unfasten his pants. The zipper drags down his groin, the sound rumbling against the soft hum of the heater.

I'm afraid my chest is going to burst as I loosen his tie, my fingers struggling against the anticipation. He watches me as if to let me make the decision.

And I do.

One button is released. Then two. I work my way down his chest. With each one freed comes another glimpse of his chest—muscled and firm—and by the time I slide the fabric over his wide shoulders, I think I'm panting.

He's glorious. A display of male perfection with tanned, smooth skin and symmetry stands before me like my own personal art show.

"There you go," he says. "You've been waiting for this since the day at the café."

I drag my eyes to his. "Don't get cocky yet. I can put my dress back on."

His hands smack against my butt cheeks and drag me against him. I look up into his unguarded eyes, my skin touching his, and watch him grin.

"Not so fast," he says. A palm slides over the round of my ass until his fingers are lying along my slit. He spreads my legs with a motion of his hand.

I gasp. My body convulses against his touch, his fingers undoubtedly wet from my arousal, and I don't know whether to be self-conscious about that or just finish melting in his arms.

"I'll promise you something," he says roughly. The tips of his fingers press against my opening.

"What's that?"

"I've been looking forward to this day more than you." He kisses me again. His free hand skims my bottom, pausing for a moment to grip the curve of my hip before working its way to my breast.

My arms dangle over his shoulders as I work my lips against his.

My brain malfunctions, unable to process the overloaded stimuli.

Lace rubbing against my clit.

Fingers dipping into the pool between my legs.

Nipples beaded into stiff peaks, begging for a tongue to stroke them.

My mouth completely overwhelmed and owned.

"Oh," I moan, letting my head fall back. He kisses down the front of my neck and over the tender skin of my chest.

Both hands dig into my hips as he kneels. His lips hover over the peak of one of my breasts, his tongue flicking as he watches me react.

My body moves under his grasp, dying for contact. For relief. *For him.*

He rolls my other nipple in between two fingers, rolling it over and over. The wetness of his tongue leaves a cool trail across my chest.

"I can't take this," I groan. My hands bury in his silky hair as he kneels before me again.

I stumble backward until my back hits a table. A motion light glows overhead.

Trevor looks up; a grin that warns me I need to prepare lights up his face more than the halogen overhead.

"You are so beautiful, Haley."

"I—Oh, my God."

His face buries in between my legs. He holds my panties to the side as he parts my body with his tongue.

My knees sag, my body giving up the fight, as he holds me in place.

"Trevor," I moan.

He licks heavily across my clit. His tongue flicks the overstimulated bud like he did my nipples. With each touch, a zap of energy shocks me.

I tug on his hair, lapping up the pleasure given so freely by this man.

Just as I can taste the orgasm, he stops.

He stands, wiping his mouth with the back of his hand as I scramble to figure out what's going on.

My body is on fire, the spot between my legs the center of the flames. I can do nothing, think of nothing other than satisfying the ache between my thighs.

"I tell you what," I say, dragging in oxygen like my life depends on it. "If you don't make me come, I'm going to do it myself."

He laughs, his eyes hooded. "Don't you even think about it."

"I'm already thinking about it," I say, cocking my head to the side. "I'm dying over here."

"Oh, really?" He drops his pants and boxer briefs to the floor. His cock stands painfully erect, a drop of pre-cum on the tip. "You think you're dying?"

"That's not helping anything," I grumble, watching his cock swell under my gaze.

My thighs clench, sticking together from the wetness. I don't realize I'm reaching down there until he snags my hand out of the air.

"I said, don't," he says, closing the distance between us. "I get to make you feel good tonight."

My knees buckle. "Then do it."

"You're so impatient."

"I hope you take this long when you're fucking me."

His eyes fly open, his mouth parting. "You're mean."

I sigh. "We've argued before, Trevor. Now let's do something we've not done before. *Please.*"

I'm aware I sound like I'm whining. Maybe I am. Maybe I don't care.

He kisses me once, sweetly this time, before finding a condom in the pool of fabric at his feet. The wrapper crinkles before it's tossed to the side, and I watch him slide the protection down his thick shaft. I rid myself of my panties as I watch the show in front of me.

"All right," he says. "Last chance to say no."

"No."

He swallows hard. "Really?"

"No, not really." I roll my eyes. "Yes. Really. Fuck. Me. Now."

A guttural sound emits from his throat as he grips my hips and sets me on the table. The metal is cool, the edges sharp as the backs of my thighs bend over them.

"Lie back." He puts a hand behind my head until I'm lying flat. One of my legs is raised, then both, and placed over his shoulders.

I suck in a breath as the tip of his cock sits at my opening. It spreads me apart, but not enough.

"Trevor—ah!"

He slides into me with one quick thrust. My eyes fall to the back of my head as my body expands around his size.

He fills me completely, even more than that, and I brace myself as he begins to pull out.

I grip the edge of the table. He pauses before pushing inside me again.

"Oh, my God." He growls as he slides out. "You're fucking incredible."

"Yes," I gush.

"Yes?" He chuckles.

"Okay. Fine. You too," I say, rolling my hips for more contact. "Whatever you need me to say, pretend I said it and—shit."

He hits the back this time, completely seated in my body, and my insides pulse around him. He groans as I tighten around his length before he moves again.

My body squeaks against the table as he finds a rhythm. The metal burns at my back, keeping me aware that I'm naked, on a table, in his dad's wife's greenhouse.

But I don't care. All I care about is reaching the climax of an orgasm that I've needed all night.

"Right there," I tell him, each syllable getting louder. "Yes, Trevor. Right there."

He picks up the pace, his cock delivering another hit as soon as I rebound from the one before. My fingers are on fire from the sharp edge of the table, my thighs heavy from the impending orgasm.

"Trevor . . ."

"Hold on," he mutters.

I do. Just in time.

"Oh, my God!" My body stiffens, my back arching off the table as a shock of ecstasy floods my body. He presses on my stomach with his hand to keep me still as he comes apart under the soft light above.

His eyes squeeze shut, his teeth clenched so hard I can see the strain in the sides of his neck. His hips thrust against my legs as he finds his moment of pleasure.

Too soon, the only sound around us is our ragged breaths. When he opens his eyes, he grins.

I'm limp, my body having given up all strength and energy. Keeping my eyes open is hard.

"Anything else you want to say?" he teases, rotating his hips. His cock, still inside me, sends a jolt of sensation through my overly sensitive body.

"No," I say, sopping up the final rays of pleasure. "That was excellent. Thank you."

He snorts, shaking his head in amusement.

His cock begins to slide out, causing a massive aftershock to ripple through my body. I moan again. He grows harder inside me. I give him a look, making him laugh before he pulls out the rest of the way.

He takes my hand and helps me sit up.

Bending forward, his lips right next to my ear, he whispers, "That was better than excellent." A grin parting his cheeks, he helps me off the table.

My body aches in a delicious throb as I find my belongings. My head is numb, unable to overthink this yet. I'm grateful for that.

"There's a washroom over there," he says, pointing to a little room to my right. "Light switch by the door."

I start to go, but he grabs my arm. I look at him over my shoulder to see a cloud over his eyes. He searches me with the care of a surgeon.

It's my heart that's on fire now as I watch him watch me like nothing else matters in this moment. It matters more because we're on this side of things, through sex, through the buildup of desire that's been taking place over the last few days.

He pulls me into his chest and wraps his arms around me. His face nuzzles in my hair as he presses a simple kiss to the top of my head. "I shouldn't say thank you because that's all sorts of wrong. But this was pretty amazing. So however I should say that, let's pretend I did."

I place a kiss on his sternum and smile against his skin. "And whatever I should say back, consider it done."

He laughs and releases me, and I head toward the washroom.

"Hey, Ohio?"

"Yeah, Thief?"

"Your ass is amazing."

I flip on the light. Before I shut the door, I peek out the side. "That's a no-go area. Just for the record."

I hear him laugh as I shut the door.

CHAPTER TWENTY-TWO

HALEY

I have no idea what time it is, but I know it's early. Way early. Too early to be up on a weekend.

"Ohio, for the love of God, get up," Trevor says.

My eyes struggle to open. But when they do, what a view they behold.

Trevor is sitting on the bed beside me, fresh from a shower. He's dressed, holding a glass of orange juice in his hand.

"Come back at a reasonable hour," I mutter.

"You're not a morning person, I take it," he teases.

"It's too early." I pull a pillow over my face.

"Is this a sexual hangover? I fuck you three times and you wake up sick? I've heard this happens."

My pillow drops to my chest. "You really think a lot of yourself, don't you?"

"I'm riding pretty high since I got to sleep with you last night." He shrugs. "Don't blame me. This one is on you."

I snuggle into the blankets, the ones covering the bed in Trevor's room. The bed in my room is untouched, and I wonder if he'll leave me alone if I get up and go in there.

I look at him.

There's no chance.

"I'm supposed to be living my best life," I grumble. "Waking up before the sun is all the way up isn't my best life."

He sighs and gets to his feet. The next thing I know, the curtains are spread open and sunlight fills the room. "The sun is all the way up. Now get up."

"No," I whine.

The blankets are ripped off me. The cold air from Trevor's need to sleep at sixty-eight degrees below zero slams into my naked skin.

"Hey," I shout, trying to pull them back up. The bastard refuses to let them go.

"Up."

"No." I cover my breasts with my forearms. "Give me my blankets."

He grins. "How about I give you something else?"

Instantly, my knees fall open. "Okay."

A single "Ha!" shoots through the air as he watches me from the foot of the bed. "I like the way you think, but no. That's not what I'm going to give you. Not right now, anyway."

"And why not?" I remove an arm from my chest and slide a finger along my vagina. "I'm wet. See?"

His eyes narrow, his jaw tensing. "Damn it, Haley."

"Then give me back the blankets."

He stays in place like he's mulling it over. I'm not sure which I'd prefer at this point—the covers or his cock. Maybe he'll relent and give me both.

Instead, he heads to the little round table by the window and picks up two narrow pieces of paper. He hands them to me.

"I'll tell you what," he says. "If you don't want to go to this thing, I will give you all the blankets and orgasms you can handle. But if you want to go, you're going to have to get up and get in the shower now."

"What is it?" I ask.

"If you'd read the tickets, you'd know."

I sigh, bringing the papers to my face. There's a lotus flower in the upper right-hand corner and another on the bottom left. Confused, I sit up in bed and focus on the text.

There's no way this is what I think it is. But it is. It says it.

I set the tickets on my lap. Urging myself not to leap off the bed and dance around the room until I'm sure this is what it's supposed to be, I take a deep breath. "Trevor?"

He looks uncomfortable. "I mean, we don't have to go. I just thought you'd like it with your new job and everything."

I spring up, bouncing into his arms. He laughs, catching me midair and bringing me to his chest.

"That's a yes?" he asks with a chuckle.

"Of course. This is the biggest flower show in the South. I had no clue it was this weekend or even that it was in Nashville this year. How did you know?"

"I didn't." He sets me on my feet. "I saw these on the counter at Dad's. Meredith was going to go before we organized the party, so she said maybe it would be nice to take you. And I agreed."

"I . . ." I squeal. "I can't believe I get to go. And you're coming with me. This is a dream."

He smiles smugly and taps me on the ass. "Then get in the shower so we aren't late. I heard the lines take forever."

I bounce on the balls of my feet, already anticipating the things awaiting me today. I start to dart out of the bedroom, but pause. "Hey, Trevor?"

"Yes, pretty girl?"

"Thank you."

I swear he blushes.

"You're very welcome."

Trevor

The convention center is packed. I'm not sure if there are more people or flowers cramming the room, or which I like less.

Various vendors are set up, most of them wedding-related, and Haley has to stop at every one. She gushes with the other women while I hang back with the occasional husband or boyfriend and talk about the weather and football like those topics will get our man cards back.

"Oh, Trevor," Haley gushes. "See this one? It's an anthurium."

"It's great."

She rolls her eyes. "Meredith had these in the kitchen last night. Don't you remember?"

"Of course."

"You do not." She shakes her head. "They represent hospitality and happiness. Must be why your dad's place felt so welcoming."

"I thought it was the bourbon, but whatever you say."

She bumps my shoulder as we meander to the next booth. "You know what, Thief?"

"What's that?"

"I think you like Meredith more than you let on."

"Meh." When she looks at me, I shrug. "It's not like I hate her. I'm just skeptical of her motivations." I watch Haley pick up another flower, a purple one this time, and think of my dad's wife. "Men do stupid shit when they fall in love. If Jake and I don't have his back, who will?"

She doesn't answer as she turns to the attendant at the table. I watch her banter with the man, his face lighting up at her questions.

The place might be packed, but everyone here is happy. Maybe Haley's right and there is something about flowers that brings out people's good sides. She turns to look at me over her shoulder. The smile on her face is so big, I have to hope some of it isn't just from the flowers, but from me.

"Do you know what this one is?" she asks, waving a flower at me. "I know you don't, so I'm going to tell you. It's a delphinium. And it's known for fun." She plunks the flower back in the container. "You need to be more delphinium-esque."

"You weren't complaining about how fun I was about six hours ago."

She shoots me a look. "That's not what I mean. I wasn't complaining about *that*."

"Good. Because I was there, all three times, and I vividly remember you yelling so loud about how amazing I am that the front desk called our room."

She blushes the color of a gerbera daisy in front of us. I lift it.

"I know this one. A daisy. My mom always had them around when we were little. No clue what it means, though."

"Good job," she says, taking the flower from me. "This one is red, so it means . . ." She puts it down and starts toward the next stall.

"What's it mean?"

She stops. "That you're unconsciously in love." She nibbles on her bottom lip. "So that's bogus, right?" Quickly, too quickly, she swipes a weird-looking flower. "This one is more accurate for right now."

"So it means something like you've been somewhere for four hours and it's time to go?" I offer.

"It's a bird of paradise, and it means something exciting is going to happen." She holds her hands to her sides. "I'm starting at the shop in two days."

"If today is any indication, you're going to do great."

"I hope so. I've been reading everything I can get my hands on about flowers so I'm prepared." She gives the flower back to the attendant. Looking around the room, she sighs. "Doesn't this just make you happy? Surrounded by all this beauty?"

I didn't have to come here for that. I've spent the last twenty-four hours by your side, and I had you in my bed.

195

"Sure," I say as we take off walking again.

We move along the last wall quietly, stopping to inspect random flowers or to talk to suppliers about interesting props. I stay in the background and watch a side of Haley I haven't seen before.

She looks like what I feel like in my office. When I'm surrounded by numbers, I feel at home. Comfortable. I know I can piece them together and have them make sense. They speak my language of logic and facts. Flowers do that for her.

Here, she's confident. Authoritative. In her element. Watching her move about this world, one I know nothing about, is the biggest turn-on.

"Not that you aren't a barrel of fun," she says, handing me a piece of a sample cookie, "but I bet Meredith would've loved it here."

I take a bite of the cookie. "You liked her, didn't you?"

"She has a greenhouse," Haley deadpans.

I laugh. "A greenhouse I fucked you in."

I'm rewarded with a flush of her cheeks.

"She also has an entire collection of Van Gogh paintings of flowers," Haley says. "What do you have to say to that?"

"He cut his ear off, you know."

"So?"

"So nothing. I was just pointing that out."

She stretches her arms over her head and yawns. Her T-shirt rises just high enough to show a sliver of skin above the waistband of her jeans. She looks like a commercial for cereal or pajamas—one of those ads where they pick the prettiest woman they can find so other women want to buy their product. That's her. The epitome of perfection.

My chest tightens like I've been hit in the stomach.

"I'm ready to go if you are," she says.

My spirits sink as I look at the clock. By the time we get out of Nashville and to Dogwood Lane, it will be almost four hours. That means it'll be four hours until I take her home. And not much longer until I return to Nashville without her.

"Let's check out that line of photographers first," I say.

"Really?" Her eyes sparkle.

"I mean, unless you don't want to."

"No, I totally want to. I just thought I was boring you to death."

I wrap my arm around her waist as we turn around. "I don't think it's possible for you to bore me to death."

And that's a scary thought.

CHAPTER TWENTY-THREE

HALEY

Neely hands me a glass to put away.

"We should be able to move in a week or so," Neely says. "The bathrooms at the new house get tubs and showers this week, and then it's just picking off little things."

I set the glass in the cabinet. "I can't believe you guys won't be living in this house anymore."

Neely frowns. "I know. And I kind of feel bad about it because Dane bought the new house for me, but you all have the attachment to this one. You have memories here."

"Yeah, but it'll be good for Mia to grow up out there and for you to start fresh in a new place as a family. Maybe you guys can get some horses. Or cows. I've always wanted a cow."

"Why?" Neely laughs.

I shrug. "They're just so pretty."

She shakes her head and fills the now-emptied dishwasher.

I swipe my phone from my pocket and check it. It's been really quiet since Trevor dropped me off at my house this afternoon. He walked me in, kissed the crap out of me, and then told me he was going to try to talk his girlfriend Lorene into renting him a room for a couple more days.

A couple more days. That's it. The house will be done, Branson and Meredith will be moving in, and life will go back to normal for Trevor in Nashville.

"How was Nashville?" Neely asks.

I sit at the island and watch her work. "Nashville was amazing. We went to Trevor's dad's party, and I met his brother and stepmom, Meredith. And then he surprised me with tickets to a floral show this morning."

"Wow. That sounds like a lot of fun."

"It was."

"How fun?" she pokes.

We exchange a knowing grin.

"Yeah, well, that's . . . that," I say.

"What's that mean?"

What does it mean? I don't know. It means I'm going to have to hope I can be the big girl I know I am when he leaves town. And I'm going to need to be strong when he forgets about me when he goes back to his other life with women like Liz.

"It means we had amazing sex and now I'm not sure what will happen," I say matter-of-factly.

The warmth I feel in Dane's house is . . . lacking somehow. I spent so much of the last almost decade within these walls—with lots of laughter and silliness—and tonight it feels chilly. Or is that just me?

For the last twenty-four hours, I've been surrounded by all things Trevor, and it's been wonderful. Now? Now I feel a little empty, and it's weird without him by my side. But it's probably good I get used to it, because his days in Dogwood Lane are numbered. I know it. It's a fact. And it's so sad.

"I guess I'm just not sure what happens when he goes home," I admit. "He's staying at the inn for a couple more days, but then he'll have to go back to Nashville."

"You could try a long-distance relationship. It's not that far, and it'll give you some time to test things out." She shuts the dishwasher and starts it. "Have you not talked to him about it?"

I shake my head. "No. It all happened kind of suddenly, I guess. And he has a thing about women being clingy. I'd die before I let him think I was chasing after him like most women do."

Neely laughs. "I like this new you."

"Yeah, well, hopefully she knows a few things the old me didn't."

"Who knows what?" Dane jogs down the stairs. "If you want to know something, you can ask me. I know just about everything."

"Oh, my God," Neely says, making a face. "You're spending way too much time with Penn."

I laugh, getting off the stool. "How much time do you guys have left out there?"

Dane opens the refrigerator and pulls out a bottle of water. "I could be done tomorrow. But realistically, probably two more days. Branson has a bunch of interior people coming and a landscape crew, I think, but those have nothing to do with me."

My heart sinks. "I figured that."

I pick at my cuticles as I wonder what Meredith will do to this house. Will it be as modern as her home in Nashville? Will she build a greenhouse here? Or will she go with something more subdued?

I'll likely never know.

"How'd things go with you and Trevor?" Dane asks.

"Good. He's a good guy. You'd really like their family. And from what I heard, you're kind of a rock star down there."

He points to himself with a raised brow as he takes a drink.

I laugh. "Yeah, you. I heard they're talking about what good carpenters you guys are. Well, you and Matt. I didn't hear much about Penn."

"Because I don't let Penn around when they call."

"Smart move," I say.

The room grows quiet. I should get up and go home, get prepared for my first day at the flower shop, but I don't want to move.

Maybe I just don't want to be alone.

A light bulb goes off in my head. *I don't want to be alone.* How many bad decisions, bad relationships, have I been in because I don't want to be alone?

It's a crazy idea, one I can't wrap my head around, but one I know is true. Being by myself always feels like a failure. Not having someone to share things with makes victories and stories a little less sweet.

Maybe that was true before, but it's not now. I can be alone. *I like me.*

I'm not withering in panic that he's leaving. I had a blast of a weekend, knowing it wouldn't be more than a fake date. And even now, I'm not devastated, knowing he's leaving. I'm dealing. And I'm doing fine.

I smile to myself as Neely nudges Dane out of the way.

"Did you decide on my idea?" she asks him.

Dane nods. "I like it. I think it'll help Mia adjust."

My jaw drops. "Oh, my God. Are you finally having a baby?"

Neely spins around and practically dies laughing. "*Finally?* Haley, we've not been together that long. And, may I point out, we aren't even married."

"You don't have to be married to have a baby."

She rolls her eyes. "No. You don't. But I'd like to be, okay?"

"Fine. You aren't technically married, even though it feels like it. So are you pregnant?"

"No," she says, leaning forward, "I'm not." She goes back to wiping a bit of spilled milk in the fridge. "Why do you always go to pregnancy?"

"Because I think it's the most romantic thing in the world," I coo. "It's two people that are madly in love, committing to bringing their bodies together to create a whole new life—*think about that!*—that will walk the world forever. It's the ultimate way of telling someone you love them."

Dane blinks. "You've really thought this out, haven't you?"

"I have a lot of time on my hands." I twist a strand of hair around my finger. "What were you talking about, anyway? What's helping Mia adjust to what?"

Neely closes the refrigerator. "We want to have a party at the new house before we move in. Just so Mia has some memories there with people she loves. And I think it'll help her be excited when the day comes to pack her stuff and sleep in a new room."

"Bring Trevor," Dane says. "I'd like to see him outside of work."

"I'll try." I fidget in my seat, wondering if he'll still be here then to invite. I hate this. I liked it so much better when I knew he'd be around.

Dane furrows a brow. "Nashville sucked?"

Neely giggles. "I think you should leave out the word 'suck,' love."

I roll my eyes. *"Anyway,"* I say, redirecting the conversation to things that won't remind me of being laid out on a table, "I'm not sure how long he'll be in town. Once the house is done, he won't have a reason to stay."

"Maybe. Maybe not," Dane says.

His hopeful attitude annoys me. "Maybe not. What would possibly keep him here? It's not like Kelly Construction has a line of projects waiting to be tackled. And even if they did, Trevor is the CFO. His job is in an office, crunching numbers."

"It is?" Neely asks.

"Yeah."

"Then why is he here?"

"Basically to build a poodle spa and make sure the house is perfect," I say, not wanting to get into it.

"The poodle spa is pretty amazing," Dane says. "There's a grooming table and a hot-tub thing for them to get bathed in. And everything is monogrammed for Buffy and Muffy."

Neely laughs. "You're kidding me."

"Afraid not." Dane grabs a cookie out of a jar and takes a bite. "In my next life, I want to be one of those dogs. But with a better name. Like Tuffy."

"Hey," Neely says, looking at her watch, "I need to go get Mia from Keyarah and Madison's house. I told Susan I'd bring the girls here for the night so she and her husband can have a date night."

They banter back and forth. I check my phone again. The home screen is blank. Again.

"You can always bring them to me," I offer. "I have nothing going on."

"You aren't seeing Trevor?" Dane asks.

"Apparently not." I swipe my phone like it has offended me and shove it in my pocket.

"Wanna talk about it?"

"Nope." I sink onto the stool again and let my irritation settle. "He doesn't owe me anything. We had a nice weekend. He'll go home. If I get upset about that, then I'm the jerk."

The door opens. Then closes. Then a knock sounds through the room.

The three of us exchange a look before Dane walks around Neely and twists the doorknob. In walks Penn.

"I knocked," he says immediately.

"Good boy, Penn," Neely says, patting him on the head. "Do you want a cookie?"

"Yes, please."

"I was kidding." She grabs her keys off the hook and blows Dane a kiss. "Be back in a little bit."

"Love you," Dane calls after her.

"Love you, babe."

The door closes as Penn walks to the cookie jar. He retrieves a large sugar cookie.

"Help yourself," Dane mutters.

"She offered it," he says.

"She was kidding," Dane says.

Penn shrugs, taking a bite of his cookie. "So what's happening over here?"

"Not much," I say. "I'm just getting ready to leave too."

Penn turns to face me. For the first time in the years I've known him, he doesn't smile. Or laugh. Or have something quick-witted on his tongue. He simply cocks his head a bit to the side. "Okay."

"Okay, what?" I ask.

"Why are you leaving?"

"So I can go home and get ready for bed. I just got back in town this afternoon, and I'm tired."

He chomps down on his cookie. "You went with Trevor last night, right?"

I nod.

"How'd that go?"

"Fine."

"Went pretty shitty if you're answering it with 'fine,'" he notes.

I blow out an irritated breath. "It went fine, Penn. It was nice. We had fun."

"Did you have sex?"

"I'm not answering that." I pick up my purse and head for the door. "Good night, Dane."

I don't know what transpires behind me, but I hear a lot of whispering. By the time I'm at the door, Dane is by my side.

"Hey," he says, stopping me.

"Yeah?"

"Don't let him get to you."

"Penn? Or Trevor?" I ask.

He grins. "Both?"

"Penn is just a fool. I shrug him off."

"But Trevor?" he pokes.

I think about his handsome face. Strong body. Gentle touch. Hard kisses. Sweet words.

"He's harder to shrug off," I admit. "But maybe we'll figure it out long distance. Or maybe it'll be over when he leaves. Time will tell."

"You know what I think?" Dane asks.

"No."

"I think two things. First of all, you seem a lot more composed about this guy. Watching you with Trevor isn't like watching you with the hippie."

I sigh. "We're back to the hippie again?"

"He's the baseline. Or he was," Dane says. "I think Trevor is now."

"Dane . . ." I groan. "This isn't helping."

He puts his hand on my shoulder and gives it a squeeze. "I know it doesn't feel like it is, but it is."

"How? It just feels like you're sprinkling some salt in my wound."

"Do you remember how I let Neely go?" He drops his hand.

"Yeah. Twice," I point out.

"Yes. Twice. Thanks for reminding me." He grimaces. "Anyway, if I would've admitted to myself that I loved her a hell of a lot earlier, then maybe I could've gotten off my ass and fixed our shit before I did."

"Trevor and I don't have shit to fix. He doesn't want to be tied down, and he lives in Nashville. It's ethos and logistics. And there really is no love involved, Dane. We've spent five minutes together and barely know each other. I'm probably a fun time to him, and I have to be okay with that. I am okay with that, because he's been fun too. So take your 'first of all' out of our equation. Please."

"But I had a 'second of all.'" Dane starts walking back to the kitchen.

"Dane, come on. There isn't—"

"I think I found a reason for Trevor to stay," he says.

"What?" I ask, my breath catching in my throat.

"You. Maybe you're the reason he'll stay."

He disappears around the corner before I can say what's really in my heart. That Trevor Kelly made himself clear. Yes, he suggested Liz saw more in his expression than she'd seen from him, but that doesn't change a man. And I need to be content to accept that.

Sorry, Dane. I doubt I'll be any man's reason to stay. Even if I am awesome.

CHAPTER TWENTY-FOUR

HALEY

I glance at my phone and giggle. A shirtless selfie of Trevor sits in my text messages, the result of losing a bet last night. He's making a duck face, standing in front of a mirror, and showing off his delicious six-pack just for me.

I don't know what the bet was about, but Jake shot me a message and told me an incoming text was imminent and I could thank him for it later. I also don't know how Jake got my number, and I didn't ask when Trevor came over last night for a quick make-out session.

Our rules are gone. Broken. Never to return. Even if I wanted to reintroduce them, it wouldn't work. I don't want to, anyway.

The chimes on the front door of Buds and Branches ring. Aerial, the woman who owns the gym Neely runs, comes in with a bright smile.

"Haley," she says. "I didn't know you worked here."

"It's my first day. What can I help you with?"

"My niece is having her tonsils taken out, and I wanted to send her some balloons and a couple of flowers. Nothing fancy, just something a twelve-year-old would like."

"How's that age?" I ask. "Mia will be there soon, and every day I feel like she's growing up on us. Wanting to be with her friends and not hanging out at home with her ex-nanny. Pushing her daddy's buttons. Seeing how far she can push Neely."

"Twelve isn't bad. I remember with my girls that fifteen was a doozy. You have a few years yet."

"Thank God." I venture over to the cooler. "So I love lilies, but they're pretty fragrant. That might not be good if she's having her tonsils out. Your throat is hooked to your nose." I make a face. "What about sunflowers? The yellow is cheery, and they don't really smell like anything."

Aerial grins. "Sounds great."

"We have a cute unicorn vase in the back. Want to use something like that or just a clear one?"

"Unicorn. Definitely."

"Just a sec."

I head to the back and grab the unicorn vase and arrange the sunflowers until they're a burst of pure happiness. I'm just placing the last flower when my phone buzzes in my pocket. I pull it out.

Trevor: Good morning, Ohio. Thinking about you this morning. A lot. And last weekend. Even more.

Me: Good morning, Thief. Thinking about last weekend. A lot. And what tonight could bring. Even more.

Trevor: I like the way you think.

Me: Ha.

Trevor: I'm in town. If you aren't busy, I'll stop by? I can even buy a flower if I need to.

Me: I'd love to know which you'd pick.

Trevor: Since it's your first day at work, I'd pick bamboo for good luck.

Me: Well played.

Trevor: See you soon, pretty girl.

I do a little dance before grabbing a couple of balloon options and heading back to the front.

"Haley, that's so cute," Aerial gushes. She holds the vase up in the air. "Is that a penny in there?"

"Yes. The copper is an acidifier, so bacteria and gross stuff won't grow as easily."

"I didn't know that."

My stomach flutters. "I learned it at a flower show this weekend."

"Fun." She selects the balloon she wants, and I ring her up. Once she's paid, she heads out the door. But before she gets out, someone else walks in.

"Penn Etling, what are you doing in here?" I laugh. "I didn't know you knew this place existed."

"I need some help and I figured you were the girl to ask."

"If this has anything to do with something dirty . . . ," I warn.

He grins. "I have another project for Meredith, and I need to plant . . ."

"What?"

"I don't know what to plant. She didn't include specifics and Dane said to plant bulbs that will come back every year, only I didn't know plants even did that and I'm not telling him that." He leans on the bar. "What do you suggest?"

"Definitely tulips," I tell him. "Tulips might be my favorite flower of all. We don't sell the bulbs here, but they probably do at the hardware store."

"Okay. What else?"

"Crocuses are nice. You could do daffodils, but they're kind of boring, if you ask me."

He stares at me. "Could you text me this? Because I'm going to forget."

"Then why didn't you text me to start with?"

He winks. "Because I never, ever miss a chance to see your face."

"Oh, boy," I say with a sigh. "You are a handful."

"I'm about three handfuls, if we're measuring that way. Or seven inches—"

"Can you not?" I say, smacking his hand. "I'm at work, Penn."

He rolls his eyes. "Fine. But you will text me this, right? Like now. I need to go get the stuff right now."

Something prickles at the back of my mind as I watch him. There's something off, something not quite right, and I don't know what it is.

"How's the house coming?" I ask. I know the answer. Most of it, anyway. I just can't keep myself from asking and trying to prepare for the inevitable.

I need to talk this out with Trevor. I need to see if anything has changed after our night in Nashville, but I'm scared to ask. I'm terrified to come across as pushy. No matter what else I do, I refuse to be viewed as clingy.

"We're done." He shrugs. "The house is what we call substantially complete. That means our work is done, but there might be little things here or there that need to be hashed out. But we won't know that until Branson comes and tells us what he wants."

"Can't Trevor do it?"

Penn bites his lip. "He already did."

"Oh."

I can't look Penn in the face. Despite the fool he usually pretends to be, I know he'll try to make me feel better if he thinks I'm upset.

Am I upset? I don't know. Everything is too confusing.

"Hey," Penn says, his voice softer. "Are you all right?"

I look up just in time to see Trevor walking by the front window. He sees me through the glass. A soft grin plays on his lips, and I melt into a puddle of goo.

He pulls open the front door and stops when he sees Penn.

"Hey," Penn says. "We were just talking about you, Kelly."

"Yeah?" he asks, looking between Penn and me. "What's going on here?"

"Penn needed some advice on flowers, actually. I think I have him pointed in the right direction."

Trevor nods, still unsure. "Hey, Penn—if you're going to be around for a few, I'd like to meet up with you at the café. Just a few things I want to see if you can do before Dad gets here."

"Sure. I can head over there now and give Claire hell until you make it over," Penn says.

"Sounds good. Be there in fifteen or so."

When Penn is gone, it's then Trevor who makes his way to the desk. I busy myself organizing notes from a call earlier about a wedding because I don't want to look at him. I'm not sure what to say.

"Hey, you," he says, breaking the ice for me.

"Hi."

"How's it going today?"

"Good. I really love it here," I say, sighing happily. "It feels good to walk in this place, you know? I love being surrounded by all this beauty."

Trevor laughs. "I'm happy for you."

"Me too."

Silence creeps around us, a weight that sinks into the room. It's large and oddly shaped and impossible to get comfortable with. Trevor feels it, too, because he shifts his feet like he does when he can't figure something out.

"So you're done at the house?" I ask. My throat is parched, making the words sound like they're said over sandpaper.

Trevor nods. "Yeah. They finished over the weekend."

"What's this mean for you?"

I really want to know what it means for me. For him and me. For us. If there's an 'us,' and God, I hope there is.

He picks up a pen and twiddles it between two fingers. "I'm not sure. We probably need to talk about it."

"Probably so."

The air stales between us, the energy that typically barrels from him to me, and vice versa, gone. In its place is a stiff, delicate situation that neither of us seems to want to deal with.

"Haley . . ." He scratches his head. "This is really complicated."

"Is it? Because it doesn't seem like it has to be from here."

He sets the pen down. "What do you suggest we do? You live three hours away from me. Your family is here. My family and my job are there."

I shrug. "I don't know. I only know people make things work that they want to work."

He looks at me warily. It sends a pang of panic over me, and I grab on to the desk to keep from marching around the corner and kissing him. Because kissing him won't help. Not in the long run.

A card that says "Love Is Forever" hangs on the rack just over Trevor's shoulder. It's surrounded by a handful of other cards with various sayings, but it's the one that sticks out to me. Probably because that's the problem—love isn't "forever" to Trevor Kelly.

Can I deal with that? Am I willing to?

"Maybe you're right," he says finally. He strolls to a display and picks up a little potted bamboo plant. He checks the price and sets it on the counter next to a twenty. "I want to buy this for you."

"You don't have to do that."

"Can you hush and ring me up so I can get out of here before Penn forgets he's meeting me?" He laughs.

I get his total, then his change, and hand him a receipt. "Here you go, sir."

"Thank you." He stuffs the bills in his pocket. "May this little plant bring you good fortune."

I hope so.

He checks his phone. I watch his brow furrow and his jaw set. I try to memorize every line in his face. Just in case.

"You're staring again." He grins as he catches me off-guard. "What are you thinking?"

I walk around the desk and stand in front of him. "Can I ask a favor of you? Before you go back to the city?"

His eyes darken. "Sure."

"Dane is having a party at his new house. It's a pre-housewarming party so Mia feels more comfortable when they actually move in." I suck in a hasty breath. "And I'd like you to come with me. As my plus-one."

I think he's going to say no. I see it on his face. As I start to tell him not to worry about it, he surprises me by smiling.

"You know what? Yeah. I'll go. I'd love to," he says. "Lorene has a group of coon hunters coming in this week, so I'm going to have to get out of town at some point soon. But I'd love to go with you. You can count on it."

I nod, afraid to say anything because I don't know what words will come out of my mouth. Either a "Thanks for coming with me," or a sob that his answer gave me more questions and no answers.

He kisses my forehead, and I don't know how to take that. If I overthought it, I might conclude it was an apology kiss.

No, I'm not ready for that. Not yet.

Trevor

"Just got word you wrapped everything up down there." Jake's chair squeaks in the background. "How's it feel?"

"I don't know, but it sounds like you need a new fucking chair."

The sound stops. Jake blows out a breath. "Okay. I'll bite. What's wrong?"

I roll-stop through the intersection by the post office before remembering I'm supposed to talk to Penn at the café. I check my mirrors and then blow a U-turn in the middle of the road.

"Wow," Jake says. "This must be good."

"There's nothing good about any of this, jackass."

"Easy there, little brother. What's going on?"

"You know," I say, "I liked it better when I didn't have a conscience. When I didn't give a shit whether a woman liked me or not. When I'd sleep with someone one weekend and maybe never talk to her again."

"Okay. Haley. Continue."

I blow out a breath and slide the truck into the café's parking lot. But I don't get out. Instead, I think of having her next to me in the hotel room. Because that's going to fucking help everything.

"For the record, you were not that way," Jake says. "You've always had a conscience, just never been in love. And now you are, if I'm guessing."

"Oh, fuck you."

"Fucking is the problem. Not me. But man, if you'll just be honest with yourself, it'll help."

"I have a decision to make here, Jake."

"Want my advice?"

"Not really."

He chuckles into the line. "Well, you called me, so I'm calling bullshit on that."

I rest my head on the steering wheel. "Everything here is wrapped up."

"Yeah. I know. We covered that."

"So I'm coming home."

"Okay. I expected that."

I heave a breath because I don't know how to explain. I don't want to explain it or to care to explain it, but the truth of the matter is I fucking care. A lot. And I can't just shake that shit off like it's a girl I met at a café, eating doughnuts.

Every girl I've had before, I've known there would come a day when I wouldn't see them again. It was inevitable. It was fine. It was expected, even. So why the thought of going home without Haley kills me is so fucking confusing.

"You know, we live in a day and age where you can travel distances fast. And we have things like text messages and video chat and email. It's almost like the other person is right there," Jake says, patronizing me.

Says the fucker who has never tried a relationship, let alone a long-distance one.

I climb out of my truck, needing the fresh air. "Damn it, Jake. It's not that simple."

"Why isn't it?"

"What happens a year from now when I don't want to be with her anymore?" I ask.

"What happens a year from now when you aren't and you wish you were?"

"Stop playing devil's advocate with me and answer the fucking question."

"I did answer the fucking question. You just don't like my answer." He sighs. "She's really fucked you up, hasn't she?"

I hate him for saying it. Hearing it like that makes it so real. So true.

"Something like that," I grumble.

"Why don't you just come home and see her on the weekends? Try it out for a few weeks or months and see what happens? It might fix itself."

He doesn't get it. Hell, I barely understand it myself.

There is nothing to fix. I'd see her every other month if that was all I could have, but that's not the problem. The problem is there's no reason to do it. We've known that from the start. She'll be expecting it to last forever, and I'll be looking for a way out in six months. It's how I work. It's how we work. It'll never work together.

"It's not like I don't understand the concept of dating, Jake. I've been there. Done that."

"So? What's the issue, then?"

I look at the door of the Dogwood Café. A couple of weeks ago, I walked in there and saw her bent over that bar. Little did I know that moment in time would rock my world to the core. Little did I know that my heart would even want to be rocked.

My chest is so tight I can barely breathe. I can only relax when I'm with her, and I can't be right now. Because I really can't be when I have to go home and leave her here.

For my own good, but also, more importantly, for hers.

I can't promise her what she wants and needs. What she deserves is the whole world. I won't be the guy to break that promise. I just won't make it.

"I'm going to ask you a question, but you have to promise me something," I say.

"Okay. What?"

"You can't laugh at me or think I'm a pussy."

"I'll try," he teases.

"Jake . . ."

"Fine, fine. I won't make fun of you on the phone. Deal?"

I groan. I wish I could hang up now, but I need his opinion. I'll have to make do.

"Fine," I say. "Do you believe in love?"

"Are you seriously asking me that?"

"Does it sound like I'm serious?"

He sighs, that damn chair squeaking again. "Okay. Do I believe in love? Yes. I do."

"Why?" I press.

"I don't fucking know. Why not believe in it? It even makes sense scientifically, if you think about it."

"Why?"

"Well, it bonds people together, I guess. It gives you a reason to wake up. It keeps a couple together to raise a family or to have experiences that are more satisfying." He pauses. "Why? You don't?"

I pace a circle, my boots crunching the gravel. "Yeah. I do. But here's my problem with it: I've never experienced a love that didn't end. And I haven't seen it either. And if you haven't seen something, does it exist?"

"You don't think Dad loves Meredith?"

Apart from Saturday night, Dad and I have never talked about emotions. He's never been particularly emotional, so why start now? Does he love Meredith? I don't fucking know.

"Maybe. But Dad married Mom and that ended in war. Meredith was married before and that failed. Look at my first serious relationship—that landed Tera in the hospital," I say, my heart breaking for her. "Why did that happen? Because I didn't feel like I was in love with her anymore, and she couldn't take it."

"Trev . . ."

"What if I do that to Haley? What if I decide it's not for me and something happens to her? I couldn't hack it, Jake. I'd be done." I shiver, my stomach threatening to expel Lorene's biscuits and gravy that I had for breakfast. "I just don't know if I can take that responsibility."

"You're the only one who knows, little brother."

Fuck. All I know is that hurting her would break me. Surely that can't be love.

It's lust. She needs someone who is all about love. All about lifelong love and commitment. And that's . . . that's not me.

"I can't commit to that with her." I turn to see Penn standing at my truck, his hands over the bed. My stomach twists and I force a swallow. "I gotta go. I'll call you later."

"Bye."

CHAPTER TWENTY-FIVE

HALEY

"H ey," I say.

I step onto the porch and close the door behind me. Trevor kisses the top of my head before taking my hand and guiding me down the sidewalk.

The friend kiss again. Okay.

"Thanks for coming with me," I say. My voice wobbles more than I'd like, but I'm doing my best to keep my composure. Every day, every hour, that passes is a moment closer to him leaving and me not having a resolution to whatever it is we are, Or aren't.

"Absolutely," he says. "In you go."

The truck door opens and I climb inside. I set the vase of flowers I arranged earlier for Neely on the floor between my feet, and by the time I'm situated, Trevor is climbing in.

The conversation he suggested we have yesterday hangs over us like a dark cloud. I feel it lingering about, threatening to ruin everything.

I don't know whether to bring it up or to let Trevor do it. As he flips on the engine, I figure it might be best to wait until the party is over. I'd rather not see my friends with mascara tears, and even though I knew who Trevor was going into this sexual relationship, it hurts. But at least I'm happier in myself and I'm still awesome.

But I might still cry . . .

"Did you design those?" he asks, nodding to the flowers.

"Yeah. They're pretty, huh?"

"You did good, Ohio."

He pilots the truck onto the road. I turn the heat up on my side and rub my hands together in front of the vent. There's a chill I can't shake, but I think it radiates from inside me and no amount of heated air will fix it.

"Turn here," I say.

"So why are they moving?" he asks. It's a clear conversation starter, and I hate that it's so forced.

"Dane has lived in the house they live in now since before Mia was born. Now that Neely is in the picture, he thought it would be nice to have a house they could all see as home." I shrug. "It's pretty sweet, actually."

"He seems like a good guy."

"He really is."

We drive quietly out of town. The sun hovers over the horizon, painting the sky the most beautiful colors. Trevor bites a fingernail, something I've never seen him do before, and I wonder if that's a good sign or a bad one.

I've thought about our impending conversation all day and popped antacids like they're candy. Whether it's out of necessity or because I'm that desperate, I can find some hope in things. He came into the shop today. He's going with me tonight. He wouldn't do those things if he didn't see *something* for us together. It wouldn't make sense, and if Trevor is anything, he's logical.

Besides sexy. He's so fucking sexy.

He glances at me out of the corner of his eye and smirks. "You're staring again."

"You're cute again. What do you want me to do?"

He reaches over and grabs my thigh. He gives it a gentle squeeze. "Thanks for inviting me tonight." His tone lacks any enthusiasm whatsoever.

"Thanks for being so excited about it."

He laughs, removing his hand. Instantly, I miss it. I want to take it off the steering wheel and put it back on my leg. Or arm. Or face.

Damn it.

"Is this it?" Trevor points at a farmhouse on the right. "Never mind. The sign makes it clear."

We pull into the driveway and park behind Penn's truck. Trevor jumps out and opens my door and pulls me into him before my feet hit the ground.

He smells amazing, like leather and pine. I wrap my arms around him and bury my face in his chest. He holds me tight, gripping the back of my head and pressing it into him. My body relaxes as his heartbeat plays beneath my cheek.

"I know you want an answer," he says quietly. "I don't want you to think I'm avoiding you or the conversation."

"But aren't you?" I ask, my chest burning like it's on fire.

"No." He shakes his head. "We have to figure out where we stand. I know that. I'm not stupid."

"Is it something you have to think about? Or do you know?"

He lowers his face and kisses my head, letting his lips linger. "I don't really want to talk about this right now."

"That doesn't sound good." I fist his shirt in my hand and steady myself. *Be strong.* "But we'll talk about it later. After the party?"

He kisses me again. "Yeah. We'll talk tonight."

I fight a lump in my throat as I pull back. He gives me a soft smile that, if I thought about it long enough, could be defined as sad. Or foreboding. Or the exact opposite spirit from what the bamboo was supposed to deliver.

Shoving it out of my brain, I focus on getting through the next couple of hours. At least here, I'm surrounded by my people. That's good.

I take his hand, his palm enveloping mine, and start toward the house. "I want you to know that this party won't be anything like your dad's. So temper your expectations, please."

He laughs, squeezing my hand. "Most parties aren't like my dad's because most men aren't married to a Meredith."

"I thought you and Jake put the party on for your father?" I ask.

"Oh, we did. Just like Dad had the house here built for her but she sent drawings and designs down to incorporate. Meredith has a way of getting what she wants."

"I respect that."

"Trust me—if I could figure it out, I'd do it too."

I grin to myself. If he only knew how much he could get away with just by flicking that smirk or touching an arm. It's probably for the best he doesn't know.

We take the steps. I give a courtesy knock and then walk on in.

Dane, Neely, Matt, Penn, and Susan are standing in the kitchen. Pizza boxes from Mucker's are open in front of them along with water bottles and two-liter containers of soda. Mia's, Keyarah's, and Madison's laughter filters downstairs as their feet pound on the floors above.

"Hey," I say as we enter.

"How are you, Haley?" Susan walks over to us, a little shell-shocked as she takes in Trevor. "I'm Susan."

"Hi. I'm Trevor Kelly."

"It's nice to meet you."

Trevor smiles and walks on by to say hello to the guys. Susan mouths, "Oh, my God," as he passes. All I can do is giggle because I get it. I feel the same way.

"Want some pizza?" Neely asks. "We have all kinds. More kids will be here in about thirty minutes. We thought we'd get here first so we can actually hear each other talk."

I grab a slice, even though my stomach threatens to reject it just from smelling it. Trevor comes up to my side and pours himself a glass of soda.

"What's up, Matt?" Trevor asks, screwing the top back on the two-liter bottle.

"Not much."

"I was telling my brother about the deck you built. He had me grab some pictures to take back with me."

I avoid Neely's gaze and take a bite of pizza instead.

My heart thumps wildly in my chest, my blood rocking through my body. *He's leaving.* That's one variable down.

"Hey, Trevor, come back here," Dane says, opening the back door. "If you like to fish, you have to see this pond. Completely stocked with catfish. Don't tell my lady, but this is the reason I really wanted to buy the house."

"I love to fish . . ." Trevor follows Dane outside, Matt on their tail.

As soon as the door closes, I shake my head. "No," I say, waving off the questions Neely and Susan are poised to ask. "I don't want to talk about it."

"Has he still not talked to you?" Neely asks.

"We're supposed to talk about it after we leave here." I feel my energy fade into the room. "I don't know what to think."

"But Nashville isn't far. You could totally see each other on the weekends," Susan offers. "Who really sees their guy during the week, anyway?"

I look from one to the other, to an unusually quiet Penn standing by the door.

"Yeah, but I don't think that's the problem," I say. "It's more than that."

"Maybe he's just unsure how to handle it," Susan suggests.

"Maybe." I realize I forgot the flowers in Trevor's truck. "Hey, I brought you something, Neely. I'll be right back."

I step outside, grateful for the quiet. All their questions—spoken and unspoken—overwhelm me because this is not up to me. If it were up to me, I'd figure it out with Trevor because I really like him.

A lot.

More than I've liked anyone and in a different way.

In a better way.

In a way that probably doesn't matter.

My feet slow as I realize all the time we've spent together meant something different to me. He might like me, but he was just having fun. I was, too, but I did what I always do . . . start *falling in love*.

Oh, dear Jesus.

My hand lies on the front of Trevor's truck as I blink back a tear.

"Hey."

I jump when Penn comes around the back of the truck and sees me. I sniffle, wiping at my eyes just in case.

"Hey, you," I say. "What are you doing out here?"

"I came to talk to you."

"Penn, now's not the time."

He leans against the truck and looks at me. His eyes are as serious as they get, his face—which is usually full of mischief—free from any shenanigans. It makes me nervous.

"I know you think I'm a big goofball," he says.

I smile. "Aren't you?"

"Yeah. More or less. But sometimes, even this goofball has something he wants to say."

"Okay."

"Do you remember the first day I met you?" he asks.

"Yes. I believe I was pushing Mia in a stroller and you made a very inappropriate comment about my butt."

"Sounds about right." He grins. His arms cross over his chest as he looks at me with a seriousness I didn't know Penn could manage. "I'm an idiot when it comes to women. You know how I roll."

"If that means you knock them over like dominoes, then yeah. I got you."

"Nice analogy. That makes me look fancy." He shrugs, shoving off the truck. "But one thing I never do is play them."

"I know you don't, Penn. No one thinks you want anything from a girl but sex. Hence the reason I've never gone to dinner with you."

He grins, his cheeks flushing a little. He's adorable in a boy-next-door kind of way, and for as much crap as he catches from us and doles our way, he's resilient. He's loyal. He knows we'd all do anything for him because he'd do as much for us. That's the beauty of Penn Etling—he'll drive you to the brink and then pull you off it before you fall.

"Look, this is none of my business." He works his neck back and forth. "Fuck it. I'm just gonna go back in."

My smile fades as a chill creeps over my bones. There's something he's not saying, and I need to know what it is. Even if it hurts . . . and I think it might.

"Penn, what's wrong?"

He squares his shoulders to mine. "You really like Kelly, huh?"

"I do."

He chews on the side of his cheek. "This is why I don't pay attention to shit. Then you gotta know shit. Then you gotta decide what to do with it."

I force a swallow. "What do you know, Penn?"

He takes a deep breath. "I don't know anything, really. I just don't think Kelly is the kind of guy that's gonna stay with a woman long term."

I lift my chin to distract him, and maybe me, from the way my heart splinters into a thousand little pieces. "How do you know this?"

"I'm not judging him for it, Hay. I'm the same damn way. But the problem is, it's you on the receiving end, and I'm gonna have a helluva time watching that."

"Maybe it won't end like you think." *But if even Penn can see this, why am I holding on to hope?*

"What do you think is gonna happen?" he asks.

I shrug. "I don't know. I'm hoping he goes back to Nashville and we figure out how to see each other and we can build on it from there. I really think we can make it work, and I think Trevor wants it to too." A bubble of panic begins to burst in my chest. "I know he says he doesn't want commitment and all that, but don't most men say that?"

"I guess. I do. But I *really* don't want it."

"I don't think he's wanted it either. But every man has to find a girl that changes things for them. Am I right? I hope," I say, grimacing. "I sound like a damn idiot."

"You do not." Penn struggles with what to say. It physically manifests itself in the rigidity of his shoulders and the strain in his neck. "I hope you get everything you want out of life. And if that includes Kelly, then I hope he realizes what he's got and reels you in." He kicks at a rock.

I put my head on Penn's shoulder and sigh. He pats the top of my hand with his heavy palm, being as gentle as he can be. It's not what I thought I'd be doing tonight, taking comfort from the guy who drives me crazier than any other, but it's what I need right now. I'm glad Penn knew it and offered his friendship to me.

"You're all right, you know that?" I ask.

"Yeah." He leans his head on mine. "And if you ever find yourself in need of a night out, don't forget that I'm patiently waiting my turn to woo you."

I snort, pulling my head up. "You don't want to woo me. You just want to sleep with me." I retrieve the flowers from the truck.

"That's not true," he says as we start back to the house. "So you know, I'd take you to a nice dinner. Tell you how pretty you are. Then I'd sleep with you. You'd get more out of it than just a lay."

I laugh as he opens the door for me. "How thoughtful of you."

"I'm really underestimated."

"That you are."

I watch him walk ahead of me and make a note I owe him one. He didn't have to do this—take time to come talk to me so I could walk back in with a smile on my face—but he did.

He'll make a good catch for someone one day.

CHAPTER TWENTY-SIX

TREVOR

I stand just around the corner of the house, unmoving. I need to go back inside, especially because Haley and Penn have returned. But I can't. My feet won't move.

That's probably for the best since I want to put a fist down Penn Etling's throat. Not because he's wrong. But because he's right.

They say the truth is sometimes hard to hear, and that's certainly accurate this time around.

"I just don't think Kelly is the kind of guy that's gonna stay with a woman long term."

My teeth grind together as the weight of Penn's words trickles through my mind. The bastard is right. I've never been that guy. I haven't wanted to be. It's against my code of conduct.

Why stay with a woman when you know how badly it'll end? When she wants a house and kids and a commitment of forever and you can't guarantee that? Tera's face, tear-stricken and pale, slides through my mind, and my stomach lurches.

I gag, imagining Haley looking at me in the same way, all because I changed my mind. All because I told her I was just learning about myself and realized I had it wrong and it wasn't fair to either one of us to stay in a relationship that wasn't right.

That I didn't want to resent her for making me not take certain jobs or not live in certain places all because I told her I wouldn't years before.

That I didn't want to break her heart, but if I didn't, I'd obliterate it because I'd already checked out.

Fear paralyzes me as reality crystallizes in my mind. The little games I've been telling myself—thinking I could figure it out, see her a couple of times a month, that she isn't like other girls, who expect the impossible—end in a checkmate.

I lose.

Because even if she did buy that line of bullshit, she deserves more. She deserves to get what she wants out of life, just like I do. And if I pull some wool over her eyes to keep her for myself when I'm not sure I can return the favor, that makes me the worst.

I'm already pretty fucking bad for keeping it going this long.

The door opens again and I hear steps on the porch. I peer around the corner to see Haley looking toward the barn.

"Hey," I say, walking toward her. "I was looking for you."

It's a lie and she knows it.

Maybe Penn's words put her on guard, but there's a shield between the two of us that slices me to the core. That's not how it's supposed to be with us. It feels so wrong.

It is so wrong.

But isn't this whole thing so wrong?

"Where have you been?" she asks.

"I went down to the pond with Dane, then came back out to look for you. Must've missed you inside," I say.

She nods. "Mia's friends will be showing up soon . . ."

Here it is, the opening to have the conversation that will make me feel like the biggest asshole in the universe. She wants it now. I don't blame her. Getting it over with is preferable to milking it over the evening.

But if I yank the bandage off now, I'll have to go. And if I have to go, there's a ninety-nine percent chance I might not ever see her again.

I swallow back a layer of bile.

"Do you, um, want to go for a walk?" I ask.

"No. I want to talk right here."

"Okay." I force a swallow. "I'm heading back to Nashville in the morning."

She nods, her jaw tense.

"I mean, I have to work."

She waits for the rest of it. The bomb to drop. The part where I kill both of our dreams with a couple of quick, pussy-mumbled lines before running to my truck and getting the hell out of here.

But as I look at her, the woman who has captured my attention unlike any other, I can't do it. I can't walk away from her. I can't lose her—not entirely.

Thinking I'll never hear her laugh again or have someone call me "Thief," to wrap my brain around the idea of never waking up next to her again, makes me physically ill.

How can someone you just met a few weeks ago already mean more to you than some people you've known your whole life? And why does that have to happen?

"I want you to be honest with me," she says.

"I'm always honest with you."

She swallows. "Do you plan on seeing me again?"

"Yes. Of course. I'll come here or you can come to my house."

Her shoulders sag in relief. "Okay."

"Okay." I head toward her, needing to touch her—needing reassurance that she's real and I'm real and this is happening.

Before I get there, she holds out a hand.

"I . . . I need to know," she says. "What am I to you?"

"What does that mean?"

I force a swallow down the narrow tube of my throat. My heart pounds in my chest, the vein in my neck throbbing as I shift under her pointed gaze.

"It means just what I'm asking," she says.

I stop in my tracks. "We don't have to put a label on it, Haley."

She runs a hand down her face. "No. We don't. You don't have to call me your girlfriend or say we're dating. But I need to know what I mean to you."

"I don't understand."

She drops her hand. There's a chill to her eyes as she takes me in. "I'm going to be honest with you, Trevor."

She pauses as she searches for words. Every second she doesn't speak feels like a lifetime as I try to come to terms with the words I think she's going to say.

I will her not to. I silently plead with her to not go where I think she's going, to just let this thing be whatever it is.

I can't do this. I can't ruin her like she's going to make me do.

"Haley—"

"I'm falling in love with you."

She blurts the words before I can object. My blood turns to ice.

"No, Haley."

She blinks back tears. "I know I signed the napkin," she says, laughing as she chokes back a sob. "And I know I promised you that I understand you just needed me to help you fill a spot of time in your life—"

"Haley, stop. That's not true."

My heart twists in my chest so hard I think it might stop beating. I want to hold her, caress her, kiss away all her tears, but I can't do that. It'll only make it worse.

"It's not?" she asks. "I know you like me. I see it in your eyes and feel it in the way you touch me. But if you won't admit that, I need to know."

"I do like you, Haley. So much. But . . . you don't love me."

"How do you know?" Tears drip down her cheeks as she watches me try to keep it together. "How do you know what my love feels like when you won't accept it? Heck, you won't even entertain the idea of it?"

She's right. I won't. Even if I did, I'm not sure it would change anything.

A girl like her doesn't love a guy like me. Not really. She just thinks she does because she's a glutton for punishment.

"You fall in love when you're ready," I say. "Not when you're lonely."

"You think that's it? You think I think I'm in love with you because I don't want to be alone?" Her brows lift as she processes this. "How dare you say that to me?"

"It's true. You are so much better than me," I tell her, fighting back a lump in my throat. "You have this huge heart, this dry wit that makes me insane, and a laugh that I'll always remember. I can't give you that."

"You won't try."

I shake my head. "I'm not there. Maybe someday I'll figure it out. Maybe someday I'll be like my dad and fall madly in love. But right now, I'm not there."

"You let me fall for you."

Guilt settles in my soul. It burrows nice and deep, rooting its way into my psyche.

I think back on the moments I didn't leave her alone. The night we made out like high school kids. The day I couldn't help myself and not visit her at the flower shop. They were choices I made well after we broke our contract, and I kept pressing. I couldn't help it. Because I'm a fucking moron.

"You know how you say you fall for the wrong guy?" I ask.

She nods.

"We fall for the people we think we deserve. You need to figure out what it is about you that makes you think you need someone like me."

Her eyes go wide, the wind knocked out of her. "Fuck you." She shuffles her feet. "You want a little truth, Trevor?"

I don't, but I nod, anyway.

"You know how you say women cling to you and won't go away?" she asks.

I nod again.

"It's you that does that to them. You break them down until they think it's safe, and then you say you've had enough and watch them wallow. I think you get a kick out of that."

"Are you serious?"

I watch an anger settle over her features that has my name written all over it. I can't blame her, but I want to. It'd be a hell of a lot easier thinking this was her fault than knowing it's mine.

"I am." She throws her shoulders back. Black lines streak down her pretty face as she sets her jaw in place. "Goodbye."

"Haley, wait." I take one measured step her way, but the look she gives me stops me in my tracks. "Let's talk."

"We've talked." She tucks a strand of hair behind her ear. "I'm not mad at you. I don't blame you for this. But I want you to think about how to not do this to someone else."

"I—"

"You warned me. I know," she says, cutting me off. "You told me what to expect and didn't make any promises. But that doesn't make this okay. I asked you not to touch me, to woo me, to say things that made me think I was beautiful to you. You overstepped that boundary, even when I asked it for my heart's sake. So no. There are no more words, Trevor. You've made your choice. So leave." She grabs the door handle. "And a word to the wise. Get out of here before Dane comes out."

"Haley . . ."

She disappears inside the house, and it's like she took the light with her. It's like standing in darkness, but it has to be this way. There's no other choice. If I give in to my hedonistic tendencies again and go after her, it'll only make it worse in the end. And there will be an end. There always is.

CHAPTER TWENTY-SEVEN

HALEY

"Don't go out there." I march inside, vision blurry, and head straight to the refrigerator. "Dane. Penn. Stop."

"What did he do?" Dane's voice is colder than I've ever heard it. "I won't ask again, Hay."

"Good. Don't." I take a half-drunk bottle of wine from the fridge and pour a glassful. I cringe as the alcohol burns my throat and settles into my already acidic stomach. "That's over."

Penn turns to face the wall with his phone in his hand.

"Hey. Mia wants ice cream . . ." Neely stops as she rounds the corner and takes in the scene before her. "What happened out here?"

"It seems as though Trevor and I are no longer a thing. Well, we probably never were and now he'll expect me to beg for attention like Liz, but if he thinks that, he doesn't know me well." I take another long drink.

Neely comes up to my side and pulls me into a hug. The adrenaline starts to wear off. I'm suddenly tired, so tired, and I sag against Neely.

"I lost the bet, Dane." The tears start again. "Guess you get to pick my next three dates."

Penn turns to face me. I expect him to make a comment about getting one of the three slots, but he doesn't. He just looks at me with a frown on his face.

"Oh, come on," I poke. "You don't even want to date me now?"

"I'd be the luckiest son of a bitch on earth," Penn says quietly. "But no. Because you deserve better than a guy like me or that rich fucker that's fixin' to get his teeth knocked in."

"Don't you dare." I stand straight, my stomach sloshing with wine. "He has the right to do whatever he wants."

"Sure, he does. So do I," Penn says. "He made you cry. I'll kill him."

"I've cried before. Odds are, I'll cry again." I pace around the kitchen, well aware I look like a crazy person. "Why do I do this to myself?"

Dane pats my shoulder. "We've had this discussion. The bet, remember? But this one isn't on you."

"Yes, it is. He didn't lie to me. Maybe he reeled me in, but I took the bait. I took it happily. Three times in Nashville," I say over my shoulder to Neely. "I took it and ran with it happily."

A flash of anger burns through Dane's eyes before he looks at Neely. "Did you say Mia wanted ice cream?"

"Yeah."

"I can go," Penn volunteers.

"Nope," Dane says, grabbing his keys off the counter. "I need some fresh air. Thanks, though."

"Fresh air better not include getting in Trevor's face, Dane. Please. It's not worth it," I plead.

He ignores me and leaves without saying goodbye.

My thighs ache from the adrenaline burn. I climb onto a stool. Everything inside me drops into the seat. I feel like I weigh an extra hundred pounds.

Penn comes over and wraps his arms around me. "Haley, I'm sorry," he says.

"Not your fault."

"No, but that doesn't mean I can't feel bad for you." He flinches. "Am I developing feelings? What if I get a conscience? This could be bad, guys." He gasps, letting me go. "I could turn into Matt."

I laugh, the act releasing a little of the sadness in my heart. "That wouldn't be the end of the world."

"For you. It would be terrible for me."

Neely refills my wineglass and hands it to me. "I'm sorry this hurts so much."

"Well, if nothing else, I learned a few things." I sniffle.

"Like what?"

"Like how to get off in the missionary position. How to handle myself when I'm jealous. How to stand up for myself when I want something, and what it feels like to fall in love." I bring the glass to my lips but don't drink. The burn of unshed tears fills my throat instead. "What it feels like to be rejected."

"Fuck him," Penn says.

"I thought you liked him?" Neely asks.

He rolls his shoulders in a small circle. "I did. Now I don't."

"Penn, this is my fault," I say. "He didn't lie to me. He didn't promise me anything he didn't follow through on. I just went all in like I do, and he didn't."

A knock at the front door makes me jump. I hold my breath, hoping, even though I shouldn't, that it's Trevor. Penn waves Neely off and marches to the front door. His fist is clenched to his side as he pulls it open.

Claire bursts in. "Where are you? Oh, friend." She rushes to me, throwing her arms around me. "I'm so sorry."

"How did you even know?" I ask.

"Penn texted me to get over here. He didn't say why, but he didn't have to. Trevor leaving was the only thing I could think would hurt you bad enough for Penn to bother with texting me." She looks at him over the top of my head. "Thanks, Penn."

He looks at Claire, Neely, and me one at a time. "I'm losing it. Something is wrong with me, and I don't know how to fix it. It's like I'm growing a heart." He sticks his lip out and wobbles it. "I don't want it. Take it back."

We laugh, watching Penn act like he's in shock.

"Let me say," Claire says, sitting beside me, "that I hate this. But as I was driving over here, I realized I'm not really worried about you."

"Gee, thanks."

"I'm not. I have been every other time you've had a breakup, but not this one. You'll be fine this time, strangely enough."

"Yeah, Claire's right," Neely chimes in. "I get what she means. You're taking this super well."

I don't know about that.

There's a black hole in my heart. I can feel the hollowness. It's deep, gaping, maybe even seeping. It hurts like a bitch, but I'm aware of one thing—nothing is going to fix it. Not now. Not yet. Not until I can at least wrap my head around what's happened.

"My friend Grace is coming from New York soon," Neely says. "Maybe we can all go somewhere, *not Nashville*, and have a girls' trip."

"I'd love that," I say.

"Wait," Penn says, cutting in. "Grace. Is she the one you were telling me about? Hot little body. Dirty mouth."

"That's Grace."

"When does she come in?" he asks with a grin.

Neely rolls her eyes. "I'm not sure. Soon. But you should probably stay away from her."

"Why?"

Neely laughs. "I can't figure out if you'd be oil and water or get along like a house on fire."

"Neely, pal," Penn says, heading for the door, "you just guaranteed I'll be looking her up."

"Where are you going?" Claire asks.

"I'm going to make sure Dane found the ice cream, because I'm pretty sure Lorene doesn't sell it at the Dogwood Inn." He shrugs. "Later, babes."

Claire sits beside me and swipes my wine. "I want to see your house and be super excited for you, Neely. But I need a drink first."

The room grows quiet for everyone but me. I hear Trevor's voice roll through my mind, telling me I'm staring. Calling me a pretty girl. Asking me what I'm thinking.

Liz was wrong. He might've looked at me differently, but not like she thought. Or I hoped.

There'll be no more staring, Thief. Not anymore.

Trevor

"What's wrong, honey?" Lorene looks up as I walk by.

I sit across from her in one of the oversize chairs by the fireplace. She continues knitting, working the yarn through sticks that remind me of something Godzilla would've used to eat Chinese food. They clink together, the sound oddly comforting.

My emotions are spent.

This is why I don't do this. Exactly fucking why. I can't win. I never win.

"If you don't want to tell me, you don't have to," she says, reaching over and patting my hand. "But I've lived almost ninety-one years. I know a little something about a lot of things. Unless it's computers. I don't know a thing about them."

I settle in and watch her work for a while. It's almost hypnotic and I appreciate the distraction. Finally, I face reality. "Were you married?"

"Yes. For fifty years. Geoff was a good man. A very good man. I miss him every day of my life." She smiles. "He left me twenty-six months before he passed, you know."

"He left you?"

She nods. "He divorced me. The fool was seventy years old and filed papers to end our marriage." She chuckles to herself. "I told him if he wanted to leave, he could. Fine by me."

I lean forward, my elbows on my knees. "I'm confused."

She laughs. "Oh, honey. There's nothing to be confused about. We got married when we were twenty at the courthouse. My daddy didn't like him, so he wouldn't come. But Mama did, and his parents, and we said our vows in front of the good Lord. We didn't have fancy weddings back then like they do now. But it wasn't about that back then. It was just about finding the person to hold on to when the storms got bad because, back then, they got bad in a hurry."

Her needles fly against each other, picking up speed.

"We battled through a war, three kids, hard times and easy ones. He was the great love of my life, and I'll never say a bad word about him." She looks up at me with a half smile. "Except he's a dumbass for divorcing me." She drops her needles. "At seventy years old. Who does that?"

"Yeah. I'm not sure." I make a face. "Did he get remarried? I mean, the guy had to have a reason, right?"

"Oh, he had one. He said he never got to experience life without me and wanted that chance before he died. I blame the doctor, to be honest. Had him convinced he had cancer, and of course, he didn't." She blows out a breath. "You can't trust a doctor these days, Trevor. They're all about the money."

"Okay."

I shake my head, trying not to laugh, because I know she's serious. Not laughing is easier than I expect it to be because I realize I have no humor in me. All I have is a place where I used to be happy.

Damn it.

"So what's going on with you, hon? You've walked in here every day since the day you came and got a room and been the most pleasant, happy man. Today you look like you want to be anywhere but here. And by here, I mean anywhere but inside your skin."

I roll that observation around. *Anywhere but inside your skin.* I sigh and hope she's wrong. Otherwise, I'll go back to Nashville and still feel like I left a part of myself here in this *quaint* little town that my poodle-loving stepmother led me to.

A grin ghosts my lips as I realize I didn't just think of her as my dad's wife, but as my stepmother.

I really am losing my damn mind.

"I had to make some tough decisions today," I say.

"Mm-hmm."

"And I don't really like having to make the ones that make me feel like this."

"First things first: you don't have to do anything but die and pay taxes. I'm assuming you're up to date with Uncle Sam."

I nod.

"And you're clearly alive. So that's kind of a bit of a fib you're telling right there, Trevor."

"That's a cute little ditty, but there's more you have to do in life, Lorene."

She sets her needles down. "Like what?"

"Like . . ." It shouldn't be as hard to come up with a list of things you have to do. There are a lot of things. "Like doing what is right."

She scoffs. "That's subjective. Life is not black and white, and it's not even black to everyone. Sometimes I'll see something as black and you'll see it white. Doesn't make it any less black to me because you don't see it that way."

"Right and wrong is pretty straightforward."

"Ha."

"I mean it," I say. "Generally speaking, most things that are right are right and wrong are wrong. There are exceptions, sure, but more or less it's not up for debate."

She raises a brow that looks like she stenciled it with a crayon. "So did you harm a child?"

"Of course not."

"Did you hurt an animal?"

"Really, Lorene?"

"Did you lie to someone's face to cause them harm? Because sometimes you have to tell a little white lie. I know people say you don't, but you do."

I shake my head. "I didn't."

"Then the only other thing you could've done that would've been unequivocally wrong is taking something that wasn't yours."

Thief.

"Trevor?"

"I had to break it off with a girl today," I say softly. "A girl I care a lot about."

My face falls. I avoid her eyes and look at the floor. The edges of the rug are a whiskey color, and they remind me of the flecks of gold in Haley's eyes.

"You had to, huh?" Lorene asks.

"Yeah. I had to."

"Oh. Okay." She takes off again in her rocking chair, her needles clashing together in a quick tempo.

I wait for her to say something more, to ask me for details, to pressure me into spilling my guts, because I fucking *need to*. But she doesn't.

"I expected more from you." That simple one-liner slams into my chest with the force of a wrecking ball.

"What?"

"You've been the biggest help to me while you've been here. I was telling my friends at the salon on Saturday morning how I'd be as proud as a peacock if you were my grandson." She sighs sadly. "And to hear you say you did something you aren't proud of because you *had to* . . . I know you, boy. No one makes you do anything."

"It's for her own good," I argue.

Her eyes flip to mine. "That's the weakest argument you could make."

"It's true."

"And why is it in her best interest for you to walk away? Does she love you?"

I shrug.

"Do you love her?"

I don't answer.

"I fed Geoff, nursed him when he was sick, held his hand on his deathbed even though the man ended our marriage and hurt me in a way I'll never be able to explain if we sit here for the next hundred years. Want to know why?"

"Why?" I say, my voice hoarse.

"Because love doesn't end. Because that piece of paper that says we were no longer married didn't climb inside me and cut the line from my heart to his."

I hang my head again.

The piece of paper in the form of a napkin that Haley and I signed didn't keep me from hurting her either. Maybe I'm as bad as Geoff.

I flinch as stomach bile threatens to come up my throat.

The weight of the world presses on my shoulders, and I think I hear the wood crack in the chair from all the pressure. Maybe it was my heart cracking instead.

Lorene scoots to the edge of her rocker and sets her project on the coffee table. "If you're running from love, Trevor, you better stop while you can and go back and get it. Because I'm telling you the truth when I say you can't outrun it."

The wind vanishes from my sails. I sag against the chair. "What if I change my mind?"

"Then you do." She laughs. "Geoff changed his and I survived." She reaches across the space between us and takes my hand in hers. There are brown marks marring her papery skin, her veins bright blue. "You're a bit of a pistol, you know that?"

I grin.

"If a woman is going to be around you long enough to fall in love with you, she's going to be strong enough to let you go if that's what you want."

"But what if—"

"What if the inn burns to the ground tonight while I'm asleep in it?"

"All right, Lorene. There are lines you don't cross." I shake my head, my frustration growing.

She shrugs, not giving a second thought to my comment. "Well, you can what-if yourself to death. Keep it up, and you'll find yourself on your deathbed someday, wondering what-if, and you'll be out of time. A hundred years goes by like the blink of an eye."

My heart is heavy as I get to my feet. It already feels like a lifetime since the conversation with Haley, when in reality it probably hasn't been an hour.

I kiss Lorene's hand and then her cheek, and watch her eyes swell with tears. I fight a tug in my chest as she pats my hand.

"Thank you, Lorene," I say. "Thank you for your hospitality. I appreciate it more than you'll ever know."

"You're welcome," she says through unshed tears. "If you ever need a place to stay, you find me. Even if it's coon-hunting season."

I shake her hand, the lump in my throat preventing any words from coming out. She nods, understanding, as I place her palm on her lap.

"Goodbye," I say.

"Goodbye, honey."

CHAPTER TWENTY-EIGHT

TREVOR

I'm almost to the end of the driveway when a familiar truck pulls in beside me. The window rolls down, and it's Dane staring back at me.

The look he's giving me rips at my pride. I might as well be the dirt under his boots right now.

"Great," I mumble. I hit the button and feel the wind fill the cab. "Hey, Dane."

"Trevor." He works his tongue around his cheek, as if he's trying to decide whether to give me the speech he's rehearsed or just rip into me off the cuff. "Are you heading out?"

"Yeah. I need to get back to the office."

He taps a beat on his steering wheel, gazing off into the distance. He brings his hand to his mouth and runs it along his jaw as I squirm in anticipation of what's next.

"You aren't the guy I thought you were."

I flinch. "What did you say?"

"I have a really good ability to pick out bad people. It's one of the few good things I got from my father. But I'll tell you, you had me fooled."

"Dane . . . ," I stammer.

"You fucked with Haley."

"I didn't. Not like you think."

He grins. It's not a gesture of friendliness or an invitation to set the record straight. It's a warning, pure and simple. A warning I read loud and clear.

"Here's the deal," he says. "I don't give a flying fuck if you did it like 'I think' or not. All I know is I watched you chase her, and now I'm watching you walk away."

I sigh, looking at the road ahead and wishing I'd left a few minutes before. I don't need this guilt trip. I'm tripping enough on my own.

He's right. She told me up front—fuck, she practically begged me at first—not to pursue her. She took a line from my playbook and was one hundred percent clear about what she wanted. I disrespected that. *Motherfucker.*

"If you leave, don't come back." He levels his final shot with the sobriety of a judge.

Message received.

I want to tell him how happy I am that she has him to protect her. But why would I do that? He knows how to treat his family, someone he loves. Hell, he does it better than I do.

My stomach sinks as his words pile on top of my own lamenting and Lorene's advice. I wonder if I'll ever be able to climb out from under it.

"Thanks for all your work on the house," I say, trying to make some progress before I leave.

He puts his truck in drive. "Fuck you." I get another go-to-hell smile before he hits the gas and blows dust all over my truck.

"Fuck you too," I mutter, rolling up the window.

I crawl through Dogwood Lane. The post office's flag blows in the breeze. Jennifer is outside Buds and Branches, washing the windows. I wave. She waves back.

I blow out a breath as I pass the road where the dog lies in the middle of the street before coming upon the café. I slow, peering in the windows as I slide by.

My body is pulled to the parking lot, desperate for some kind of positive connection to a place I've grown to really like. But I keep going. Because it's all I can do. It's all I know how to do.

⁂

I pull my phone from underneath my pillow. The screen lights up when I press the button on the side.

Nothing.

Not a call or a text or an alert that someone sent me an email.

Nada.

I roll over on my back, the room dark. Three blankets are piled on my body, and I smile as I think of what Haley would say about the temperature of the room.

She hates it cold.

She hates all the blankets.

She hates me.

If this was the right thing to do, why does it feel so wrong? Why does it feel like someone sawed my chest in half and gave a part of it away and now I'm expected to act normally even though I can't breathe?

It's my own fault. This was my choice.

I swipe around the screen until I find my dad's name. It's late, but not too late to wrestle some advice out of the old man.

Laughing at the level of desperation I've reached, I listen to it ring.

"Hello," he says.

"Hey, Dad."

"Trevor. What's going on, son?"

"Nothing. Just got home a little while ago. Thought I'd check in."

"I'm getting ready for bed. Meredith and I are heading down to Dogwood Lane next week, and we have a lot of preparations to work on. I figured you'd still be there when we got to town."

My heart sinks. He's going to Dogwood Lane, a town where I left a piece of my heart.

"I have work to do here," I say.

"Jake said you were doing a good job of handling it online. And having Natalie there helps, of course."

"Yeah."

The line goes quiet. My mind is in Dogwood Lane, in a little house with no room in the kitchen and a living room with a fireplace. It's with a woman with a penchant for doughnuts and pizza and blanket-less nights.

"Are you going to tell me what's wrong?" he asks.

I'm surprised he knows anything is wrong. It's not like he and I have ever had some deep, emotional connection.

"I think I'm having a midlife crisis," I say with a laugh.

He laughs heartily too. "If I'm having one, as you say, then you can't have one too."

"I don't know how else to explain it, Pops." I sit up and rest against the pillows. "I'm the same guy I've always been. Doing the same things I always have. Making decisions under the same rules I always use, and right now, it all feels . . . wrong."

"I thought you were in love with her."

"What? I'm not in love with Haley," I say, dismissing it immediately. I stand up and pace the room, fighting the urge to yell into the darkness.

"Maybe you are. Love changes people, Trev. It makes you a different person."

"But I like who I've always been."

"Then go be that guy and do it without Haley."

I grimace, hating that he thinks those are my options. "I'll opt for Plan C, please."

"There is no Plan C, and there's no Plan B either. There's Plan A: fall in love or regret it your whole life. As a matter of fact, that's wrong. You don't get an option to fall in love. You only have the option to accept it."

I contemplate that. "But what if you accept it and then you decide you don't want it anymore?"

"Is this about Tera?"

"Not completely."

He sighs. "What happened to that girl isn't your fault. You were as kind and as respectful as you could've been. And honestly, you were right to get out of that relationship. What if she would've killed you?"

"Dad."

"Things happen." He groans as he moves. "If you want to walk away from a relationship, then you aren't in love with that person. It's really, truly that simple."

"But what if there are extenuating circumstances?" I press.

"Like if she becomes a serial killer? Or drug addict? Or is married to someone else?"

"Have you been watching daytime television with Meredith?"

Dad laughs. "The pleasures of retirement."

"I'm worried, Dad. For real."

He laughs again. "If something like that happens, then you still love the person. You try to help them. Sometimes you have to walk away, but it's not to go be with someone else or because you're bored or because you just want new pussy."

I grimace. "Don't say 'pussy.' It's . . . weird."

"Okay. Because you want to screw someone new. Better?"

"Let's just not bother trying to word that right. Let's move along."

"All right. You're going to have to figure out how it's easier to sleep—beside the woman you love or without her. And if you really think you'll mess her up that much that you'd rather sleep alone, then you don't love her. So the answer is simple. And on that note, I'm going to go because I'm in love with a beautiful woman that's currently in my bed waiting on me."

I lie back on my bed and hear the air conditioner kick on. I grin, knowing Haley would be objecting and wishing she were here so I could listen to her complain.

"Night, Dad," I say.

"Good night, son."

CHAPTER TWENTY-NINE

HALEY

I prefer the sexual hangovers. This one is definitely not that.

The coffee takes too long to brew. Each second that passes feels like an eternity. I pull the cup from under the spout before it's finished, and hot liquid spills onto the counter. It's sad that I don't even care.

I miss him already. The two phone calls last night and three texts didn't help because I couldn't return them. I just couldn't. Despite needing to hear his voice and hoping he'd say that he was wrong and sorry, I couldn't do it, because I deserve more.

It's a weird feeling, prioritizing yourself. It's not something I've ever done, and I'm not quite sure how to walk the line. What I do know is it feels good, empowering even, to know what I want and do the things I need to do to get it. After all, wanting love isn't the most ridiculous thing in the world.

Tossing some creamer in my cup until the brew is a perfectly golden color, I take a sip. The fluid washes down my throat, clearing out some of the leftover tears from last night.

A knock at the door makes me jump. My heart scampers in my chest, my thoughts immediately going to Trevor. Gripping my mug like it's my job, I almost jog to the front door. I don't even check the peephole before I tug it open.

"Oh. Hey," I say when I see Dane on the other side.

He gives me a tight smile. "Just checking on you. How are you today?"

I let the door open all the way and pad back to the kitchen. I hear it latch and Dane's footsteps fall behind me.

"Want some coffee?" I ask.

"Nah. I'm good. Grabbed some already from Claire."

I nod. "I think I'll go by for a doughnut today. Sugar never killed anyone."

"Actually, it does. All the time."

"Well, smart-ass, the chances of it killing me before this heartache does aren't good."

He pulls out a chair and sits. His boot taps against the floor. The sound feels like little nails pounding into my skull.

"Can we not do that?" I ask as I sit across from him. Pulling my robe tighter around my body, I curl my legs up under me. "What are you doing today?"

"I have some paperwork to finish. Just . . . stuff."

"You can talk about the Kelly house, you know. It's fine."

I take another sip of my drink, hoping the taste of the coffee will carry away the taste of Trevor's last name. It feels heavy on my tongue, bitter against the sweetness I once associated with him.

Dane leans against the table, a worried look on his face. "I want to apologize to you, Hay."

"What for?"

"Neely and I talked last night, and I shouldn't have gone after Trevor. I should've stayed out of it."

"You were just trying to do what you do—protect everyone. This time, it was me."

"Yeah. You're right. I was trying to protect you, but Neely pointed out how disrespectful it was too."

I lift the mug to my lips. "How's that?"

"It was selling you short." He sighs and leans back in his chair. "Sometimes I forget you aren't the little girl who showed up here to take care of Mia. You're an adult. A capable woman that can take care of herself, and me going after Trevor yesterday insulted that, in a way."

Reaching across the table, I lay a hand on top of his. "You didn't insult me. But thank you for saying all that. It helps."

"It's true." He takes his hand out from under mine. "I just hate to see you hurt. You're such a good person."

"I hate feeling like crap, too, but if he wants to go, let him go."

Dane's eyes go wide at my words, and quite frankly, mine do too. I didn't realize I was going to say that, but putting it into the world frees something inside me. I shrug and take another drink.

"Wow," Dane says.

"I know." I laugh, the pitch filled with a sadness I can't shake. "But I learned a lot over the last few weeks, so it wasn't a total loss."

"Like what?"

"Like how to negotiate an agreement. And how the rich live. And what I want my greenhouse to look like someday." I smile to myself. "Someone once told me that things were only a waste if you don't learn from them. I learned from this. It'll come in handy one day."

He shakes his head and gets to his feet. "I have no idea what has happened to you, but I like it." He leans over and pulls me into a hug. "You're gonna be fine, aren't you?"

"I am," I say, leaning back.

"That's good. And what's even better is not seeing you in bed with chocolate slobber hanging out of your mouth like you did when Joel broke up with you."

"Screw Joel," I scoff. "What was I even thinking?"

"I asked you that a million times. You said you loved him."

My spirits sink as I remember my feelings toward Joel. I thought the sun set on him. He was the epitome of what I wanted in a man—or so I thought. I probably would still be thinking that to some degree if I hadn't met Trevor.

With Trevor, it wasn't just about him. I liked him because of how he made me feel about me too. I felt like I could do anything, be anyone, and that I deserved good things. All things except him.

"What are you going to do today?" Dane asks, bringing my thoughts back to the present.

"I'm going to see Claire and get a doughnut. And then going to work. I want to figure out how to build a cold frame for vegetables this winter." I blow out a breath. "I saw this greenhouse in Nashville that was pretty spectacular and figured I could build a tiny version of it."

Dane grins. "Well, if you need help, let me know. Mia and I would love to help you."

"You're the best."

"I know." He tosses a wink my way before heading to the door.

"Hey, Dane?"

"Yeah?"

"Thank you for believing in me. It means a lot."

He doesn't say anything, but he doesn't have to. A smile is launched across the room before he leaves.

I look at my coffee and then back to the door. Some fresh air might do me some good.

Then again, so would going back to bed.

With a yawn, I head to the bedroom.

Trevor

The computer glow burns my eyes. It probably doesn't help that I've been sitting here for almost twenty-four hours, trying to lose myself in facts and figures. The only figure I can think about consistently is Haley's.

Jake walks in, not bothering to knock. If I had any energy at all, I'd be pissed. I don't.

"What?" I ask.

"Are you still fucking here?"

"Is that a real question?"

"No. The real question is, why are you still fucking here?" he asks, sitting in a leather chair across from my desk. One leg props on the other, his socks a stupid red-and-black checker that makes me want to comment on them. But again, I don't.

I look at my brother. I don't want to talk about this with him. Or anyone, for that matter. I just want to talk to Haley, and she won't fucking answer.

Not that I blame her. I wouldn't answer my calls either.

"So Natalie says you fell in love," he says.

"Natalie apparently wants to be fired."

He laughs. "Nah, I think she wants your job when we finally commit you."

"So, so funny." I toss a pen on the desk. "Did you come in here for anything besides to rag on me?"

"No."

"Then get out of here."

He sighs, lacing his fingers behind his head. "Want to go to dinner?"

"No," I say, shoving away from my desk. "I don't want to go to dinner. I don't want to leave the office. I don't want to take a break and steal candy from Natalie's desk."

"Then what do you want to do?"

I brace myself against the desk. I want to listen to bad jokes and fight over the thermostat and figure out where to take Haley for dinner.

That's what I want. The thing I can't have.

I hang my head.

"All right," Jake says, getting to his feet. "I'll let you be. I'll be in my office for a bit if you want to talk."

I nod but still don't look at him. I don't even look up until he's gone.

I lean back in my chair. I can't keep sitting here, pretending I'll somehow raise my head and have forgotten about her. But I don't know what to do.

My mind goes back to the last time I saw her.

"It's you that does that to them. You break them down until they think it's safe, and then you say you've had enough and watch them wallow. I think you get a kick out of that."

My heart twists in my chest as I remember her words. I don't get any pleasure out of hurting her or anyone. As a matter of fact, it might just hurt me worse than it does her. All I'm guilty of is taking her heart.

Taking her heart . . .

I did take it. I took it because it was mine. It is mine.

She's mine.

I spring to my feet, my breath coming out in rushed waves.

I love her. I think. No, I do. I have to. I can barely breathe without her. I can't imagine not talking to her today or seeing her on Christmas. I can't imagine not spending her birthday with her next year or not having her at my side at the next party I have to attend.

I love her. I'm fucking in love with her. That's what this ridiculousness is.

Well, hell.

What do I do now?

I consider going to find Jake but nix it just as quickly. I almost call Natalie, but that crosses a line I'm not ready to broach. My fingertips stroke the top of my desk as I realize the only other person I have is my dad . . . and Meredith.

Fuck it. I grab my phone and dial her number.

"Hello," she says.

"Hey, Meredith. It's Trevor."

"Well, hello," she says. "Is everything all right?"

"No. I mean, yes. But no."

"Okay . . ." She laughs. "I'm not following you. Are you looking for your dad? He's golfing this afternoon."

I shake my head. "No, actually. I called to talk to you. I need some advice."

"Is this about Haley? Because if it's about anything other than love, fashion, or flowers, I'm probably not your girl."

"It's about Haley."

"Go on . . ."

CHAPTER THIRTY

HALEY

The morning is bright. Too bright. Everything is too bright these days.

I take my sunglasses off as I walk into the café.

"Hey," Claire says. "Look at you, up bright and early again."

"I have to work in a few minutes." I climb onto a stool, then promptly scoot over one to the right. "It's . . . wet."

"Sure." Claire holds up a finger and disappears into the kitchen. She comes back with a cinnamon roll on a doughnut plate. "Here. I swiped this one for you earlier. The fire department ordered a couple of dozen, so the kitchen made a special batch. They got two dozen minus one."

"Thanks, Claire Bear."

"Anything for you, Love Pie."

I should eat it. Especially considering all the trouble Claire went to in order to get it for me. But my stomach feels full despite not eating much of anything these last couple of days.

The two empty seats, the ones Trevor and I sat in the day he came in for a doughnut, haunt me. It sucks, but it'll get easier. Maybe one day I will even be able to look at them fondly.

That day isn't today. Today, I can almost hear our laughter. See his smile. Smell his woodsy cologne.

"Haley?"

I whip around, even though I know he's not there, *to find him there.*

My body leans his way, my heart stuttering in my chest. So many emotions run through me because he's not just the balm to my wound—he is the cause of the wound.

There are bags under his eyes. His usually perfectly styled hair is shoved under a baseball hat. The lines around his mouth are sagging.

Damn it.

Tears well up in my eyes as I deny my body the contact it relishes. I spin back around and face the fork on the wall.

He sits beside me. "There's enough room for two Jesuses here."

I don't want to smile, but I do. Sort of. "What do you want?"

"To talk to you."

"Hey, Claire," I say. She looks at me from the kitchen. She's standing off to the side where Trevor can't see her. She holds up a knife in one hand and her other hand, palm up. I roll my eyes. "I need my check."

"Does that mean we're going outside to talk?" he asks carefully.

"That means I'm leaving. You can do whatever you want."

"Haley, don't be like this."

I summon every ounce of grace I can find. Digging deep, blocking out the fracture in my chest from crying so hard when I fell asleep last night that I couldn't breathe, I look at him.

And wish I hadn't.

His eyes are clear, open for me to see the emotions swirling around in them. I blink faster, scooting the unshed tears away from the brink of falling. But I can't look away.

He holds my gaze like only he can, pleading with me without any words. It reminds me of what Jen said about couples who make it and how they can communicate in the quiet moments.

I'll have to tell her she's wrong.

"Your bill is covered," Claire says, stopping in front of me.

"By who?"

"Don't worry about it." Her gaze flips cold as she looks at Trevor. "Do you want something more than to torture my best friend?"

"Claire . . ." His shoulders fall. "I'm sorry."

"Don't tell me, fuckhead. Tell her."

He shrugs. "She doesn't want to hear it."

"I want to hear it less." She narrows her eyes as she walks away, leaving me alone with him.

I rise from the stool. "I need to go."

"Please, talk to me."

"No."

I hoist my purse on my shoulder and head to the door. Sunglasses cover my eyes as I step into the light and walk as fast as I can without overtly jogging to my car. I grab the handle, but his hand presses on the top of my car door to keep me from opening it.

"Go away," I say.

"Just hear me out."

"I already heard you." I spin around to face him, knocking his arm off my car in the process. "There was an element of finality in the words you've already spoken, Trevor. There's nothing more to say."

"Stop talking."

"Fuck off."

He starts to grin but wises up just in time. "You're so mean."

"Me?" I let out a little shriek in disbelief and pull open the door. The force makes him step away from the car as I climb in.

"Does this mean we aren't friends?" he asks.

"What do you think?"

"You aren't answering my texts or calls or emails, so it's not looking good."

My heart softens. I turn on the engine and shut the door. Staring out the windshield, I wonder if something might be wrong. He's not evil. He wouldn't come back to torture me . . . would he? Would he really come back to be just friends with me?

I told him flat out I was falling in love with him, which is his biggest fear, and yet he's here. But do I care? I don't know. I do know I don't want to do *this* anymore.

I roll down my window warily. "Is anything wrong?"

"A lot of things are wrong."

"Let me rephrase that: Is anyone hurt?"

He narrows his eyes. "Yes."

I roll mine. "Let me rephrase *that*: Is anyone dying?"

"No."

"Good, then. We have nothing to talk about." I shift the car into reverse.

"Haley. Stop."

"You stop." My heart hardens again. "I listened to you. I trusted you. I believed in you. And I got treated like Liz."

His face goes pale.

"That's what *you* did," I tell him. "You treated me just like one of those women you told me fawn all over you and won't let you go and blah blah blah." I take my foot off the brake. "Guess what? I'm not them. Maybe I was with Joel. Maybe I was kind of pathetic because I didn't want to be alone. But now I like myself, Trevor. And maybe I have you to partially thank for that. So thank you. And goodbye."

"Haley . . ."

I roll up the window and let the car back out. He stands in front of my car and watches me back away.

I don't know how long he stands there.

I don't look back, because I'm not doing this anymore.

❧

My purse hits the counter. "If Trevor Kelly comes in today, I'm throwing him out." I look at Jennifer as I take my sunglasses off. "I'm not kidding."

"Trouble in paradise?"

"Trouble in something, but it's not paradise." I slip off my jacket and fold it. I place it on top of my purse and then slide my things under the counter. "Speaking of paradise, when do you go to Hawaii?"

She finishes up an arrangement she's working on before looking up at me. "Next week. We got the finalized itinerary last night from the travel agent."

It would be so nice to lie on the beach with some sun and alcohol and no worries or boys.

"I've always wanted to go to Hawaii," I say.

"We went once. On our honeymoon. It was the most amazing time."

"The farthest I've ever been is Austin, and that's because my dad had some kind of work thing there. We were there for a week, and it was so hot. That's about all I remember."

She lifts the vase in front of her and inspects it more carefully than she usually does. She sets it in the cooler in the front. When she comes back, her smile has faltered.

"What's wrong?" I ask.

"I have three things I need to talk to you about."

The hair on the back of my neck stands up. Maybe I'm just on high alert, but something feels wrong. "What?"

"First, I have a delivery I need you to make today. Can you do that?"

"Sure."

She nods. "The next thing is that I got word this morning that the library lost their funding and the doors will close next week."

I grip the edge of the counter, my eyes bugging out. "No."

"I'm sorry."

Tears fill my eyes as I think of Sandra and the others. They'll be crushed. And what happens to children like Nathaniel who count on the library for books?

This can't be happening.

"Oh, my gosh." I cover my mouth with my hand. "What is wrong with the world?"

"Many, many things. The older you get, the more you'll see."

My hand slides up to cover more of my face as I think of Sandra. "I bet they're devastated."

"I thought maybe we could make them something today and take it over. When my heart hurts, flowers make me feel better, if only for a little while."

"Yes. Absolutely. Let's use bright colors and keep the arrangements simple so we can make more of them."

She pats my hand. "You're such a sweet soul. You know that?"

I bite my lip as I remember Trevor calling me mean. "Well, that's up for debate."

She comes around the counter so she's standing next to me. She leans against the wood, facing me. "I have one more thing."

"Okay," I say, straightening my shirt. "What is it?"

Her lips dip. "The shop sold this morning."

"The shop? What shop?" I gasp. *"This one?"*

She nods.

"You sold Buds and Branches?" I look at her like I misheard her, even though I know I didn't. I'm just blindsided. "Why?"

She frowns. "The Realtor Tom had talked to called this morning. A buyer came through. They wanted a price and I tossed them a number and they took it. I'm supposed to meet with a Realtor this afternoon, which is why I can't take the delivery."

I'm torn inside. A part of me is excited for Jennifer. The other is devastated for me.

"They said to keep operating as normal until the deal goes through. Apparently, they're buying a couple of shops, so they're being packaged together or something. I'm not sure. But I'm sorry to have to tell you that after you just started."

"You know what?" I say, shaking the negativity out of my brain. "This is amazing for you. Tom will be thrilled, I'm assuming."

"Oh, yes. This made his week. His year," she says. "But still . . ."

I square my shoulders and lift my chin. "Don't worry about me. I'll be fine. Maybe the new people will keep me. And if not, maybe I'll go back to school and become a botanist. Or a landscape architect. I saw some awesome things from them at the flower expo."

She pulls me into a quick hug. "The world needs more people like you."

"I think it needs men like me so women like me don't get burned."

She gives me a sad smile. "Let me check something real quick." She disappears in the back before returning with a pink-and-white arrangement. "This can be delivered anytime today after nine. It's after nine. Why don't you take it now so we can work on the library stuff when you get back?"

"Perfect. Where's it going?"

"Mount Zion Road. The Kelly residence."

I take a step back, convinced the universe hates me today. My body sags. "That's Trevor's family."

"It's for a Meredith Kelly. Do you know her?"

I nod.

I wonder if he's told his family we aren't together. And are Branson and Meredith in town already?

I groan.

This is going to be so, so awkward.

"Can you do it?" She looks at her phone. "The Realtor is calling. I really need to grab this."

"Go," I say. "Just . . . go. I got this."

I think.

CHAPTER THIRTY-ONE

HALEY

The house already looks different.

Men work in the yard, putting in shrubs and trees. A porch swing has been hung, and a plaque reading THE KELLYS is mounted prominently by the doorbell. Meredith definitely went a little more casual, not quite as fancy, with this house. It's perfect. So perfect.

I step out of my car, checking for any sign of Trevor, and take the arrangement out of the back seat.

Just deliver it to whoever you see first and get the hell out of here.

"Haley, hello."

I look over my shoulder to see Meredith walking toward me. A little white poodle is nestled in her arm. She's the image of contentment, of the life I hope to have for myself—minus the poodle. Tears flick the corners of my eyes as I wonder if I'll ever find it.

"I'm so glad to see you," she gushes. "This is Buffy. Muffy is inside, eating her breakfast."

I stick my hand out for the dog to get to know me. She licks me immediately and tries to jump in my arms. Meredith loves this.

"Oh, look at that," she says. "She likes you. Here. Hold her for me while I take the flowers into the house." We exchange bundles. She examines hers while mine licks my face. "I'll be right back. These are outstanding. I love the fullness of this arrangement."

"Thanks. Jennifer did it."

"She's good," she says, winking.

I look at Buffy. Little yellow bows sit on her ears as she wags her tongue in my face. "What about you? Are you good?"

The poodle barks in response, her body shaking from excitement.

I laugh. "You're a good ego boost, you know that?"

Meredith returns quickly, a smile splitting her cheeks. "Here. Come to Mommy." She opens her arms and the dog leaps into her chest. Meredith nuzzles her under her chin, scratching her belly as she looks at me. "I was hoping you'd take a walk with me, Haley."

"Oh," I say, surprised. "I, um, I need to get back to work. Jennifer is on her own, and there are a lot of things happening today."

Meredith smiles, undeterred. "So a short one, then?"

I want to say no. I need to get back to the shop and away from all things Kelly. But Trevor's words ring through my mind, that Meredith always gets her way, so I relent to get it over with.

"Well . . . okay."

We traipse across the yard parallel to the house. I've been here a hundred times to drop things off for Dane or to let Mia see him when he was working late. But I've never seen the far side of the house now that the porch is up.

"Oh, wow," I say as we round the corner.

I can imagine the view from the top of the deck and how far you can see. It would be the perfect place to sit and read a book or watch the leaves turn colors.

"What I want to show you," she says, "is even better than this."

"Is that possible?"

Her baby-blue eyes shine. "Yes."

The grass is soft, my shoes sinking into the ground as we plod our way down the side of the hill. My brain is muddled with the loss of

Trevor and the uncertainty of the flower shop. I suck in a breath and tell myself I'll battle through today because I always do.

"How have you been?" she asks.

"Okay."

"I heard Trevor is an idiot."

"Yeah."

She smiles at me. "You know, Branson and I dated when he first got divorced from the boys' mom. It was this torrid love affair, a fling that had my head spinning. And then he stopped seeing me out of nowhere."

"Why?"

"Heck if I know." She tickles the dog under its chin. "I was devastated. He'd talked about marriage and I'd told him I can't have kids and I was ready to do the damn thing. And then he pulled the plug. I was . . . well, destroyed. I don't know what else to say."

My heart aches for her. She'd be a great mom, oozing love for Branson, her dogs, and everyone around her.

"I'm sorry to hear you can't have kids," I say.

"I'm lucky to be alive. I'm able to live and love and have my puppies and maybe adopt one day. I don't know. Branson is a lot older than me, and I don't want to put pressure on him to raise a baby at this point in his life." She shrugs. "It's a discussion we'll have someday. Hopefully once we settle in up here."

We walk a little farther until the house is out of sight. There's a stand of trees to our right, and Meredith leads me around them.

I glance to my left and think the road must be close. "Aren't we almost by the road?" I ask.

She nods. "We are. There's an access point to it, actually, right around this bend."

I furrow a brow, not remembering ever seeing that from the road. As we make the turn around a grove of pines, I gasp.

"Oh, my God. Meredith! This is amazing." My jaw hangs open as I see a little cabin, not much bigger than a standard living room, nestled into the stand of pines. It has a little chimney on top and a wall of windows that overlooks a valley in the back.

"It's a sweet little place, isn't it?" she asks smugly.

"Sweet? It's perfect."

I walk a circle, taking in the beauty of the space. It's nestled against a grove of trees, but the view on the other side is breathtaking. It's absolutely spectacular.

Meredith points to a spot off to the side, beneath some of the windows. "Tulips will come up there in the spring. And crocuses. But no daffodils."

"Oh, that's perfect," I say. "Daffodils are so boring."

I stop moving and look at the sky. Something prickles the back of my mind.

Didn't I say that same thing to Penn?

"I think I helped choose those," I say.

"You did, which is ironic, given the circumstances."

"Why?"

"You'll see. Come on." She flashes me a smile as she sets the puppy on the ground. Waving a hand for me to follow, she starts toward the little house.

I can't move. I'm not sure why. My mouth goes dry as I will my feet to move, following her until we're on the porch.

"Penn has been working on this for the last week or so," Meredith says. "It's not finished by any means. The outside is complete in case bad weather hits early this year, but there's still a lot to do."

"You'll really enjoy it in the spring," I say carefully. My chest flutters, my stomach flipping at the look in her eyes. "It'll be a great spot to curl up with a book."

She takes a deep breath. "You'll have to let me know."

I take a step back until I'm against the railing. I look at her and then at the house, then back to her. Buffy barks behind me, but I barely hear her.

"Meredith, I don't understand."

"There's a note inside, if you want to read it. And if you're still too tender to do this, that's fine too," she says softly. She looks at me with the kindness only someone who truly cares about you can show. "Trevor has been a big baby."

I blink quickly but am unable to fight the tears.

"I'm not telling you what to do," she says. "That's for you to decide, and whatever you decide is the right thing. But maybe go in and check the place out and see what you think."

I can't think straight. I can't comprehend anything other than I might be sick.

"Before I say anything," I say, my mouth full of cotton, "what *is* this place?"

"To be honest, it was originally supposed to be the poodle spa. Then I realized how inconvenient that would be and decided to incorporate it into the house. That left this place half-built with no purpose." She scoops up her puppy. "Trevor called the other night to mope, and I was trying to talk some sense into him. A few ideas sprang to life, and . . . he thought maybe this was a place you would like to use."

I can barely swallow. "I don't know what to say."

"You don't have to say anything. And there's no pressure. But I will say, I have no friends here and thought that even if you and Trevor don't work out, or if you make him wallow a little bit, it would still be nice to have you around." She bites her lip like she's afraid she overstepped. "You're nice and maybe, you know, we could be friends."

"Wow, Meredith. Of course, I'd like to be your friend. But this . . ." I look at the house again. "This is just . . . a lot."

She laughs. "I know."

Curiosity gets the best of me. "Can I look inside?"

"Absolutely. It's yours, after all. If you want it." She heads down the steps, cuddling Buffy. "I'll leave you alone. If you need anything, please shout."

"Meredith?"

"Yes?"

My heart pounds in my chest as I look back at the little white-and-green building. "Is Trevor in there?"

She smiles softly. "No. He didn't want you to feel like you had to take him if you took this. This is a no-strings-attached kind of thing. He just thought you'd love it."

I nod as she heads across the lawn. The breeze flutters by, the air clean and crisp. It's so quiet, so still, that I almost cry. Not just because it's beauty realized, but because no one is here to see it with me.

Taking my time, I walk to the building and climb the three little steps. The bronze handle opens easily and I gasp.

My words come floating back.

"I'd put a little place somewhere like that. With a great view of the sunrise and a field with tons of wildflowers. There'd be a room with windows like this and a woodstove because there's nothing more romantic than that. And a claw-foot bathtub nestled in a corner and tons and tons of bookshelves."

He listened. He really listened.

The windows reach from the floor to the ceiling. A fireplace sits in the corner with river rock framing it up the wall. Bookshelves line every wall that isn't taken up by a window.

Blinking back tears, I close the door behind me.

It smells like new construction and cedar and is warm and cozy. A cream-colored sofa faces the fireplace, and a table with a marble top sits beside it. A room opens to the right, and I peek inside to find a claw-foot tub and another fireplace. It's more finished than I realized.

"Oh, my God," I whisper, stepping inside the bathroom.

On an open shelf are a stack of towels. I take a washcloth and dry my face, clutching it in my hand like it's a life raft. The tears keep coming as my heart pines for Trevor.

I miss him. I miss him so much, and I can't understand why he did this if he doesn't want me.

As I reenter the living room, I see an envelope with my name scrawled across the front in blue ink next to a bouquet of camellias.

My fingers fumble the paper, tears streaking down my face, as I unfold it.

Ohio,

I had no idea how much my life was going to change when I dropped into the Dogwood Café the first time. I just wanted a cup of coffee. Claire talked me into a doughnut. You talked me into giving you my heart.

Because it's yours. I didn't realize that until lately. Or maybe I did know it before but couldn't understand. It's hard to understand things you haven't experienced before.

There are a lot of things I want to do in my life. None of them I want to do without you. I bought a flower shop this morning (okay, two), and all I wanted to do was tell you.

I don't blame you for not talking to me. And I hope you don't feel any pressure from this. It's yours, whether you want me or not. (But please want me.)

And when it comes to the flower shops, I hope you'll help me with them. Meredith talked me into buying them. She said it's good for my karma and promised to step in and help out if you want no part of it. (Please want a part of it.)

The camellias mean "my destiny is in your hands." Nice touch, right? I hope you aren't feeling mean anymore.

Trevor

"Damn you," I say, clutching the letter to my chest.

"Does that mean I have to get Meredith to help me with the stores?"

I swing around at the sound of his voice to find him standing in the only room I haven't explored. My knees go weak as he catches me in his arms.

"I'm still mad at you," I say into his chest. I breathe him in and feel his heart thumping as wildly as mine. "*Very* mad at you."

"But *very* attracted to me too. Right?"

I roll my eyes. "And *very* annoyed with you."

"Yeah, I get that one." He pulls back and looks me in the eye. "I don't expect you to do anything. I want you to do whatever makes you happy. Whatever you feel is the right move for you."

I wad up his red sweatshirt in my hands and keep him close to me. I give myself a moment to truly feel what I feel.

The longer I stand, the more I know.

"How I feel has nothing to do with this place," I say softly. "Or . . . did you really buy two flower shops today?"

He winces. "I have a meeting in about an hour to sign the papers. I know shit about flowers, so this should be fun. And Jake's thrilled, let me tell you."

I sigh but nestle myself against him again. "It has nothing to do with that or the camellias, but those were a nice touch."

"I saw them at the flower show. I had that in my pocket for a rainy day."

I can't help but laugh.

"We can take this slow," he offers. "Or fast. Or however you want to take it."

He pulls me off him, much to my dismay, and holds me at arm's length. His eyes shine as he looks at me.

"I left you because I was scared. I was scared of what I was feeling and what that meant and what that might mean. But I realized shortly afterward that I'd already hurt you. And then I went home and lay in bed and realized something else: I was more scared of never holding you again than I was of anything else."

"Trevor . . ." I wipe a tear off my cheek.

"Someone very wise told me that when you find the right person, you hold on to them for when the storms of life get bad. I know now that I can't even imagine going through the good times without you, let alone the bad."

I laugh, brushing tears as quickly as they fall.

"I want to do this right, Haley. I want you to want me. I hope you'll choose to trust me enough to need me, and I need your love. I thought for a long time I didn't need love, but I do. And I need it from you, and even more, I need you to accept mine." He swallows hard, his throat bobbing. "This feeling I'm scared of? It's me, falling in love with you."

There's no stopping the tears that flood my face. He's blurred from my vision as I openly cry.

I don't try to fight it. Don't try to stop it. Don't try to do anything but believe that I'm capable of handling the choices I make.

He hands me a napkin.

I, TREVOR KELLY, PROMISE TO MAKE YOU, HALEY RAYNOR, FALL IN LOVE WITH ME EVERY DAY. AND I PROMISE TO FALL IN LOVE WITH YOU OVER AND OVER FOR THE REST OF MY LIFE.

Tears blur my sight as I look up at this gorgeous, flawed, perfect man. "I love you, Trevor."

"And I love you, pretty girl."

EPILOGUE

HALEY

The bustle inside the newly minted Buds, Branches, and Books is beyond chaos. People come in for hot chocolate and to see what's been going on behind the blacked-out windows for the last two months.

Christmas songs play softly on the speakers, a tree sits in the corner with little pieces of paper with the names of kids who need help this time of year. It's more than I ever wanted it to be, and to see it finished, a plan coming to fruition, makes me want to burst at the seams.

"I told you this was going to be a hit." Trevor wraps his arms around me from behind, nuzzling his face in the crook of my neck. "I'm so proud of you, Ohio."

"It's because of you." I turn my face and brush my lips against his. "I'd tell you that you're pretty special, but you already know that."

"Yeah," he jokes, "I do."

"Hey," I say, waving as Neely walks in with another woman. "This must be Grace."

The short woman with beautiful eyes gives me a warm smile. "This place is adorable," she gushes. "And yes, I'm Grace. It's nice to meet you."

"I'm Haley, if you didn't know. And this is Trevor."

I look at my man. The pride on his face as he looks down at me makes my heart skip a beat.

"Nice to meet both of you," Grace says.

Neely looks around the store, her eyes wide. "Haley. Seriously. This is amazing."

"Thanks. I'm pretty proud of it."

"You should be," she says. "It's such a great thing for our town."

Someone tugs on my hand. I look down to see Nathaniel peering up at me with a marshmallow stuck in his hair. "Miss Haley. Can I have more hot chocolate, please?"

"You sure can, buddy."

"Let me take him," Trevor says. "You talk to your friends." He takes the boy's hand and whispers something conspiratorially, making the child laugh.

My heart swells so big I think it's going to explode. The more I learn about Trevor, the more I love him. He's even sweeter with the kids than he is when he insists on taking Lorene to lunch on Saturdays. Watching him grow closer with his father and learn to like Meredith has been endearing, but the thing I love most is none of those. It's the way he cares about everyone around him.

He stops to help people when they're broken down on the side of the road. He leaves crazy tips for servers at restaurants when they go out of their way to be kind. He makes my coffee every morning and brings it to me in bed to help start my day off right.

It might've been his face that caught my attention and his wit that drew me in, but it's his heart that keeps me around.

"If they grow men like that down here, I'm moving in," Grace says, snapping my attention away from Trevor. "No offense, Haley. Or rather, congratulations."

I can't help but laugh as Neely sighs dramatically at her friend.

We stand in the middle of the entryway, at the point where the flower shop intersects with the new library. Of course, Meredith wasn't about to let the town go without books. I think she blinked her eyes twice at Branson before he demanded I expand, on his dollar, and create something special. Although, having watched them together for the last two months, I can see that it's not Meredith being manipulative, really. Branson simply loves her, and in that love, there is the desire to please her and make sure she's happy.

"Did you and Trevor work out where you're going to stay this winter?" Neely asks. "The last update I got was a very dirty, sexually explicit answer from Trevor at the café."

"For now, Trev will have to spend upward of a week in Nashville at the office. Most of the other stuff he can do from here or Natalie can do. She got a raise. A big one," I say.

"But where are you staying?" Neely asks. "Your house? At the Love Nest?"

"You have a love nest?" Grace raises a brow. "Damn it. This place is a utopia."

I laugh. "We're staying at the Love Nest," I say. "It's just the two of us, and Trevor hated my kitchen."

"I don't blame him there." Claire comes up behind me and hugs my neck. "This place is awesome, friend." She steps around me. "Sorry. I'm late. Long story and you don't want the details."

"Are you sure?" I ask. "Your stories are usually pretty great."

"Totally sure." She glances at Grace. "Hi. I'm Claire."

Neely laughs. "Claire, this is my friend Grace. Grace, this is the one and only Claire."

"It's nice to meet you." Grace's eyes go wide as she looks toward the entrance. "And which one of you lovely ladies is going to introduce me to *him*?"

We all turn to see Penn walking in. His swagger is on point tonight as he pops an invisible collar with his large, tattooed arms. And then he sees Grace. His jaw hangs open for a half of a second before he recovers.

"And yet again, no one called me." Penn saunters up, a short-sleeved shirt over his chest despite the cold. "It's like you guys hate me or something."

Grace smiles, batting her lashes. "I don't know you, so I don't hate you. Yet."

Penn grins a killer smile. "Let's fix that. I'm Penn Etling."

"And I'm Grace."

"No last name?" he asks, cocking a brow.

"Not until the third date."

Neely laughs. "Seriously. Stop while you're ahead. You two would kill each other."

"It might be fun." Grace winks at Penn, and we watch Penn almost melt on the spot.

Our attention is redirected by the sound of a bell. We turn to see Trevor at the checkout desk.

The patrons quiet down, sipping their hot chocolate and coffee and waiting on Trevor's speech. My body tingles as I watch him look around at the faces of Dogwood Lane that came to support our project.

"On behalf of Kelly Construction, Incorporated, I'd like to thank everyone for coming tonight," he says. "I'd like to personally thank everyone that contributed to this night's success, specifically my father and stepmother, Branson and Meredith Kelly. They couldn't be with us tonight because a poodle was sick."

The crowd laughs.

"And the biggest thank-you of all to the love of my life, Haley Raynor. You, pretty girl, are an inspiration."

The crowd *oohs* and *aahs* at Trevor's sweet words. Lorene gets to her feet and claps, beaming as her favorite person in the world heads my way.

My eyes leak as the handsomest man I've ever seen smiles at me. I leave my circle of friends and wrap my arms around Trevor's neck.

"You just stole from me again, you thief."

He flinches. "What did I do now?"

"You stole my heart."

"I thought I already had it?"

I shrug. "There was a little part holding out. Just in case. Don't worry—you have me so tangled up in you now, you'll never get away."

He studies me, his eyes narrowing. "When I saw you in the café, I was scared to touch you."

"But you did."

"Then I touched you and I was scared to have you."

"You did that too."

"Then I had you and I was scared to love you. And now I love you and it's like winning the best prize in the entire universe." He rests his forehead on mine. "No, the best prize will be when I finally convince you to have my baby."

I bury my head in his chest and try not to swoon. I couldn't love him more if I tried.

"Love me forever, will you?" he asks.

I pull back and look him in his gorgeous blue eyes. "Says the man afraid he won't feel the same way twenty years from now."

"That was before."

"Before what?"

He looks at me and grins. "Before you. Before I knew what love was."

I melt into his arms, the frenzy of the room fading out. In this moment, in this man's arms, I realize what true love really, truly means. It involves trusting in the person to hold your heart close to theirs and never tire of that job. It involves sacrifices too. And we all know that basically means that if your girl wants the doughnut, then your girl gets the doughnut. *Now that's true love.*

ACKNOWLEDGMENTS

I'd like to thank a few special people who helped make this book happen.

First and foremost, I'd like to thank God for His blessings and the ability to do what I love.

I'd also like to express my appreciation to my family for their patience, love, and support. Saul, Alexander, Aristotle, Achilles, and Ajax—otherwise known as my world—thank you for being you. I'm so lucky to call you mine.

I've been blessed to have the world's best parents, Mandy and Dennis, and in-laws, Rob and Peggy. I love you all so very much.

Kari March, Tiffany Remy, Carleen Riffle, and Kim Cermak make everything possible. You are my backbone. Thank you for your unfailing friendship.

Thanks to Marion Archer for her tireless energy and exceptional kindness, and to Becca Mysoor for her love and answering all the phone calls.

Hugs to Mandi Beck for making sure I laugh every day and to S.L. Scott for always being ready to bounce ideas around.

Jen Costa and Susan Rayner never fail to encourage me and provide the best kind of friendship a girl could want.

Ebbie Moresco, Kaitie Reister, and Stephanie Gibson are the women who keep my groups running. You are all the best. I couldn't do it without you.

And to Haley, the girl who makes me laugh over pizza and fajitas. I love you. Even if your taste in music isn't that great.

Sincere gratitude to the bloggers who continue to show excitement for my stories.

And to my readers: Thank you for choosing to pick up my books. I appreciate and acknowledge you.

Don't miss a release! Sign up for my Amazon Live Alert or text the word "adriana" to 21000.

ABOUT THE AUTHOR

USA Today bestselling author Adriana Locke lives and breathes books. After years of slightly obsessive relationships with the flawed bad boys created by other authors, Adriana created her own. The author of the Landry Family and Gibson Boys novels, and *Tangle* and *Tumble* in the Dogwood Lane series, Adriana resides in the Midwest with her husband, sons, two dogs, two cats, and a bird. She spends a large amount of time playing with her kids, drinking coffee, and cooking. You can find her outside if the weather's nice, and there's always a piece of candy in her pocket. Besides cinnamon gummy bears, boxing, and random quotes, her next favorite thing is chatting with readers. She'd love to hear from you! Look for her at www.adrianalocke.com.